OTHER MOONS

OTHER MOONS

Vietnamese Short Stories
of the American War
and Its Aftermath

Translated and edited by
Quan Manh Ha and Joseph Babcock

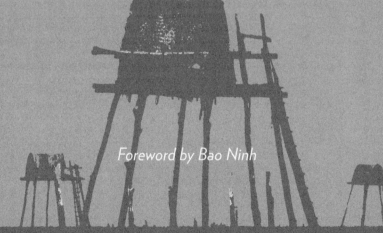

Foreword by Bao Ninh

Columbia University Press / New York

Columbia University Press wishes to express its appreciation for assistance given by the Pushkin Fund in the publication of this book.

Columbia University Press
Publishers Since 1893
New York   Chichester, West Sussex
cup.columbia.edu

Library of Congress Cataloging-in-Publication Data
Names: Ha, Quan Manh, translator. | Babcock, Joseph, 1985- translator. | Bảo Ninh, writer of foreword.
Title: Other moons : Vietnamese short stories of the American War and its aftermath / translated and edited by Quan Manh Ha and Joseph Babcock.
Description: New York : Columbia University Press, [2020]
Identifiers: LCCN 2019055643 (print) | LCCN 2019055644 (ebook) | ISBN 9780231196086 (cloth) | ISBN 9780231196093 (paperback) | ISBN 9780231551632 (ebook)
Subjects: LCSH: Vietnam War, 1961-1975—Vietnam—Fiction. | Vietnam War, 1961-1975—Influence—Fiction. | Short stories, Vietnamese—Translations into English. | LCGFT: Short stories.
Classification: LCC PL4378.82.E5 O84 2020 (print) | LCC PL4378.82.E5 (ebook) | DDC 895.9/223340803581—dc23
LC record available at https://lccn.loc.gov/2019055643
LC ebook record available at https://lccn.loc.gov/2019055644

Columbia University Press books are printed on permanent and durable acid-free paper.
Printed in the United States of America

Cover image: © Tran Tuan Viet / Gettyimages
Cover design: Lisa Hamm

CONTENTS

FOREWORD

Writing About War Is Writing About Peace

BAO NINH

Since 1995, when the United States normalized diplomatic relations with Vietnam, Americans have been visiting Hanoi, and many of them are veterans who fought in the American War. A veteran myself, I am able to have open conservations with them. I like the way American veterans talk about the war because they are sincere and straightforward, always saying what they think.

Although individual Americans may perceive Vietnam and the Vietnamese people differently, they are usually all surprised by the fact that they encounter no hatred from their "former enemy" in postwar Vietnam. Even two decades after the end of the war, it was hardly a forgotten past in 1995, when Americans first started visiting our country, because the remnants and catastrophic consequences of the conflict were ubiquitous throughout Vietnam. So why did most Vietnamese people treat American veterans as friends rather than enemies? Australian and South Korean veterans—U.S. allies during the war—whom I met were also astonished by the Vietnamese people's peaceful attitude, and they wondered how the Vietnamese could possibly change their attitude toward their former enemy so quickly and easily; they found this difficult to comprehend. But if one reads the history of Vietnam, one will realize that this is by no means incomprehensible.

From its birth over two thousand years ago up through the last few decades of the twentieth century, Vietnam has continuously fought against foreign invaders, all of whom were far more powerful than the Vietnamese, militarily. Therefore, whenever Vietnam was invaded, the country had to bear great calamities: the land was reduced to ashes; death was everywhere. After each war ended, in order to survive, the Vietnamese not only had to work hard to rebuild houses and villages but also had to try their best to free themselves from the nightmares and catastrophic psychological devastation caused by war.

That meant we had to learn to quickly "close down the past." In order to achieve this goal, we needed to reconcile with our former enemies and hold no hatred toward them, because hatred is poisonous. If we kept holding resentment in our hearts, we would be killing ourselves, our fellow citizens, and, more broadly, our country. Resentment or hatred would make the country sink permanently under the weight of the horrifying and tragic memories of the war. Hatred would make us unable to live a normal life: we would be devastated physically and psychologically, and we, as well as our children, would never be able to live happily. This is a valuable lesson that the Vietnamese have learned throughout centuries. Generations have been practicing this philosophy—a philosophy of loving peace and harboring no xenophobia. These are defining characteristics of the Vietnamese people.

Antixenophobia might seem to be paradoxical in the Vietnamese people, but I think it is an admirable trait. The Vietnamese have fought several wars, but they love peace and are essentially peaceful people. We are neither militant nor vainglorious about our victories. We are courageous in fighting against foreign invaders, but we treat foreign people with respect. We are known for our nationalism, but we do not practice the narrow form of nationalism prevalent elsewhere in Asia.

It is our love for peace and antixenophobia that make us more open-minded and eager to learn new and useful things, especially from other cultures, even from our invaders. This is evidenced in the relations between France and Vietnam from the nineteenth through the first half of the twentieth century.

From 1858 to 1954, France invaded and colonized Indochina—Vietnam, Laos, and Cambodia. That was one hundred years of hatred, violence, and exploitation. The Vietnamese rebelled against the French colonizers, and in turn, the French suppressed the Vietnamese revolutions violently and brutally. But during the nearly century-long French occupation, Vietnamese society, which was influenced by French culture, was able to free itself, relatively speaking, from the feudalist system that had dominated Vietnam for thousands of years. French Enlightenment thinkers such as Voltaire, Rousseau, Montesquieu, and Diderot had a great influence on Vietnamese intellectuals, who eventually turned away from Confucianism. The French Revolution of 1789 promoted freedom, equality, and human rights, all of which were later introduced to Vietnamese society and, as a result, weakened the domination of Confucianism over Vietnamese culture.

The Vietnamese also adopted the Roman alphabet from Europe. At the end of the nineteenth century, with no hesitation, we began using the Roman alphabet rather than the logographic *chu Nom* system composed of Chinese characters. *Chu Nom* had been used in Vietnam for several years, but it was rather complicated and difficult to learn, write, and read. Therefore, for years the majority of the Vietnamese population was illiterate. The Roman alphabet, which the French colonizers used, was easy to learn, use, and print. Getting rid of *chu Nom* and adopting the modified Roman alphabet (*chu Quoc Ngu*) used in modern Vietnamese was considered a great cultural and linguistic revolution.

And literature, in fact, was this revolution's greatest beneficiary. Young Vietnamese poets of the New Poetry period in the first half of the twentieth century—who were, for the most part, educated in French schools—used *chu Quoc Ngu* to write poetry and were no longer bound by the Chinese language and the outdated *chu Nom* system. Vietnamese novelists and poets of this period learned the quintessence of French Romantic and realistic literatures, and between 1930 and 1945 they produced several great literary works and introduced Vietnamese literature to the Western world. I consider this the golden period in Vietnamese literature, especially prose fiction. Novels written in this period were influenced by great French authors, and one can see the absence of the classical Chinese prose movement in them. The language they use is more familiar, the characters are easy to relate to, the plots are more interesting, and humanism is promoted. Two prominent authors from this period are Vu Trong Phung and Nam Cao, whose fiction is as great as any world masterpiece, even today.

In the autumn of 1945, Vietnam gained its freedom from the Japanese imperialists and the French colonizers. But soon after that, Vietnam was at war again. There were three consecutive Hot Wars in the second half of the twentieth century: the Vietnamese-French War (1945-1954), the American War (1960-1975), and the Sino-Vietnamese War (1979-1990), also known as the Border War with China. Then there was, of course, the Cold War—the global ideological battle between communism (from the former Soviet Union) and capitalism (from the United States).

When the country was at war, literature suffered the same fate. Vietnamese authors, whether voluntarily or reluctantly, wrote to serve the country's revolution against foreign invaders. They were considered "soldiers on a cultural battlefield" who used their pens as weapons to destroy the enemy. Therefore, they had to put artistic and literary values aside and quickly produce revolutionary works that conveyed the spirit of fighting. These works are often characterized by blood, fire, and hatred.

Vietnamese literature from the period 1945-1990 was also influenced by the dictates of "socialist realism." Socialist realism, or Stalinist and Maoist propaganda literature, dominated literary production and artistic expression in communist countries, including

Vietnam. As a result, Vietnamese literature lost its traditional beauty and gentleness and alienated itself from global modern literary trends.

The concept of "realism" in the term "socialist realism" is, in fact, a kind of antirealism. It glorifies socialism and denounces everything that is contrary to or different from socialism and its ideology. It rejects individualism and advocates for collectivism; thus, it is intended to be the literature of the masses. Although there are a few good—even great—literary works of socialist realism, oftentimes these works are heavily politicized and read like political documents that have been "literaturized." Socialist realist fiction tends to be tedious, dry, vain, and xenophobic. During the Cold War, Vietnamese readers had access only to this kind of literature written by socialist writers from the Soviet Union, Eastern Europe, and China.

Vietnamese readers eventually lost interest in literature produced under the paradigm of socialist realism, and nothing written with this political ideology is known outside of Vietnam. Even today, with conditions much different than those in the pre-1986 period, not many contemporary Vietnamese works have been translated into other languages, and many have been rejected for publication in the West.

In fact, since 1986, especially after the collapse of the communist bloc in 1990, Vietnamese authors have courageously freed themselves from literary restrictions imposed by politics and by the government. The pioneers of this newer style of writing are Nguyen Minh Chau and Nguyen Ngoc, who were once considered important Vietnamese socialist realist authors. They wrote articles, gave talks, encouraged Vietnamese authors to boycott political literature, and called for reform, otherwise known as *Doi Moi*.

Doi Moi refers to reforms started in 1986 in order to help the Vietnamese economy transition to a market economy by abandoning the cooperative economic model. Although these reforms primarily targeted the economy, they had a sweeping, positive influence on all other aspects of Vietnamese society. Human rights, freedom of speech, and freedom of artistic expression all benefited. Censorship of the media and publishing became less strict compared to that of the pre-1986 period. Vietnam started to open its doors to the world, and literature written by American, British, French, German, Spanish, and Italian authors—both classic and contemporary works—were now translated into Vietnamese and published in Vietnam. This was a great opportunity for Vietnamese writers, especially the younger generation, many of whom are featured in this anthology. They include Ta Duy Anh, Nguyen Ngoc Tu, Suong Nguyet Minh, Thai Ba Tan, Nguyen Van Tho, Vo Thi Hao, and Nguyen Thi Am.

A common characteristic in the work of this younger generation of Vietnamese writers is their rejection of socialist realism. This is evidenced especially in their works about a very old topic, and the focus of this anthology—the war—which was once considered a strength and a source of pride in the Vietnamese socialist realist tradition. Writing about the American War in Vietnam, these young writers of the post-1986 period condemn war, whereas authors of the pre-1986 period had glorified it. Before 1986, even well-informed writers had sometimes written propagandistic epics about the war and heroism. For example, Nguyen Minh Chau's story "A Crescent Moon in the Woods," which is considered a "gentle" story and portrays mostly realistic characters, still romanticizes the tragic war with America. Although it is well liked by many readers and is taught in Vietnamese high schools, it is still a work of what I could call "socialist half-realism." In contrast, Thai Ba Tan's story "War," which is rather simple and not as famous, successfully and subtly addresses the cruelties of war and the misfortunes that the Vietnamese people—men and women, soldiers and civilians—experienced.

I am arguing here that the literary reform since 1986 and the topic of war and its aftermath are a return to the theme of humanism that has always existed in Vietnamese culture and literature for thousands of years. Because Vietnam's history is associated with war, most Vietnamese magnum opuses, like Nguyen Du's *The Tale of Kieu*, Dang Tran Con's *The Song of a Soldier's Wife*, or Nguyen Dinh Chieu's *Luc Van Tien*, are related to war. Although the wars depicted in these texts are not real battles—no winning or losing, no swords or guns—the stories are about people and their sorrows, tragedies, and suffering caused by war. Similarly, most contemporary works about the war are not directly about the conflict itself but about how people lived and suffered during and after the war.

And this holds true for many of the stories in this anthology. The characters in the stories collected here are common people—soldiers, civilians, peasants, men, women, and children; they are neither generals, nor high-ranking military officers, nor heroes. The reality of the country and the war are seen through these characters, their lives and their fates.

Unlike writers of socialist realism, contemporary Vietnamese authors write about the war to oppose war rather than to promote or advocate for it. In other words, they write to express their love for peace and promote cross-cultural understanding and global love.

ACKNOWLEDGMENTS

Collaborative projects like this one always depend on the gracious help, participation, and support of dozens of people. We would like to thank, first and foremost, the twenty authors whose work appears in this anthology. We realize that placing one's writing in the hands of others is an act of trust, and we feel honored and privileged to have had the opportunity to translate and share your art with a wider audience.

We had trouble initially contacting some of the authors represented here and relied on the generous help of friends and colleagues, including Le Van Han, Le Trung Binh, Vo Thi Le Thuy, Ta Duy Anh, Suong Nguyet Minh, Quoc Phuong, Truong Hanh Ly, Do Han, and Truong Thi Thanh Binh. Without your diligence—and, in some cases, amateur detective work—this project never would have become a reality. A big thank you also to our friend Nguyen Thi Minh Hanh, who was always willing to help wrangle copies of Vietnamese-language books.

We are deeply indebted to Bao Ninh for committing his writing time and energy to composing the foreword to this anthology, and for his generosity in welcoming us into his home in Hanoi last summer.

A special thank you to Wayne Karlin, who was generous enough to read an early draft of our proposal and manuscript. We were buoyed throughout the final stages of this project by your continued support, encouragement, and advice.

Thank you to everyone at Columbia University Press, especially Christine Dunbar, Christian Winting, and James R. Purcell, for their work on and commitment to the project. It is thanks to editors like you that often-overlooked short fiction in translation like this has a chance to reach a wider audience.

We would like to acknowledge the generosity of the Humanities Institute at the University of Montana and the Unit 18 Professional Development Fund at the University of California at San Diego for funding our project-related trips to Vietnam.

And finally, a big thank you to our parents, Dinh Thi Hai, Noel Harold Kaylor, Richard Babcock, and Gioia Diliberto for their support and encouragement. We love you and can't thank you enough for everything.

INTRODUCTION

A Note on the Selection and Translation of Stories

QUAN MANH HA AND JOSEPH BABCOCK

The American War in Vietnam was an extremely controversial and complicated event in the context of both Vietnamese and U.S. history. In our selection of the stories collected in this anthology, we have tried to be as inclusive and diverse as possible in terms of both the author's background and the content, style, and themes present in his or her work. Still, some readers may notice that only one perspective on the conflict is represented here—that of the war's victors, the Vietnamese communists based in the northern capital city of Hanoi.

Since the end of the war in 1975, the Communist Party of Vietnam has maintained tight political control over the country. Today, Vietnam remains a single-party state, with tight controls and limits on freedom of expression, the media, and the arts. These extend, of course, to the publishing industry, where all literature, including works of fiction, is subject to censorship and the demand—sometimes unspoken, but always firmly understood—that all published work adhere to the tenets of Party orthodoxy. This includes narratives concerning the war against the Americans, a war seen by the ruling Communist Party as a struggle to reunite the two Vietnams, North and South, and shake off foreign control.

Virtually all literature about the American War published in Vietnam adheres to this narrative.

We believe that it is important for readers to keep this strictly controlled publishing environment in mind when first approaching the twenty stories collected here. Given the restraint placed on these authors in terms of what is viable for publication about the American War in Vietnam, the artistic and thematic diversity represented by their work is even more striking.

By referring to the conflict as the "American War," we are adopting the terminology most commonly used in Vietnam, *Chien tranh chong My*. The war is sometimes referred to in Vietnam as the "Resistance War against America," *Khang chien chong My*, but this is often shortened simply to the American War. Outside of Vietnam, people usually refer to the conflict as the "Vietnam War." Of course, it would not make sense for the Vietnamese to refer to the *Vietnam* War. Despite the persistent use in the West of the word "Vietnam" as a stand-in for the conflict itself, Vietnam is, first and foremost, a country, not a war.

Outside of Vietnam, the conflict is also sometimes referred to as the Second Indochina War. The *First* Indochina War was Vietnam's earlier struggle for independence from French colonial rule, which lasted from 1945 to 1954. At the end of that conflict, the Geneva Accords split newly independent Vietnam at the 17th parallel into North and South. According to the agreement, the split was meant to be temporary, and the country would be reunified for national elections in 1956. That never happened. Instead, the United States began promoting South Vietnam—known also as the Republic of Vietnam (RVN) or the Government of Vietnam (GVN)—as a legitimate country, a "democratic" alternative to Ho Chi Minh's northern communist government based in the capital city of Hanoi. By 1960, forces opposed to the government of South Vietnam had united under the Hanoi-supported National Liberation Front (NLF), known colloquially and often derisively as the Viet Cong.

By 1965, the conflict had become an all-out war, with the United States eventually committing hundreds of thousands of troops to fight alongside the Army of the Republic of Vietnam (ARVN) to preserve the newly formed country of South Vietnam, and the North Vietnamese Army (NVA) and the NLF fighting to expel the Americans and reunite the country under a single, communist government. In 1973, with American loss of life in the conflict totaling nearly 60,000 and no easy end to the fighting in sight, the United States withdrew militarily from Vietnam and began cutting financial and military aid to the South. The Republic of Vietnam collapsed two years later, in 1975, as communist forces reunified the country by taking control of the southern cities, including Saigon, which they renamed Ho Chi Minh City.

For Vietnam, the impact of the war was devastating. According to the best available estimates, 3 million Vietnamese died in the conflict, roughly 7 percent of the country's total population at the time; 2 million of those killed were civilians. Over 300,000 Vietnamese soldiers were still missing when the war ended, and hundreds of thousands of farmers and their families were displaced from their homes in the rural countryside. American bombs had left sections of North Vietnam in ruins, and U.S.-manufactured chemical weapons had, quite literally, poisoned the soil and environment across many southern provinces.

The two decades immediately following the end of the war were extremely difficult for Vietnam and the Vietnamese people. Harsh U.S. trade sanctions—intended, some historians argue, to "punish" communist Vietnam for having won the war—kept the country staggeringly poor through the mid-1990s. The communists imprisoned thousands of people, mostly southerners who had been involved with the Americans or the former South Vietnamese government, in austere rural "reeducation" camps where they were held sometimes for upward of ten years. During this period, millions of Vietnamese refugees—again, mostly southerners, many of whom had worked for the defeated regime—fled the country as "boat people." Those who survived the dangerous journey would go on to build vibrant diasporic communities in places like Southern California, Canada, Australia, and France.

The twenty stories collected in this anthology all address aspects of this conflict that consumed Vietnam for much of the latter half of the twentieth century: the effects of exposure to Agent Orange, one of the most toxic chemical weapons used by the United States, on one peasant farmer and his family; the bond between a North Vietnamese soldier and his fiercely loyal pet dog; the use of psychics in the continuing search for the bodies of missing soldiers; the lingering effects of conscription on romantic and family relationships in the countryside; the treatment of veterans in an economically depressed postwar society. The stories presented in this volume range from the intensely personal and specific to narratives that deal with larger national trends of remembrance, trauma, and healing.

In Vietnam, these stories are some of the most frequently anthologized and popular pieces of short fiction about the war. Their original publication dates cover a wide range, from 1967 to 2014, offering readers the opportunity to explore how Vietnamese narratives of the war have (or in some cases, have not) changed through the decades. Some of these stories originally appeared in mainstream Vietnamese newspapers and literary magazines like *Thanh Nien* (*The Youth Daily*), *Nhan Dan* (*The People's Daily*), and *Van Nghe Quan Doi* (*Military Literature Magazine*), and others were published in popular anthologies such as *Tuyen truyen ngan doat giai cao: 30 nam doi moi, 1986–2016* (*Selected Award-Winning Short Stories: 30 Years of Reforms, 1986–2016*) and *Truyen ngan hay ve khang chien chong My* (*Best Short Stories About the American War*). Many are frequently taught and critically discussed in Vietnam, and several are considered canonical. Yet none of these stories, despite being so popular and widely read in Vietnam, has ever appeared before in English. *Other Moons*, therefore, represents a unique opportunity for American audiences to learn about how the Vietnamese people continue to think about, commemorate, and generally process the conflict that consumed their country for so many years.

Many of these stories provide a firsthand glimpse of the experiences of Vietnamese soldiers both during and after the war. The canonical story "A Crescent Moon in the Woods" by Nguyen Minh Chau depicts a group of tired North Vietnamese Army truck drivers sitting around a fire and telling war stories until one of them captivates the group for hours with his deceptively simple tale of love, fate, and courage. The narrator of Nguyen Van Tho's "Unsung Hero" walks readers through the details of his life on a remote jungle base—days spent fishing, foraging, tending a small vegetable garden, and recovering from the occasional bout of malaria. For Vop, the tragicomic main character of Mai Tien Nghi's "The Louse Crab Season," memories of his time as a soldier are almost idyllic compared to the ignominious treatment he experiences in his hometown after an accident leaves him castrated. Similarly, in Nguyen Trong Luan's "The Corporal," the narrator relays the story of Xuan, the daughter of a poor peasant in his hometown who spent years fighting bravely in the war only to return to her village, marry a "dull-witted" man, and eke out an existence foraging for manioc roots. Despite her commendable military service, Xuan's lack of education and social connections limit her options in finding a comfortable job, suggesting the continuation of traditional class tensions—the peasant agrarian class versus the land-owning educated elites—in postwar socialist Vietnam.

The counterpart to the soldiers' experience is the drama that unfolds on the home front while they are away. In "War" by Thai Ba Tan, "Ms. Thoai" by Hanh Le, and "The Most Beautiful Girl in the Village" by Ta Duy Anh, the setting is the domestic front, where wives are expected to wait patiently and faithfully for their husbands to return from the battlefield. When things do not go exactly as hoped—in the case of "Ms. Thoai" a rape, in "War" an unexpected pregnancy that may have been immaculate, and in "The Most Beautiful Girl in the Village" a marriage that never materializes—the characters' lives are changed forever. These stories present a compelling moral landscape in which the suffering of the women is treated as both tragic and heroic, while the men are portrayed as stubborn and cruel. For these characters, it is not the horrors of actual combat that linger years after the fighting has ended but the obsession, resentment, doubt, jealousy, and pain of perceived betrayal that end up defining the rest of their lives.

In our selection of the stories, we have made a concerted effort to include authors from a variety of personal and professional backgrounds. The group of writers represented here are a mix of both well-known, full-time authors (Bao Ninh, Nguyen Van Tho, Suong Nguyet Minh) and writers who carve out time to create their fiction around the demands of their day jobs. Mai Tien Nghi is a middle school math teacher. Nguyen Thi Am works for a company that sells agricultural products. Luong Liem is the full-time director of a local association for victims of Agent Orange. Lai Van Long is a beat reporter for the *Ho Chi Minh City Police News*. Most of these writers are veterans of the war with the Americans, though several are from the later generation, born in the mid- or late 1970s, such as Nguyen Ngoc Thuan, Nguyen Thi Mai Phuong, and Truong Van Ngoc. Some of them are members of the prestigious national Vietnamese Writers' Association—the Party-sanctioned organization that decides who is "officially" considered to qualify as a *nha van*, a writer—while others are relatively unknown outside their local province, far removed from the official publishing apparatuses in Hanoi. The majority still live and write in Vietnam. The exceptions are Nguyen Minh Chau and Hanh Le, neither of whom is alive today, and Vo Thi Hao, who now lives in asylum in Germany.

Readers may notice that out of twenty authors included in this anthology, only five are women. This gender disparity reflects the fact that the vast majority of Vietnamese fiction about the war is written by men. Although women did serve in the army in various capacities during the war, the rate of conscription was much higher among men. Therefore, most authors who are veterans of the conflict and are concerned with exploring war-related themes in their short fiction are male. However, several female Vietnamese authors have had considerable international critical and commercial success writing about the war: two of the most internationally popular works of Vietnamese nonfiction about the conflict were written by women—Le Ly Hayslip's memoir, *When Heaven and Earth Changed Places*, and *Last Night I Dreamed of Peace*, the diary of National Liberation Front doctor Dang Thuy Tram, who was killed in an American attack in 1970—and the most internationally popular war novel after Bao Ninh's *The Sorrow of War* is female author Duong Thu Huong's *Novel Without a Name*.

Some readers might also note that the anthology does not include voices from "the losing side," the Army of the Republic of Vietnam (ARVN), or those who supported the former South Vietnamese government and American intervention in the conflict. There are several reasons for this. First, these narratives are already widely available to English-speaking audiences in the form of exile or diasporic literature published outside of Vietnam. Diasporic Vietnamese literature often favors the ARVN/South Vietnamese perspective. Those who fled the country as refugees in the postwar years tended to be people who had supported the South Vietnamese regime or worked with the Americans and their ARVN allies. There is also the practical reality of the tightly regulated publishing landscape in Vietnam. Still today, over forty years after the end of the conflict, stories sympathetic to the ARVN side are not published in Vietnam, let alone widely read or anthologized. Some short fiction by former ARVN soldiers has been self-published online, though usually under a pseudonym, making it difficult to even find the author for the purposes of securing a "right to translate" agreement. Despite the logistical hurdles, this might be an opportunity for a future translation project: an anthology of online dissident writing about the war.

We have also made a point to include voices here from the three main geographic regions of Vietnam, the north (*mien Bac*), the central region (*mien Trung*), and the south (*mien Nam*). With Hanoi usually considered the cultural and political center of the country, Vietnamese literature and state-controlled publishing have tended to favor the war writing of northern writers, work that often focuses on depictions of pastoral village life and traditional village culture. Southern and central writers often present a different experience of the war by focusing on issues unique to their own experience: life alongside the American soldiers, brothers forced to fight on opposite sides of the conflict, the seizing of private property in the postwar period. Nguyen Ngoc Tu's "Brothers," Nguyen Thi Thu Tran's "An American Service Hamlet," and Lai Van Long's "A Moral Murderer" are all examples of stories written by southerners that enrich the corpus of Vietnamese short fiction about the war because they address issues not normally found in short fiction written by northern writers.

Bringing a short story from its original Vietnamese into English poses a number of challenges. To begin with, the Vietnamese language does not have simple, generic pronouns like the English "you" or "she" or "they." Instead, Vietnamese speakers use a system of relationship-dependent pronouns—*anh*, *em*, *chi*, *chu*, *chau*, *ong*, and *ba*, among others—that change according to the respective ages of and the relationship between the speakers. But attempting to translate these pronouns into English would have resulted in something like, for example, "How is sister today?" or "How are you today, sister?" We felt this sounded unnatural and stiffly formal, whereas the pronouns in the Vietnamese original often convey familiarity and friendly rapport between speakers. We have chosen, therefore, not to represent the original Vietnamese pronouns in dialogue with an attempt at literal translation. The only exception is the title for "Brother, When Will You Come Home?." Without the Vietnamese pronouns, of course, we lose some of the associative information the characters communicate. Thus, when necessary, we have tried to indicate the relationship between speakers in other ways. This usually meant the addition of small identifying phrases to the description of some characters, like "brother-in-law" or "my sister," or adjectives like "older" and "younger."

We have also had to wrestle with the inevitable fact that some Vietnamese phrases lose their associative and cultural richness when rendered into English. One example is the term "ve que," which appears at the beginning of Nguyen Trong Luan's "The Corporal" and acts as the initiating frame for the rest of the story. Ve que is a common fixed phrase in Vietnamese that translates as "to return to one's hometown." The Vietnamese would never say "di que," or "to go to one's hometown." The concept is always conveyed using the verb ve, "to return," suggesting the speaker's deep connection to his or her ancestors and the land where he or she originated. The English word "hometown" also does not carry the same cultural weight as the Vietnamese word que, which is often used as shorthand to mean "the countryside." Ve que, therefore, implies returning to a simpler, less hectic, rural life.

This is just one example of several challenges we encountered during the translation process. The editorial note at the front of each story is meant to help cover any lost associative ground similar to this, as well as to provide some cultural and historical context. We have opted to include the notes rather than attempt this contextualizing work within the text of the stories themselves in the service of offering a reading experience in English that hews as closely as possible to the experience of reading the story in its original Vietnamese.

Written Vietnamese can also sometimes feature small regional differences. For example, the word for "bowl," as in "a bowl of rice," is different in the North versus the South, as is the word for "spoon." Northern Vietnamese tends to use more formal phrases of greeting and expressing thanks; southern Vietnamese is generally considered more informal. We have tried to maintain these regional differences in the tone of our translations as best we could, though the editorial note for each story will also help regionally locate the author for readers unfamiliar with these more subtle linguistic differences.

In all of these translations, we have tried to remain as faithful as possible to the Vietnamese original. Preserving the integrity of each author's artistic vision was always the priority. This included maintaining the aesthetic uniqueness of each author's use of language and voice. In some cases, the resulting English sentence or phrase felt redundant or wordy, and we were forced to make minor adjustments to the sentence structure or the phrasing to make the English more readable. However, these adjustments were always informed by the author's style and in keeping with the aesthetics of their cadence, tone, and word choice.

One final note on the text: we have opted not to include the diacritic markings on Vietnamese words that remained in the English translation. We believe these markings would have proved distracting to most readers, and those who are familiar with the Vietnamese language can easily infer the appropriate diacritics for each word.

OTHER MOONS

1 / UNSUNG HERO

NGUYEN VAN THO

Nguyen Van Tho, who sometimes writes under the pseudonym Thu Nguyen, was born in 1948 in the northern province of Thai Binh. He is a veteran of the war with America, which he fought in for nearly a decade, from 1965 to 1975. He has written several books, including six short-story collections, one novel, and four works of nonfiction, and has won several awards from the Vietnam Writers' Association, though his work is not well known outside of Vietnam. Many of his short stories deal with the experiences of the common soldier; his characters are often *bo doi*, the enlisted men of the North Vietnamese Army. "Unsung Hero" is in this vein, with the addition of a new, unique type of soldier—the canine combatant. The original Vietnamese title of the story, "Vo danh tran mac," emphasizes the anonymity of the dog at the center of the story, especially in the context of the normal cultural rituals for honoring a war hero. Nobody will celebrate this special soldier, the narrator suggests, despite his selfless acts of courage and heroism.

I was about to leave the village when I heard a voice coming from the ground. It sounded like a weak kind of shriek, a sound we heard a lot in the war. But it wasn't that. Bombs from a C130 night patrol plane had destroyed the village. Everything was burnt. The tree in front of me had been ripped up by gunfire. I kicked away a fallen branch and saw a pair of sparkling eyes staring out of a dark hole in the burnt ground.

For a few seconds I was just confused. I shouldered my gun. It was a kid, about eight or nine years old, and he was holding a dog. The kid was clearly dead—his head smashed, neck twisted against the side of the hole at an awkward angle. He was staring straight up at the sky, eyes white and stunned. His blood had dried black all over his hands, which were clutching this puppy. I almost had to break the kid's fingers to get the dog loose.

We named the puppy Lu. Don't think that this was some trendy Western name. It was just like the other common names for dogs— Ven, Leu, Eu. We knew that it would sound Western if we called him LuLu, so at first we avoided this and only called him Lu. But he didn't know his name—he was only a puppy, after all—so we had to repeat it twice, and then it just became our habit to call him LuLu.

He became the seventh member of our squad. We shared our food rations with him. Lu was too weak and skinny to find food himself, so we mixed rice with water to make porridge that he lapped up. If I happened to catch some small fish in a nearby creek and then stewed them with wild tamarinds, I'd let Lu taste a little of the sauce.

In secret, of course, so the rest of the squad didn't find out.

"I wish we had milk and egg powder like back in '54," said Bao, who was from Hang Thiec Street in Hanoi.

This was an unrealistic daydream. The truth was we didn't even have enough salt. We used to hoard the stuff like treasure. Sometimes I'd take a little pinch and put it on my tongue. It felt incredible.

So obviously we couldn't even think about sugar or milk for the dog. But Lu got stronger anyway. After three days he started running around our camp, and eventually he started jumping up and down to greet us when we'd come back from patrol. He got healthier and put on weight. His fur, which was yellow with black dots, had been patchy and bare before but began to grow back, thick and shiny. He was quick now, and energetic, just like a normal dog. We were living deep in the jungle, which was lonely and isolating. It was nice having Lu around. About a month after I'd first pulled him from the bloody hands of the dead kid, we heard him bark for the first time—"Arf...arf...arf!" Lu had been practically dead when I found him. Now his barking echoed against the cliffs and the thick jungle foliage.

It made me feel something that was difficult to put into words.

We were all soldiers from Hanoi. There was Hanh, the experienced squad leader who had fought everywhere, North to South. Then there was me, and Hoang, Lam, and Bao—all experienced veterans who knew about the bloody battle of Hue in 1968 and the enemy's brutal Operation Lam Son 719. There were also Tam and Khanh, both newly enlisted soldiers.

Each of us had a different relationship with Lu. For example, Tam was usually the one who fed Lu, and each time he'd pet his head and say things like, "Hurry up! Faster! Six bowls, six bowls!" in this kind of sing-song voice. Even though Tam was a skinny guy, he lusted after food, whether he or Lu was the one eating it.

Hanh was different. He was quiet. Sometimes he'd sit with Lu for hours, just scratching his head or rubbing his back. Lu would get silent and move his ears, as if he were listening closely to what Hanh might say. I wondered if maybe Hanh had told Lu what he'd told only me, about his sister who spent her days, year in and year out, unloading sacks of coal, fish sauce, and heavy dyeing yams from boats at the Black Ferry Pier. Hanh had been born into a poor family. His parents died when he was young, and he'd been raised by his sister. He'd spent his childhood pulling bark from medicinal jungle trees to sell at the market. A person like Hanh couldn't live a carefree life like someone whose parents had been state officials or longtime Party members. Maybe it was because Hanh had been through tough times that he was so frugal. He'd never waste even dirty old gun-cleaning rags or a smashed manioc that he found in a field, which he would mix with his daily rice for a little extra food.

Enlisted soldiers like us came from all sorts of backgrounds. Hoang, for example, was the opposite of Hanh. His family was very wealthy. Hoang claimed that his parents sold government rice and his family ate very well. He'd had plenty of pork sausage to eat growing up. When he ate chicken, he said, he only swallowed the juices, not the meat itself. Maybe he only bragged about his family because he was as hungry as the rest of us. I knew that Hoang's mother and my mother were friends. Back in Hanoi, my mother sold clothes at Dong Xuan Market, in the center of the city. I remembered Hoang's mother vividly—she had dark skin and often wore an expensive-looking jade necklace.

Hoang liked to tease Lu. He'd pull Lu toward him by the tail, and Lu would shriek miserably and then be mad at Hoang for a few days afterward. But Hoang could also be very generous, throwing Lu scraps of fatty meat when we'd managed to catch a wild porcupine.

But Lu was closest to me. On cold nights he'd jump up onto my bunk and sneak under the blankets, warming my feet.

⁄⁄ ⁄⁄ ⁄⁄

The rainy season in the highlands that year was awful. It rained for several days straight, destroying all the transportation roads. Vehicles from the North couldn't get to the front. Rice rations were reduced. At the beginning of the rainy season, the ration was five grams; then, as the season progressed and the rain got worse, it went down to three grams, and then eventually to only two grams per person. When we received our share and untied the little sack, black rice weevils jumped out. We had to rinse the rice carefully to get rid of the bugs, and the good, big grains would wash away in the creek water and we'd be left with only the tiny grains. But if we didn't wash the rice carefully, it would taste bitter.

The situation with the manioc that season wasn't any better. They were black and full of fungus. Fortunately, we didn't have to fight the enemy at that time. Instead we spent our days guarding the battalion's armory, doing farm work, and sometimes patrolling the worn walking paths that ran along the river on the outskirts of the base. We couldn't complain, though—at least we still had something to fill our empty stomachs, even though taking care of the farm was a lot of work. Where we'd set up camps wasn't like the northern villages we'd fought to protect in '54. Back then it had been easy to hunt animals to eat, as if they'd been caged. In the highlands there were some owls, squirrels, rats, and mouse deer, but we weren't allowed to shoot them, otherwise we might give away our position. So we set up traps instead and went fishing. If we actually wanted to shoot an animal, we had to walk an entire day, until we were far enough from the camp. And anyway, hunting animals was not our expertise. But we ate everything we could catch, including tough and unpleasant-smelling meat from crows and parrots.

When it was the right season for bamboo shoots to grow, we looked for bamboo rat holes and dug until we found the little furry rodents. Lu would help, sniffing the ground and using his front legs to signal where there might be a rat hole. We all craved something fishy, so in the dry season, when the creeks became more shallow, we managed to catch snakehead and catfish. If we wanted to eat bigger fish we had to walk farther, to a strong-flowing river with deeper water.

Near the border, we found some Laotians and traded them our new double hammock and one-half kilogram of salt for a fishing net that was over twenty meters long. The net worked in places where the water was calm, or where a creek merged with a river.

We also used dynamite to catch fish, cutting the fuse short and using only a small amount of TNT so that when it exploded in the shallow water it only made a quiet, bubbling sound. When we saw the water boiling, that's when we'd jump in and grab the fish. There were a lot of white *bangana behri* fish in the rivers in the highlands, and when we used dynamite to catch them, their white bodies would float on the surface of the water. We had to be quick or the fast-moving river would carry them away. Our mouths, feet, hands—we used every body part we could to carry the dead fish back to shore.

While we fished, Lu ran alongside the riverbank, barking loudly, which annoyed me.

Later, as we sat around the fire baking the fish, Lu was well behaved. The fish smelled very good, but Lu sat patiently watching the baking fish fat drip on the fire. He knew to expect the baked fish tails that we always gave him.

"You did nothing except bark," I said to Lu once, getting annoyed with his patient groveling. "You're a dog. You do nothing, but you want to eat like a king. You're ridiculous—do you know that?"

Lu knew that I was serious. And I could tell from his face that he was scared and remorseful. His ears dropped and his eyes were wet and downcast. He came over and started licking my hand in a beseeching way.

I believed that dogs could understand human language, even though they couldn't speak themselves.

Two months later, when we were once again out catching fish with dynamite, Lu jumped into the water with us and carried a big fish in his mouth back to shore. Then he floated downstream another 300 meters to catch another one. We were stingy because of our hunger, but after that performance we had to give Lu an entire fish to eat.

Time flew by and eventually the rainy season ended. It would be time to harvest the farm crops soon. The rice stalks were heavy with solid grains and the corn had turned full and milky. By this point, Lu had grown into a big, strong dog. He'd become helpful. At night he chased away rats and squirrels and even monkeys, who were fast and smart. Every day he took part in the soldier's work that had become the routine of our lives. He was both friend and comrade.

%. %. %.

It was in the following rainy season that the battalion suddenly ordered soldiers to help a company that was fighting back an invasion in the border area. Because our entire company relied on our camp farm for food, someone had to stay behind to take care of the crops, and the squad leader chose me.

"You'll stay here with Lu," he told me.

Looking after the farm wasn't as dangerous as fighting, but I knew that it would be boring and lonely. I wanted to go with the other soldiers, but I had no choice.

"You and Lu get along well, and he listens to you," the squad leader said, tapping me on the shoulder. "So you'll stay here. It's my order."

The next day, Lu and I saw everyone off at Ben Rung as they crossed the river.

At night I slept in a hut near the farm to keep an eye on the crops. It was comfortable enough, except the nearest source of water was far away. Then, three days after my squad left, I came down with a malaria fever. This was common among soldiers who had been sent to the highlands. I took some pills, but they didn't seem to work. The fever got worse. I lay on the straw mattress in the hut feeling miserable and unable to eat even a small bowl of rice. Even though I had no appetite, I craved something sweet, so I went and plucked a few young ears of corn and a pumpkin to eat. I knew that Lu was hungry as well, but I couldn't cook anything for him. He didn't have a fever and was healthy, so he'd be fine.

Probably animals could deal with hunger—at least better than most humans could.

By the third day of the fever, the water in the bamboo containers had run out. I was so thirsty. That night, the fever knocked me out and I had a terrible dream. I was sitting in our house in Hanoi. My mother was across from me—I saw her clearly. My grandmother was sitting next to me and I felt her caress my hair; then she started to sob. When I woke up, the full moon lit up the night sky with bright yellow clouds. One of my arms hung off the side of the bed. In my dream, I'd torn off my sweaty old soldier's shirt. I sat up in the moonlit darkness, bare-chested and trying to breathe.

It was okay, I told myself. That wasn't actually my mother. Lu was in the bed next to me. In the light from the moon his eyes looked blue, and I could see that he was staring up at me anxiously. He licked the sweat off my face and chest. Lu seemed to understand how miserable I felt—he put his warm mouth against my neck and pushed my head back onto the straw pillow, as if he were putting a child down to sleep.

I thought about death. The night went on. Even if I didn't die from the fever, I would die of thirst. I forced myself to get up and walked out among the crops to collect some young corn, hoping to maybe suck the water out of the ears, and I dragged a canteen to the edge of the jungle where I knew there was a small creek. But the ground became steep and hilly all of a sudden and I fell and rolled down into a shallow ravine, knocking my head against a tree trunk.

I have no clue how long I lay there unconscious. When I finally opened my eyes again, Lu was right next to me. He latched on to the hem of my pants with his mouth and tried pulling me out of the ravine. But it didn't work, the fabric just ripped. I thought I would probably die, and it made me weep all of a sudden, lying there in the ravine, thinking about such a pitiful, lonely death.

Meanwhile Lu started running around me anxiously. Then he stopped and started to howl. It was the first time I'd ever heard a domestic dog howl like a wolf. I'd read books that said wolves howled on quiet moonlit nights to attract a mate. I wondered who Lu was calling. I wanted to talk to him. He probably wanted to talk to me too. Looking into his eyes, I could just tell.

In that terrifying moment, when I was fully aware that I would die, I had no fear. I closed my eyes—I was only semiconscious—and imagined that my soul was leaving my body. With arms extended, I flew above the dense jungle foliage, back toward Hanoi.

Then all of a sudden I felt a strange shaking. It was a sensation I wouldn't experience again until years later, when I was on an airplane flying abroad for the first time and the plane hit an air pocket that caused turbulence. When I opened my eyes I saw that a group of people were using jungle vines to carry me across a deep canyon. They looked like Montagnards. At some point, I remembered vaguely, we'd patrolled this area. It was a natural border between the two mountains that an average person could never manage to cross by themselves. Once we reached the other side, they gave me some water to drink. It was the sweetest water I'd ever tasted.

They were a Montagnard family who lived on the far side of the mountain. There were three of them—an elderly man, his wife, and their daughter, all living in a stilt house under a tree. They also had a dog that had a Montagnard name I couldn't pronounce. Lu must have come here looking for help, I figured. Actually, he'd been here before, though I hadn't realized it. The Montagnard dog was pregnant; her hard swollen belly was covered with nipples.

The Montagnard family gave me a bitter leaf medicine that made me want to throw up. I also ate a kind of root vegetable mixed with honey, and some ground corn stewed with meat. I didn't speak their language and they didn't speak Vietnamese. I wasn't sure exactly

why this family was living in such isolation, since the Thuong or
La Vang ethnic people normally didn't live like this.

I stayed with them for several days as my fever started to sub-
side. One day an enemy plane flew very close, crossing the empty
space between the mountains, and the husband pulled his wife
and daughter behind a big rock to hide. The elderly man had long
black hair that reached his shoulders, and his body was as lean as a
khoop tree after a farm fire—I noticed this clearly as he stood next
to their lean-to hut slicing strips from a hanging chunk of dried
meat. He'd throw the meat at the dogs—Lu and his female friend
were fed well.

After five days, when I started to regain some strength, I learned
from the Montagnard man how to trap animals. His trapping tech-
niques were simple yet effective; it wasn't surprising that his house
was full of hanging cured meat. He taught me how to chop down
bamboo trees to make sharp stakes. Lu and his friend helped us
track the animals, sniffing out their muddy prints on the sides of
tree trunks. We chose narrow paths where wild animals crossed
and planted sharp bamboo stakes that were as high as a deer's chest.
We also collected ant eggs. There were lots of ant colonies scattered
around the jungle, little mounds made of leaves that we sliced open
like a melon, letting the eggs fall and collect on a piece of banana
leaf. Ant eggs smelled really good and were tasty when baked in
banana leaf. I learned later that some bugs had rare vitamins that
humans couldn't produce in their own bodies. That was why I
recovered so quickly from the malaria.

After my stay with the Montagnards, I had newfound respect
for Lu—he knew where to find food and even where to satisfy his
dog's lust, but he still had returned to save me.

※ ※ ※

Over a year went by. It was now 1975. A week before Tet, our squad
was ordered to participate in a meeting. It had been a long time

since we'd reunited with the rest of the battalion, and I was happy to see some old friends. Lu seemed excited as well. He sniffed everyone he came across, trying to recognize their typical soldier's smell. He didn't know, of course, that we were about to fight a big battle. Fighting was business as usual for us. But still we couldn't bounce around happily like Lu. We cleaned our guns, adjusted bayonets, and sharpened daggers. The officers handed out extra grenades and bullets.

In the early morning, an order was issued: kill all animals, no exception. More than a dozen chickens and a pig that belonged to the combat logistics unit were transferred to the kitchen. The cook would slaughter them and chop the meat into small pieces, then mix the pieces with salt to make dried food rations.

As dawn broke, the cook came to our squad to take Lu, who had no idea what was going on. The cook slid a rope around Lu's neck and tried to pull him away, but Lu resisted, snarling, rearing back, refusing to move. Of course none of us could interfere—it was an order. Finally, Hanh told Tam to take Lu to the kitchen.

"Why me?" Tam asked. He looked at the rest of us, bewildered.

Tam and the cook started walking toward the kitchen, and Lu followed them.

I lay down on my hammock and covered myself with a blanket, but it was no use. I couldn't get the image of Lu out of my mind. After a few minutes I got back up and ran to the camp kitchen. Tam was already coming back.

"Did he kill Lu?" I asked, almost frantic.

"Not yet," Tam said. "But I can't stand looking at him."

"Follow me," I said.

We approached the kitchen from the back and saw the cook tying Lu to a tree. Lu lifted his head and stared at the cook. He had a rock in his hand—he was going to use it to bash Lu in the head. Meanwhile, Lu wagged his tail in excitement and licked the cook's wrist.

I felt heartbroken. Then, all of a sudden, I spotted a small bottle of gasoline and a thought popped into my head. Without hesitating, I grabbed the gasoline and threw it in the direction of the stove. After a few seconds, there was an explosion and smoke curled up two meters high.

"Fire! Fire!" Tam shouted.

The cook dropped the rock he was holding and rushed to take care of the fire.

I went to the tree and took out my dagger to cut the rope around Lu's neck.

"Run, run fast," I said, tapping him on the butt. For a moment his familiar wet nose rested against my neck. I could feel him staring up at me, hesitant. Then finally he ran away.

※ ※ ※

That evening a military truck came. It rained heavily, the last rains of the rainy season. As we were infantry soldiers, it was our first time being transported by truck. The rumor was that this battle would take place in the biggest city in the highlands, which was hundreds of kilometers away. We had to get there quickly. The truck started driving and plunged into the darkness of the night. But I could see Lu jumping out there in the dark, trying to run after us. I sat up in my seat, and so did Hanh and Hoang. Lu was like a shadow trailing behind us, rainwater splashing around his paws. "Go back to the Montagnard girl's family, go back to the jungle," I said to him. I turned around until Lu's shadow finally vanished in the dark.

They dropped us off about ten kilometers from Buon Me Thuot City. We walked quietly. We headed directly to the airport, where General Phu's seasoned special forces stood guard. I had no knowledge of how other units had done in previous battles in this city, but in order to seize half the airport our unit ended up losing several soldiers. The enemy, aided by A37 planes, suddenly emerged from the tunnels where they had been hiding and fought back until dawn. Hanh had a leg injury, so I brought him over to a wall at the end of the runway to take cover. We didn't realize that there was a group of enemy soldiers charging the wall. As soon as two of them jumped down and landed on the ground, Hanh and I shot them, but there were two more after them. They were so close that I hit one of them with the butt of my rifle and tried to stab the second one with my bayonet. But my attempt failed, and the tall enemy soldier jumped on top of me, knocking me flat to the ground. Within seconds, I saw his shining bayonet hovering in the air, ready to kill me. I thought that very soon I would become a bloody chunk of meat on the ground.

But fortunately, God didn't take my life.

Thump!

I thought I must be dreaming. It was Lu. Out of nowhere he suddenly appeared and jumped onto the enemy soldier, using all of his canine strength to push him away.

"Oh my God! Lu!"

That night I held Lu in my arms as I slept. He breathed noisily and licked my face and neck. I had no idea how he'd managed to run more than 100 kilometers to follow our squad. Maybe it was fate that connected us at difficult times when we needed each other most.

When I woke up the next morning, Lu was staring at me as if there was something on his mind. I didn't know what he was thinking about. If he were human, I figured, those eyes would be judgmental.

Three days later, we seized the entire city and the airport. It was an important battle. Then a few days later we received some new recruits from the North and launched an attack near the central highlands. Lu came with us. Nobody wanted to leave him behind now, even the cranky political instructor, so Lu accompanied us into battle. He helped us find a group of civilians who were awaiting death in the jungle—they'd mistakenly run away with the withdrawing troops and had gotten lost deep in the highlands. They were both Vietnamese and Montagnard, children and adults, curled helplessly next to a *sang-le* tree, their lips cracked and dry from thirst and hunger.

We marched on, toward Saigon. The enemy had stationed defensive forces on the outskirts of the city. That first day they annihilated one of our units with seven tons of bombs, but we kept fighting, all through the night. Lu was by our side the entire time.

Around noon on the second day of fighting, our squad stopped at an empty lot between two houses. Gunshots rang out all around us. There were bullets everywhere, and the air was smoky and hot from all the burning fires. While we were lying there, taking cover, a group of children came running down the middle of the street, dodging bullets. Immediately Lu jumped up and went toward them. The kids were cowering against a wall, terrified and screaming. I'm not sure what they thought, seeing this spotted dog in the middle of the burning, deserted street. With his mouth, Lu grabbed the first kid by the collar of his shirt and tried to drag him into a ditch off the side of the street. But the gunfire was everywhere, and almost immediately bullets pierced Lu's furry chest and then danced over the rest of his body.

We went over to the ditch where Lu had fallen. Trying to save the kid, Lu had lost his life. He was dead. His blood was all over the street. His four legs were stretched out in front of him and his eyes were closed, as if he were sleeping. He had no idea, certainly, why these human beings had killed him.

The fallen soldiers from my regiment were buried on a high hill, on the outskirts of the city. We buried Lu with them. No one dared stop us from doing so. Next to the grave we placed a wooden tombstone. It read, "Lu. Squad 3. Regiment 72. Died on April 16, 1975."

"Farewell," I mumbled, as I fired my machine gun up into the air. I was crying, and through the tears I saw strange images in the rising gun smoke. Battalion after battalion of fallen soldiers marching together in unison, and then Lu, galloping toward the endless horizon and disappearing among the wandering clouds in the rainy, southern April sky.

The next day we marched into Saigon. The war was over.

2 / WHITE CLOUDS FLYING

BAO NINH

Bao Ninh is Vietnam's most internationally renowned writer, known primarily for his novel *The Sorrow of War*, which was published in English in 1994. He was born in 1952 as Hoang Au Phuong in Nghe An but has lived most of his life in Hanoi. At the age of 17 he joined the North Vietnamese Army, where he was one of only 10 soldiers from the 456 in his unit to survive the war. Most of his writing deals with the lingering psychological trauma of war. Though he has won nearly all of Vietnam's top literary prizes and honors, his work is often considered controversial at home because it does not present the war effort as noble and heroic. On the contrary, Ninh's writing often treats the war as a cause of deep, ongoing psychological and emotional suffering. "White Clouds Flying" was first published in 1997 and features themes present in much of his work: the role of tradition in an increasingly modernized society, the small absurdities of everyday life, the persistent sorrow of war trauma and loss.

It was raining when the airplane took off. The sound of the landing gear retracting up into the body of the plane seemed louder than usual, putting the cabin on edge. I wished that I'd listened to my wife's suggestion. I should have canceled this trip—it was a bad day to travel, with bad weather.

Suddenly the entire aircraft lifted up into the air. Next to me, directly to my right, sat a man wearing a suit. He looked pale. His eyes were closed and his lips trembled.

Meanwhile, I clutched the armrest tightly. I felt like a tiny being who had been dangled over a canyon that was growing deeper and deeper.

"Clouds are floating in the sky! Do you see them?" said an elderly woman sitting in the window seat, to the right of the man in the suit.

Once the plane had reached a desirable altitude, it flew straight and level. The electric seat belt sign was turned off, though fluffy clouds were still flying outside the windows.

"The clouds are so close to us, aren't they?" the elderly woman said. "I can touch them with my hands, just like I touch the leaves on the trees in my garden."

The man wearing a suit opened his eyes. His lips were still closed tightly. He seemed nervous and cranky.

"I don't know why people say airplanes can fly above the clouds," the elderly woman said.

The man in the suit remained silent.

"There's no direction here in the sky, so how do we know which way to go?" the woman asked.

But nobody answered her question, so she didn't ask anything else. Instead she sat quiet and still for a moment. She was holding a rattan sack. Her small body seemed to sink deeper into the seat. When a flight attendant came past, pushing a cart down the aisle to serve the passengers breakfast, the elderly woman refused to accept her tray of food. She said she was not used to eating without a bowl and a pair of chopsticks, and anyway, she'd already eaten an early breakfast. Besides, she said, an old person like her didn't have much money. The flight attendant politely explained that the woman need not worry since the food was included in the cost of the ticket.

"No wonder it costs two million *dong* for a round-trip ticket!" the woman said. "When my son's air force friends offered me this ticket, they said it cost only a few hundred thousand *dong*. They were being very thoughtful, because in the countryside we don't talk about millions—a thousand and a hundred are already hard enough to earn!"

The elderly woman lowered her tray table but didn't put her food on it. Instead she put everything she'd been served into her rattan sack. She didn't eat anything. When the flight attendant came by again to serve drinks, the woman asked for only a glass of water.

"Are we close to the Ben Hai River?" she asked the flight attendant.

"Well," the flight attendant said, glancing at her watch, "in about fifteen minutes, ma'am, we'll be crossing the 17th parallel air zone. But we're flying over the ocean, ma'am, not the river exactly."

"When we get to that area, will you please open this round window here for me so I can get some fresh air?" the elderly woman asked.

"Oh no—it can't be opened." The flight attendant laughed.

Outside the window, the sun was shining. For a moment the wings of the airplane glittered in the bright sunlight, but it was only a short moment. The sky was still full of clouds.

I felt a little dizzy, as if I were going round and round on a Ferris wheel. It was probably the storms over the central highlands that had created air pockets, because suddenly we experienced some turbulence, which caused some commotion among the passengers in the cabin. There was a noise that sounded like something cracking underneath us.

The man in the suit struck a match to light a cigarette. Although I myself was a heavy smoker, the smoke annoyed me. He should have waited to light up until after he got off the airplane—he shouldn't have just disregarded the "No Smoking" sign right in front of him. But he was obviously scared, which explained his oblivious behavior.

Carefully, I glanced over at him. The cigarette smoke and his huge shoulders blocked my view of both the elderly woman and the window.

"Hey you, Miss Flight Attendant!" The man stood up suddenly, straightening his suit jacket. "Is this an airline or a noodle stand? An airplane or a pagoda, huh?"

"I beg you . . ." the elderly woman said quietly. "Sir, I beg you. Today is the anniversary of my oldest son's death. It has been thirty years, and now I have a chance finally to visit the place where he died."

The man in the suit hurriedly stepped over me to get to the aisle. His face was red—he looked angry and disgusted.

The elderly woman sat quietly, bent over, her skinny hands held in prayer against her chest. On her tray table she had laid out a vase of flowers, some green bananas, a few rice cakes, and three incense sticks standing in a glass of dry rice. There was a small framed photo leaning against the cup of rice.

The flight attendant hurried over. But she stopped right next to me all of a sudden and didn't say a word. She observed in silence.

The aircraft began to climb higher above the clouds, making the floor of the cabin steep. The shrine the elderly woman had set up tilted and slid to one side. I reached over to hold the framed photo so it wouldn't fall. I could see that the photo had been cut out from an old newspaper, but the pilot in it looked very young.

Smoke from the burning incense gently curled in the air above our seats. The incense emitted a pleasant smell. Outside the window was the bright, endless ocean.

3 / LOUSE CRAB SEASON

MAI TIEN NGHI

Mai Tien Nghi was born in 1954 and lives in the northern city of Nam Dinh. A veteran of the war with America, he has worked as a middle-school math teacher since being discharged from the army in 1976. He began writing seriously in 2006 and has published more than fifty short stories and two novels. His work often portrays the harsh realities of war, as experienced by soldiers as well as civilians. Mai Tien Nghi has said that he wrote "Louse Crab Season" to highlight the difficulties many veterans faced in the postwar period, once they had returned to domestic life. He is currently at work on a novel about the war that addresses the consequences for both the communist North and the former Republic of South Vietnam.

It was early evening. The sun had almost gone down already. To the west there was only a small yellowish glow in the sky. It was the end of autumn, and the weather was chilly. Cold dry winds seemed to blow constantly, and when they stopped blowing people heard the sounds of ocean waves lapping the shore like a long sigh. The ocean was sad and lonely because the exciting days of summer were over.

Near the ocean, there was a river running through the rice fields that was also lonely. Its surface looked dark purple in the twilight. A raised dike bordering the rice fields separated the sky and the water with a straight line. Along the line appeared the shadow of a man walking wearily. His silhouette looked like a scribbled question mark.

The man walking wearily at twilight was Tran Xuan Vop. He had just finished fishing in the river and was now on his way home. As he walked, Vop's thoughts turned to griping about his fate: *Why do humans suffer? Why is my life so miserable?* When Vop had returned home from his military service years earlier, his wife's thirst had been like a desert during a quick, heavy rain. Their five children were born one right after another: Ha, Ngao, Gion, So, and Vang. Vop gave them these names because they were all girls and the names seemed to match the sound of his own. Vop sweated and toiled tirelessly in the rice fields, dug up clams, hunted crabs, and cast fishing nets, but he still was unable to put enough food on the table for seven people. His children quacked like wild ducks. In fact, they were an entire family of wild ducks—one mother duck and five ducklings. Vop couldn't bear all the complaints, the nagging, the derisive comments about him being a worthless man because he failed to provide for his family. Sometimes he felt like giving up completely, but he knew this was impossible. He couldn't take his own life by jumping in the river. *If I died,* he said to himself, *all of you would be homeless.*

As he walked along the rice paddy dike, Vop all of a sudden looked down at the river. Its water was black—it resembled thick black jelly. He thought the water was very mysterious and must contain thousands of deaths. When he looked toward the mouth of the river, near where it ran out to the ocean, he noticed a floating object. It looked like a giant sea crab bobbing in the water. The crab was dead. Vop rubbed his eyes. No—it wasn't a crab, he could see now in the opaque twilight, it was a small covered bamboo boat,

floating along the surface of the water. It looked empty. It was probably someone's boat that had not been secured properly. In less
than an hour, the current would drag the boat out to sea and it
would be lost forever.

Vop ran along the dike, toward the mouth of the river, until he
was standing directly across from the boat. *Well, I should swim out
there and bring it to shore so that the owner can come collect it tomorrow,
and maybe he'll even give me a little money,* Vop thought, jumping into
action immediately. He took off his clothes, rolled them into a bundle, and hid the bundle under a bush on the side of the dike.
Wearing only his underwear, he ran toward the river. But after a
few steps he stopped. *It's so dark out now, and nobody's around,* he
thought, removing his underwear. *Besides, this type of fabric is easily ruined by seawater.* He ran back to the bush and hid his underwear with the rest of his clothes, then returned to the river and
jumped in.

Vop shuddered as his body touched the cold water. *No big deal!*
he said to himself. *Nothing is easy, certainly not earning money . . .*

He was familiar with the river water and so swam quickly and
easily over to the boat. But once he touched the oars, he paused all
of a sudden and plunged down into the water.

*It looks like someone is inside the boat. I've got to be careful, or they'll
think I'm a thief. Maybe I should just go back before they see me. Actually,
it seems like there's more than one person in there.*

Vop held the side of the boat and craned his neck to look inside.
In the dim light shining over the front of the bow he could make
out two naked bodies in an intimate embrace. His ears were full
of water, so he shook his head to get the water out. He could hear
their loud breathing, their moaning, and the occasional shriek that
reminded him of cats during mating season.

The couple in the boat were unaware of the third person watching them. The woman sat on the man's belly. Vop could see her
full, round breasts swinging back and forth as if the breasts were

dancing, and her long hair was untied. Suddenly his own body began to get hot and hard. Vop leaned in closer and continued to watch.

The woman was like a maniac. She placed her hands on the man's chest and moved her body back and forth like a carpenter smoothing wood with a hand planer. When the woman arched her back, Vop recognized who she was—a woman who lived in his neighborhood.

Your eyes are always wet and you're a horny woman, Vop thought. *Why is she having sex with her husband here? But wait—her husband has very dark skin, and this guy . . .*

All of a sudden Vop coughed. The sound rang out loudly across the river.

The couple froze. Then the man, who was lying down, rushed to the stern and grabbed the oars.

Ah, so he is not her husband, Vop thought, as he turned and started to swim away. *She's just sleeping around.*

But the man had started rowing the boat in a hurry. The oars slapped the water around Vop violently. They were like two sharp blades churning the water. One of the oars traveled down Vop's belly, practically cutting him open, but was stopped by his penis, which was still erect.

Vop sank deeper into the water. He felt dizzy and coldly numb around his belly. Desperately he swam to shore, and when his feet finally touched the muddy soil, his head felt completely empty. Looking back, he saw the boat speeding away and the oars churning fast. The boat seemed to metamorphose again into a giant sea crab as it vanished into the dark river.

Vop's stomach pain felt unbearable. He reached down to his groin.

Oh no!

The sky, the river, and the water all became one, dense and black. The pain was like an arrow piercing his entire body—stomach, heart, lungs, head. The dense blackness all around was overwhelming. Vop fainted.

※ ※ ※

It was August, the beginning of the louse crab season. After the heavy storms, thousands of louse crabs had come to shore, as if God wanted to compensate the poor villagers for his destructive acts.

In the vastness of the sea, the muscular male crabs mated with the flirtatious female crabs. As a result, millions of tiny crabs were born. They looked like little lice. The mother crabs felt no responsibility toward their tiny offspring and abandoned them to the sea. The sea was their birthplace but also a challenging place to survive. They floated among the aggressive waves, pulled every which way by the rising and falling of the tides. Their survival had to do mostly with luck. Most of the louse crabs died in the dry sand of the shore. Their tiny corpses became black, minuscule grains on the beach that together formed a long black line that resembled dry blood stains around the mouth of a fierce carnivore who had just consumed raw meat. Only a small number of the tiny crabs were pushed farther inland by the tides, where they managed to survive in the water of the river mouth.

These surviving louse crabs were very valuable. People caught and sold them to sea crab hatcheries where they would be carefully raised until the day when they would be served at fancy parties. The cooked crabs made buffet tables look even more luxurious because of their vibrant red color. Their large, strong legs looked delicious. The boiled red crabs made people whose faces already were red from drinking alcohol even more excited.

In order to catch the tiny crabs, the fishermen had to leave at twilight on days when the tide would be high. They used a tool called a *riu*—a thin net that resembled mosquito netting. They stretched the *riu* net using two long bamboo poles; the poles were bound together at one end while at the top they spread open, fanning out the *riu* net. To make the net sit deeper in the water, the fishermen put pieces of heavy lead on the upper part and stitched a three-meter-long sac to the bottom.

At high tide, the fishermen stood in the water up to their necks and used all their strength to pin down the *riu* over the seawater that poured into the river. The sac attached to the end of the *riu* struggled in the water like the tail of a giant python as the fishermen pushed forward, trapping the crabs in the net. After a few hours of this, the fishermen went to the shore, emptied the *riu* sac, and used flashlights worn on their heads to separate crabs from sea detritus. The crabs were as tiny as lice, and one needed excellent vision to see them. That's why it was impossible to catch them with bare hands. The fishermen used chicken feathers to gently and meticulously gather all the tiny crabs and store them in bottles of seawater.

All night long they repeated these steps. On lucky days they could catch hundreds of crabs. But often they came home empty-handed. Only nature could determine when exactly the louse crabs would appear. The village was happy when the fishermen were able to catch many crabs, but then the calculating market traders would lower the price and the village would make very little money. On the other hand, when not many crabs were caught the price would go up. The village people put up with cold and hunger in order to earn only about fifty *dong*.

※ ※ ※

I didn't want my daughters to live the life of a louse crab. They were girls with unpredictable fates and no clear destiny. I must live. I must persevere. But that fateful night—the night I saw the couple in the boat—had directed our lives down a treacherous path. Still, I had no choice—I kept walking, despite the thorns in my feet and the harsh words targeted at me.

When I opened my eyes after passing out that night, the sky was still black. I knew that I was lying on the dike in the middle of the rice paddy, but I couldn't stand up. My pain seemed to be caused by an invisible hook running through my private parts and latching me to the ground. I tried very hard to stand but could only sit up. With all my energy, I dragged myself across the dike, like the time back in the military when we'd learned how to roll and crawl across the ground.

I was exhausted after about ten meters and collapsed. There was some sort of buzzing sound around my ears, and I imagined that it was encouragement:

Vop, keep trying! You don't want to die here, do you? You've been able to survive after being on the precipice between life and death many times. You must live!

The image of my five children popped into my mind. Yes—I must live!

I don't know how long exactly it took me to reach the edge of the village. I knew that my five children were waiting patiently for me at home—I could imagine their dirty faces and skinny arms waving at me. I kept crawling. Maybe someone would see me if I made it just a little farther. I pulled on bushes to drag my body. Thorny plants punctured my hands. The grass beneath me was wet and slippery. I felt so cold. My teeth chattered. My body was wet. I had no clothes on. I could feel the cold spreading and worsening the pain from my groin. Exhausted, I couldn't go any farther and collapsed.

In the silence of the night, I heard the sound of a church bell. It seemed like people were coming closer. I knew that some villagers went to church early to attend morning mass.

God have mercy—they saved me!

I was only half conscious. I saw a white sheet and heard quick footsteps and hushed whispers:

"It was damaged. We must amputate . . ."

I heard the sound of scissors opening and closing, and knives clanging against a metal tray.

Even in my half-consciousness, the pain was inevitable.

%% %% %%

When I'd confronted death before, I had tried to survive. But now I wanted to die. I wanted to die because of the gossips, the judgmental looks, and my family's cold attitude. The injury that deprived me of my manhood and the fact that I'd been stark naked in the cold night were the reasons they all made fun of me.

In the hospital, they thought I was a grotesque being, even among the other unfortunate and deformed patients. The other patients moaned and complained and demanded things from their relatives and the doctors. But I had to cower in the corner like a strange animal caught by a hunter. I was surrounded by curious people who made remarks and pointed at me. Every day, my oldest daughter brought me food. The expression on her face looked cold. "Dad, please eat!" she'd bark at me. My wife never paid me a visit. I hated her frigid demeanor. I had done nothing wrong. Who would listen to me if I tried to explain? I wanted to shout, *Let me talk!* But nobody wanted to hear my side of it. Meanwhile, the village gossips exaggerated my story. They said I was worse than a promiscuous man who had his ears cut off for messing around with another man's wife. In their eyes, the promiscuous man deserved his punishment. It was the same thing in my case—they thought losing my penis was a well-deserved punishment.

I knew that I couldn't take much more of this, that I must speak up. I didn't want my children, all girls, to bear the burden of my disgrace. I didn't want other people to think badly about my family.

But how could I defend myself if nobody would listen?

I remembered a painful life lesson I'd learned during the war. For an entire month my battalion had been surrounded by the enemy. Soon we ran out of rice and salt. There was nothing but chili powder. We ate the roots of wild banana trees and continued to fight the enemy. But boiled banana tree roots without salt were bitter and tasteless. After a few days, we couldn't stand to eat them anymore. If we tried to eat the banana tree roots, we vomited. So we started to starve. We desperately craved rice and salt. Our bodies turned haggard like those of drug addicts and our limbs swelled with fluid from edema. Our cook finally came up with the idea of using the chili powder on the banana tree roots, but the following day everyone in our battalion was constipated. We went into the woods to empty our bowels, sitting there for hours so that our rectums became badly irritated. We didn't eat anything else after that, despite our hunger. We didn't want to waste precious time and energy and experience more pain.

One day, I chose a private spot in the woods to go to the bathroom. Almost an hour passed, but I was unable to go. Suddenly my legs froze—I heard footsteps approaching, and the sound of someone pushing back leaves. I thought it might be a commando, so I panicked and hid in a thick bush. But it turned out to be my battalion commander. He stopped right in front of my hiding spot.

Did he think I'd done something wrong? Had he followed me because he thought I was exchanging information with a spy? I held my breath. The commander looked around. Then, from his shirt pocket, he pulled out a small paper package wrapped in plastic. Craning my neck, I saw that it was a package of salt. The salt grains were almost as big as kernels of corn. I gulped, swallowing my saliva, which was tasteless and somewhat fishy. The commander looked around again to make sure he was alone; then he placed a grain of salt on his tongue and closed his eyes. I also closed my eyes and tried to imagine the taste of salt. But it didn't work—my throat was dry and my mouth felt hot. My thoughts turned suddenly to a fellow soldier who had died only a few days earlier. He'd been severely wounded and had lost a lot of blood. Before he died, he begged for some salt. Everyone in the battalion had cried in that moment, even the commander. But look at him now! Later, I told the head of our platoon what I had seen in the woods. That same day, I was called into the battalion command office where I reported everything in detail. Everyone listened in silence. Then the battalion commander broke the ice with a question: "You accuse me, but do you have any evidence?" Immediately they accused me of slander, impugning the dignity of our battalion commander, and spreading rumors that would dampen our unit's fighting spirit.

After this incident, though I tried very hard on the battlefield and fought bravely and was awarded several medals, I was never admitted to the Party. If I'd been a Party member, I might have been considered for a government position in my village after the war. And I wouldn't have had to live like I have.

I already knew the difficulties of trying to share the truth. If I told people what I'd seen that night on the river, who would believe me? Besides, I would have to reveal the name of the promiscuous woman, even though her husband was still alive and healthy and they seemed like a happy couple. It was only normal, I figured, that people told lies and betrayed each other for moments of carnal pleasure. If I revealed the truth, the couple would break up and their children would be homeless.

But it was impossible for me to stay silent. So I told people about it, only I didn't mention the woman's name. Nobody believed me. They said that I'd fabricated the whole story while I was in the hospital. They laughed and hated me even more.

My beloved family's cold attitude drove me crazy. After I left the hospital, my wife started avoiding me. She didn't want to talk, or sleep in my bed. She even refused to eat with me. At every meal we were left waiting for her while the food got cold.

I put up with this for about ten days. Then, finally, I told my wife the name of the promiscuous woman one day when my children were still at school. Right away, my wife ran to the couple's home to verify the story. The husband listened to what my wife was saying and became furious while his wife cried and called me names—bastard, son of a bitch, slanderer. "You were drunk that night, and I stayed home with you," the wife said to her husband. "I didn't go anywhere. This is slander! Where's the evidence? He just wants to disgrace other people!" To honor and preserve her dignity, the wife ran into the kitchen and got a rope to commit suicide. But her husband believed his wife and took the rope away from her. Within an hour the woman's husband showed up at my house carrying the rope. He didn't say a word. He just put the rope around my neck and pulled until I fell down. Then he punched my face until my nose started to bleed.

It was the same life lesson I'd learned in the military, only more intense. But back then, at least I was still a soldier. Now I'd been robbed of my manhood, and this made people think I was depraved, including my wife. She treated me now like an animal. And my children didn't want to be close to me since I was called a depraved man and a eunuch. I was all alone among my own family.

But even worse was the fact that I, as a man and former soldier, could no longer fight in the carnal battle because I'd lost my gun. There were other "depraved" men in the village, but only I had been castrated, people said, because of my so-called extreme depravity. This gave my wife the right the flirt with other men.

She was in her early thirties and still had a strong sex drive. At first she was tactful about going out with other men. But she eventually concluded that I was the one who had betrayed her, so she had to take revenge. She could never forgive me, because forgiveness was for those who could heal a broken relationship. We couldn't be happy just by sitting down, looking at each other, and saying, "I love you." Happiness also required carnal pleasure. Even if our love was pure, sex was a must.

Though I was unable to have sex, it seemed like my wife's sex drive increased tremendously. Eventually she started telling me about her sexual encounters with other men. At first they did it in private places, but then they started doing it right in my house. I felt powerless and deeply insulted. I couldn't stand it any longer and thought about committing suicide.

But I knew that I must live—live for my children. I would not let them go hungry and drop out of school. For over a year, I lived in a hut built for a duck herder out in the fields near the mouth of the river. I sent my children all the money I earned and only kept enough to live on. I didn't want to see or interact with anyone.

%. %. %.

Vang, Vop's youngest daughter, went to the village pier every day. The *riu* fishermen, after plunging themselves into the river water all night, came to the pier in the morning to sell their crabs to traders from Hai Phong and Quang Ninh. Vop was no longer a young man, but he still went *riu*ing for louse crabs every day during the season, using a pair of old reading glasses to see the crabs more clearly.

Vang didn't have school in the mornings, so as soon as she woke up she would run to the pier and meet Vop, then take some money back to her mother. Taking a break from selling his crabs, Vop embraced his daughter and smelled her hair, which was moist from the early morning mist. When Vang asked why he didn't live at home anymore, Vop got teary-eyed. "I have to live here to earn money for you and your sisters to go to school," he replied. "Why do other people live at home but still come here to catch crabs?" she asked. "Well, they are different," Vop said. He changed the subject by asking about her sisters.

Every day, Vop gave his daughter almost all the money he made from selling louse crabs, clams, and anything else he'd managed to catch in the river, so she could take it back to her mother. He kept only a few thousand *dong* to buy food. The crab season this year had been good. Vop hoped that his children would have everything they needed for school. He started to feel that maybe life was worth living after all and that he wanted to see his children grow up.

One morning, as usual, Vang went to the pier very early. The night before, she'd seen a woman talking for a long time with her mother. After the woman left, Vang's mother embraced her and said, "Tomorrow go tell your dad to come home. Do you love him?" "Yes, I do," Vang replied. Then she asked, "Do *you* love him, Mom?" Her mother said nothing, but Vang saw tears in her eyes.

At the pier the next morning, Vang waited excitedly for over an hour but didn't see her father. She wondered if maybe he was sick and ran to his hut near the mouth of the river. The hut was cold and contained only a bamboo bed and a neatly folded military blanket. Vop wasn't there. Then Vang looked out toward the river. Across the river she saw two *riu* poles and hair floating on the surface of the gently undulating water. Someone had drowned. Vang shouted and started running. The entire village rushed to the mouth of the river.

Vop was dead. After many days of *riu*ing he'd discovered a secret spot, farther back from the mouth of the river, where there were even more louse crabs. But he didn't know that when the water rose the current became more aggressive. It pushed him into a churning whirlpool in the middle of the river where his feet couldn't touch the bottom. The submerged *riu* net was like a giant python as the whirlpool wrapped it around Vop's body. He drowned standing up, like someone who had been wrapped in a cocoon.

They brought Vop's body to shore and removed the *riu* net from around him. Then they placed Vop in his small hut. Because he had died in the river, the funeral took place right there in the hut. They purchased a coffin, which was quickly made, the yellow varnish still wet. Before his body was placed in the coffin, they cut the *riu* net and used it to line the inside, so that when Vop's body was eventually dug up on the anniversary of his death, as tradition dictated, all of his bones would be there.

The large *riu* net overflowed down the sides of the coffin, leaving marks in the wet varnish. The final closed coffin looked like it was covered with a dirty black net. The undertakers looked at the coffin with disappointment since they hadn't been careful in their work.

"It's not a problem," one guy said. "The Veterans Association will come by soon to cover the coffin with the ceremonial red cloth. Don't worry."

But another sighed and said, "Unfortunately he wasn't a member of the Veterans Association, so no red cloth for him."

"But he used to be a soldier!" another said.

"I know that," the other guy said. "But after that disgraceful incident, they took away his membership."

In the golden sunset a line of people, heads bowed, walked quietly along the dike, carrying the coffin toward the village. It was as if Vop's coffin were bobbing on the waters of a human river. The mournful sounds of funeral drums and trumpets mixed with the sound of crashing waves in the distance. The river water began to rise. It was cold outside. The year's louse crab season would end very soon.

4 / BIRDS IN FORMATION

NGUYEN NGOC TU

N guyen Ngoc Tu was born in 1976 in Ca Mau, the southern-most province of Vietnam. She is known as a prolific and popular southern writer who captures the typical lifestyle and colloquial language of southern Vietnam, particularly the Mekong Delta. Her characters are often sincere, hardworking rural people—fishermen and farmers—forced to deal with the often cruel and capricious vicissitudes of life. She is most famous for her 2006 collection of short fiction titled *Endless Field (Canh dong bat tan)*, which has been translated into Korean, Swedish, English, and German and was adapted into a 2010 Vietnamese film called *Floating Lives*. The narrator in "Birds in Formation" speaks from a generational vantage point reflective of Nguyen Ngoc Tu's own—that of someone born after the end of the war. The story highlights how the war remained present in Vietnamese domestic life for decades after 1975 and the emotional and psychological challenges of uniting a country that had seen its people, sometimes even within the same family, end up on opposing sides of the conflict.

It was a day in October, around noon, and we had both skipped our midday nap, like usual. Vinh was sitting on the branch of a tamarind tree in the front yard, chewing on an unripe mango and occasionally dropping the fruit's skin on my head. His mouth was dripping with spit. This annoyed me, but I just smiled and didn't say anything. If I retaliated, I would be falling directly into his trap. And besides, if we started fighting everybody would know that we had snuck outside instead of taking a nap, and we'd get yelled at.

Because I didn't respond, Vinh eventually got bored and stopped trying to provoke me. We were both quiet. Sunlight pierced the leaves of the trees and created flecks of light around the yard. Every now and then, a breeze would blow some tamarind leaves to the ground, mixing them with the dog hair and the dirt and the flecks of light.

I was fourteen back then and had experienced countless boring early afternoons just like this one. We were at the age when we weren't interested in taking a nap or running around and playing. If Grandma hadn't begun to cry on that particular day in October, those lazy midday lulls would have slipped my mind and I wouldn't be saddened, as I am still to this day, whenever I come across a similar scene in our languid front yard flecked by the midday sun.

At first, when I heard the soft sobbing, I thought it was coming from Vinh and looked up at the tree. But his eyes were wide and he was staring back down at me.

"It's Grandma," he said.

"She's crying," I said.

Then we started calling for the adults: "Grandma is crying! Dad, Grandma is crying!"

Soon everyone was awake and had surrounded Grandma. She was still in bed. She'd probably just woken up from her nap.

"Mom," my father said. "Why are you crying? Are you in pain?"

Grandma shook her head and continued to cry. As soon as she wiped away her tears, more ran down her cheeks. We tried to comfort her, but it wasn't working. We looked at one another wondering, *Who made Grandma cry?* Then suddenly she stopped crying for a moment and took my father's hand.

"Why did you shoot my son Ut Hon?" she asked softly.

Much later in my life, after I had experienced various ups and downs, I would still swear that no words caused me more distress than my grandmother's question that day.

Everyone standing around the bed was still, except for my father, who stumbled backward as if an arrow had pierced his heart.

"Mom!"

"You shot and killed my son Ut Hon."

But Grandma kept repeating these words, which just made my father suffer even more, as if an arrow were being twisted deeper into his chest. Sometimes I cried to myself, because I felt like my father was slowly dying. Meanwhile, my mother knew nothing; she was too busy with her stall at the market. When she came home in the afternoons, she seemed surprised to find that Grandma refused to eat with us, turning her back to the table as she held her bowl and unhappily swallowed her food. She ate only what Vinh put in her bowl. Elderly people could act as stubborn and irrational as children sometimes.

Her behavior upset my father. A lot of times he would put his chopsticks down without finishing the meal. It was as if he were still bleeding from the wound caused by his mother's harsh words. He stared at her back, trying to understand. Had she seen something in a dream? Or was this merely behavior caused by dementia? Once she'd watered the vegetables we had stored in the refrigerator and planted some weeds in a water pitcher. Another time she'd looked around the table at all of us and asked, "Who are you? Why do you call me 'Grandma'?"

If Grandma had acted strange—if, for example, she'd climbed up a tree and started to sing or burned her clothes to heat a pot of water—I would not laugh, because what she did would not seem unusual. But her sobbing that day in October *was* unusual. She cried because of a war that had ended long ago. The war was over, and the wounds it had caused were now healed scars. At least that's what we thought, because when Vinh and I shot each other with water guns Grandma laughed until tears ran down her face. It wasn't until that day in October that I realized maybe she was actually crying out of sadness. Her tears were for the war in which my father and Uncle Ut Hon, Vinh's father, had fought on opposite sides.

It was difficult to understand Grandma. Some mornings she would act normal, as if nothing had ever happened. She woke up early, walked to the dining table, and ate a bowl of instant noodles that my mother had prepared before she left for the market. Meanwhile, my father still looked haggard. Grandma would ask, "You couldn't sleep? Why do you look so sad? Why are you staring at me like that?" But my father wouldn't say anything. Had Grandma already forgotten what had happened, or was she just trying to suppress her sadness?

Maybe her crying had been some sort of delirious episode, like when a drunken husband comes home and says to his wife, "My darling Diem!" even though his wife's name isn't Diem, and Diem probably isn't even a real person, just some fictional character in a film or a novel. But of course the wife becomes furious anyway.

Or like when Vinh used to point up at the sky and shout, "Look at those birds!" when really there wasn't anything in the sky, and I'd realize that he was trying to trick me again.

What Grandma had said to my father was cruel. Besides, the accusation didn't even make much sense. My father had been stationed in Saigon and Uncle Ut had been killed in a remote forest somewhere, far away from the city. My father didn't believe that he had shot Uncle Ut. But he still had to dig deep into his memory to be sure; there was a small possibility that his younger brother in fact might have once faced him in combat.

This thought ate away at my father. He wasn't able to live his life in the present. But we all tried to continue like everything was normal, even Grandma. Two months after the day she'd suddenly started crying, she was found sitting in the front yard stitching a pair of shirts. If somebody asked, "Who are you going to give those shirts to?" she would smile and respond, "To my grandchildren, Hien and Vinh." But the shirts were only about as big as an open palm.

To Grandma, time was malleable. She couldn't help mixing the present with the past. After a good sleep, she could wake up and suddenly be transported twenty years back in time. Unfortunately, I wasn't old enough to do that. Otherwise, this ability would have allowed me to forget everything and live my life as it had been before that noonday lull in October. Before that was when my father had been a happy man, always smiling and being affectionate. He seemed always to remain calm, even when Vinh would start jumping up and down and teasing me like he wanted to box. Every morning, my father used to wake Vinh and me up and we'd run to a nearby park to kick a shuttlecock back and forth. That's what our lives had been like. Then suddenly Grandma cried one day after a long nap . . .

Human emotions are too fragile.

Vinh also acted differently after what happened. His personality started to change. He became quiet and sullen and refused to look me straight in the eyes. When he slept, he turned away so his back was toward me, which made me feel uneasy. Although I was lying right next to him, I still felt like I missed him tremendously.

Vinh had originally joined my family when his mother remarried. My father had sat him down next to me and said, "This is your brother." Vinh smiled, then rubbed his snot on my face as a greeting. Vinh was short and skinny, but he always won when we competed in snuggling up against Grandma's breasts. When we were older and shared our own bed, he would jab me with his elbow every night before falling asleep. He'd always been a naughty kid. His bad behavior went beyond what my family could have anticipated. Some of his antics included throwing his piss-soaked pants into a pot of duck porridge that was cooking on the stove in the kitchen, forcing a cat to suck a rat's nipple, and peeing into the fridge because he liked the feeling of the cold air on his penis.

Still, everyone in the family loved Vinh—they even pampered him, which made me sometimes want to cry with jealousy. To Grandma and Father, Vinh was just like Uncle Ut Hon, who had also been somewhat wild. When he was a kid, Uncle Ut used to scare the adults by chasing them with a piece of burning wood. And one time he poured hot water that had been used to boil a chicken into Grandma's teapot. When he got older, he dropped out of school and got married. One night, he left his new wife out in the swamp all by herself just to prove a point that people can survive without basic necessities and still be cheerful.

Vinh was just like his father, unpredictable and impulsive. I knew that my mother didn't love him, though. I had only seen her hug Vinh tightly one time, and I'd noticed that he had a kind of confused, lost look on his face, as if he could sense that the tight hug wasn't really for him.

For my father, raising Vinh had been an interesting challenge, but of course he would never complain. He had always been Grandma's obedient, passive son. He would sit wherever he was told to sit without asking why, and he'd always been very clean and neat, like a girl.

Whenever we played together, Vinh was always the leader, and he usually won all our games and competitions. I would be hurt but try to smile anyway. I knew that I still loved Vinh. I felt this most strongly when we honored the anniversary of Uncle Ut Hon's death every year. Holding a bundle of incense, Vinh would turn around to ask my father, "Uncle Hai, what should I say in my prayer?"

"I've told you before," my father would respond. "Say something like this: Today is the fifteenth of July of the lunar calendar. We respectfully invite you to come eat the food we're offering you here." But Vinh stumbled over the words in his prayer. As he planted the incense in the cup of dry rice, his face looked sad and disappointed, and I knew exactly why. Every year he said his father's name, but there was no reply.

On the day of Uncle Ut Hon's death anniversary, Vinh's mother would usually come for a visit. Sometimes Vinh made the mistake of calling her Auntie Ut, which is what I called her. Vinh would run around playing, and then when it was time for his mother to leave he'd just stand there with his hands on his hips watching her walk away. I could tell that he was standing like that to stop himself from collapsing with sadness.

I loved Vinh, and this pleased my father. My father and Uncle Ut Hon had lived together for twenty-three years, but their brotherhood had been characterized by emptiness and regret. Vinh and I were the next generation. We could continue that brotherhood and hopefully make it into something more positive. We could fill in the old painting with new colors. I was the slow, gullible one, while Vinh was smart and wild. As my father watched us playing, though, I noticed that his eyes usually looked sad.

My father was strict; I had to behave to keep him happy. I wasn't allowed to make mistakes, even small ones. I had the sense that my father was trying to teach me something—something beyond school lessons, or how to act at home. But what was it exactly? I thought about this question a lot, even at a young age. When he started taking me with him to the weekly community meetings, I wasn't sure why he wanted me to go. He rushed me through breakfast as if we were going to get there late, even though we were always the first ones to arrive and would end up just sitting there waiting patiently for everyone else. Father seemed serious during the meeting; he listened attentively while other people yelled and cursed and complained. We were always the last people to leave the meeting room, after we'd helped put away the chairs. On Independence Day and other national holidays, my father heeded the call from the community to hang the flag in front of our house. Again, I was sure he was trying to teach me something by doing this, but I didn't know exactly what. There was also our strange next-door neighbor, an old man who every morning would brush his teeth and spit onto our porch. My father never said anything to the man, and I felt disappointed in him at first, though I realized that it was probably better to avoid confrontation. I know now that he was actually protecting me. It wasn't until my school started the process of selecting outstanding students to be recognized by the city that I learned there was a stain in my father's background: the fact that he'd fought for the South during the war. Somehow knowing this made me more comfortable. A collection of official certificates of recognition was nothing compared to the peace of mind I now felt knowing about this. But my father still seemed sad. . . .

He knew that sometimes we had to pay a huge price for a small mistake. Because of his experience, he'd always had a fear of separation. And I think he suffered from a crushing feeling of self-loathing, which one day might have consumed him, even if it hadn't been for that lazy early afternoon in October.

People also can be punished for making no mistake at all. For example, Vinh turned his back on me because of a war in which neither of us had been involved. I caressed his hair because I wanted to look him straight in the eyes and hoped he'd turn around and say something like, "Stop it, Grandpa, or I'll punch you in the face."

But Vinh said nothing. Instead he pinned me to the ground, suffocating my chest with his knees. I struggled to free myself as I stared up into his dark eyes, which were spotted with small broken blood vessels.

"Vinh," I said, trying to smile, my mouth all twisted and contorted. "Don't play like that. We're brothers."

"Brothers..." Vinh repeated sarcastically. He laughed, then finally let me go. He walked away, still obviously agitated, as I lay there trying to catch my breath. My heart sank. I went down to the first floor and quietly watched Grandma as she slept. I wondered about how much she must have suffered, knowing that her two sons were fighting on opposite sides of the war. Was it any wonder that, with her unreliable memory, she had cried on that October day and still brought it up now, seemingly at random?

"My son Ut Hon waved at you cheerfully and jumped up and down saying, 'Brother Hai! It's me, Ut Hon!' But you shot him anyway. I can see it very clearly...."

Lazy early afternoons in October returned to our neighborhood. Nobody paid attention to the intricate flecks of light that danced on the ground of the front yard. At the market, which was never really crowded with customers, Mother was busy rearranging the racks of cigarettes she sold. Father wasn't interested in flecks of sunlight. He sat quietly as he typed up a customer's request for a land purchase. His face looked withered and his hands resembled pieces of dry bone. I knew he was tormented by the question, *Did I really shoot my own brother?* When Grandma took her nap now, her face usually wore a frown, and sometimes she'd moan quietly in her sleep. It seemed like her dreams were eating away at her life. Vinh and I still secretly skipped our noontime nap. In the yard, I climbed a tree and dropped dry branches on his head, hoping that he would take the bait and react, retaliate, and maybe rub his snot on my face or punch me and call me Grandpa. Then eventually we would smile at each other and everything would be back to normal.

5 / A CRESCENT MOON
IN THE WOODS

NGUYEN MINH CHAU

Nguyen Minh Chau (1930–1989) was born in the central northern province of Nghe An and is known mostly as a novelist. He is perhaps most famous for authoring a 1978 essay in the national *Military Literature Magazine* in which he called on his fellow writers to be less propagandistic in their writing and to depict the war with more realism and humanity. "A Crescent Moon in the Woods" was first published in 1970 and made into a film in 1980; in 2014 the story was performed as a musical at the Hanoi Military Theatre. The moon is a recurring symbolic trope in Vietnamese literature, often associated with romance and unrequited love. In this story, Nguyen Minh Chau juxtaposes the idyllic love between the characters Nguyet and Lam against the cruelty and everyday drudgery of the war.

The flame crackled as it burned the wick of the candle made from an old condensed milk can filled with oil. They were deep in the woods. It was quiet except for the sounds of a flowing creek in the distance and the persistently melancholic song of two lone birds. The time was past midnight, but a dozen drivers from the oil delivery team were still awake, scattered at random around a bamboo hut, some sitting, some standing. A folded piece of corrugated cardboard had been placed around the candle to diffuse the light that illuminated their tired faces. Outside the hut, the rough country road was gutted with bomb craters and knee-deep tracks from their trucks. It had been raining all night. The rain meant an opportunity for the transportation platoon to spend some downtime together. The atmosphere inside the bamboo hut was boisterous; sometimes their laughter seemed to shake the entire woods. Was there anything in life more jovial than a night like this when the drivers from various routes returned from their assignments and gathered together? You might expect them to want nothing but rest, especially after several sleepless nights behind the wheels of their trucks. But no one felt sleepy.

Before one person had finished their story, someone else was ready to tell theirs. Their minds were full of images collected during driving trips all across the countryside. And at this moment, on this night, those images were in competition to come alive.

"Are you finished yet?" said one driver who was lying in a dark corner of the hut. "It's my turn." He moved closer to the dancing flame of the makeshift candle behind the corrugated cardboard and began:

One night in early March, my truck pulled out from the K3 Storage Unit. My assistant driver was behind the wheel that day because I had to attend a meeting with senior drivers at the battalion headquarters. I would join him after the meeting. Let me tell you a little about my assistant driver. He was a young and happy recruit; he worked very hard, but he also liked to flirt. The story I am about to tell happened back when I was assigned to the Mekong Delta routes. It was flood season, but the enemy still attacked the area regularly. They targeted the underground bunkers and the trenches, especially around the Blue Stone Bridge where we were protecting the border from the enemy. That night, immediately after sunset, it began to rain. After the meeting, I left the battalion headquarters and was waiting for my truck at the top of a hill. I had my hammock under my arm, wrapped in plastic, and a flashlight around my neck. I was smoking and felt relaxed. For a person who drives all the time, a person whose life is chained to the cab of his truck, a quiet moment like this is quite rare. I crossed my legs and leaned against a tree on the side of the street, breathing out rings of smoke and staring up at the small sliver of a crescent moon in the sky. This peaceful moment was short-lived. Soon I started to get nervous as trucks came flying like racehorses down the road in front of me. My assistant driver wasn't among them. The darker it got, the more nervous and frustrated I became.

It was usually a relief when my truck was faster than the others, even by half a wheel. And for this trip I wanted to get an early start so we'd have enough time, when we returned from the delivery, to hide our truck in the Sang-Le woods. It was safe to hide the truck there, and it was close to where my sister worked. I had already asked my commander for permission to visit her. She'd written me a letter complaining that it had been three years since we'd last seen each other. But this was just my own personal concern. I was frustrated mostly because my assistant driver had been unable to get things done.

Then suddenly I saw him driving up from the bottom of the hill. When he came to a stop I started yelling at him for being so late. But he just ignored these reprimands and quietly handed me the paperwork and a receipt, then placed in the cabin a package of peanut sticky rice and a bottle of water mixed with sugar. "Have a safe trip," he said, winking and tapping my shoulder. He crouched and jumped down from the truck. On this trip I was assigned to be the only driver. My assistant driver said good-bye and started to walk away, but he paused and banged heavily on the truck door.

"Hey, Lam. On the receipt I noted that a spare tire is missing, and I got the storage keeper's signature to confirm that."

"All right," I said. I felt satisfied with what he'd done.

"There's one more thing," the assistant driver said. "But this one isn't written down on the receipt..."

"What is it?" I asked.

"There's a hitchhiker in the back who wants a ride to the Blue Stone Bridge."

"We're not supposed to take hitchhikers," I said, annoyed again. "You know that."

He gave me some excuses for breaking this rule, which all sounded logical enough. But I was still upset with him. I was sure that the person sitting in the back of the truck was a woman. I could imagine the scene perfectly: a shy woman, holding a white hat and standing at the door of the truck, while my assistant sat up in the cab with a grin on his face, asking her flirtatious questions as he finished a cigarette. How could he agree to give some woman a ride when our truck traveled through so many dangerous areas? But at the same time, how could one have refused and asked her to walk instead?

My assistant had already left, so I decided to get going. Before starting the engine I turned around to glance through the iron screen behind me, but I saw only darkness. The cab of the truck smelled like fresh rubber sap. I had no clue where exactly in the cavernous back of the truck the hitchhiker was sitting.

"Who's in there?" I asked, trying to make my voice sound as stern as possible.

No answer. But I could hear the spare tires shifting in the back of the truck and sounds like a chicken fidgeting in its nest. I figured that the hitchhiker must have heard my conversation with the assistant and was probably too scared to answer.

"Who's back there?" I repeated, less aggressively this time.

"It's me. Please give me a ride to the Blue Stone Bridge."

My guess wasn't wrong. It was a young woman's voice. Her voice sounded clear and calm—strong and confident, even.

"Male or female?" I inquired.

"Male."

"Come on," I said. "Don't mess with me. I could order you to get off. This is an army truck."

There was silence for a moment. Then I asked, "Why do you need a ride to the Blue Stone Bridge?"

"I am a road construction worker. Your assistant checked my ID. I have some business to take care of so I need to return to my unit."

"What kind of business?" I asked, skeptical. My tone was teasing. "Are you visiting your boyfriend there?"

"Yes," she replied, without hesitating. "I'm visiting my boyfriend."

Hurriedly I started the engine. It seemed strange that she'd respond so candidly. But her voice didn't sound like she was joking. Maybe she was being honest. . . .

"Who was she?"

"Yeah—who was this young woman?"

"Where did she come from?"

The other drivers chided the storyteller to finish his story.

"Be patient," he said calmly.

From the woods came the sounds of melancholy birdsong. The driver stood up and walked toward the old condensed milk can. Squinting from the oil smoke, he bent down and blew out the blue flame of the makeshift candle. The hut suddenly plunged into darkness. He continued his story:

Don't get too worked up about the woman just yet. Let her sit with the tires in the back of the truck for now. I have to explain something else to you first.

I have a sister who is an officer in a transportation unit located very close to the Blue Stone Bridge. If you drove one of the Mekong Delta routes four or five years ago, you probably remember the busy and productive atmosphere at the Blue Stone Bridge construction area. My sister Tinh was stationed there back then. There were hundreds of women on the construction team. One of them was named Nguyet, which means moon—a very beautiful name! Right out of high school, she volunteered for the construction teams in the Mekong Delta. Tinh treated Nguyet like a younger sister. She cared for her deeply because Nguyet was a hardworking and obedient girl. In her letters to me, my sister always mentioned Nguyet. Then in one of her letters she wrote, "I have thought seriously about this, and I've decided that I want to introduce you to Nguyet. She is very special, and it is difficult to find a woman like her these days." In another letter, she was even more insistent: "When I told Nguyet that I wanted to introduce you to her, she blushed. She didn't say anything, but if I talk about you, especially about how you ran away from home to enlist in the military, she listens closely. Try to come up here as soon as possible. I can tell that Nguyet is looking forward to meeting you."

Back then, I was an assistant driver and often drove in the North. I made a few trips down to the Mekong Delta and visited Tinh, but I had never met Nguyet. In my letters to Tinh, I usually included a few sentences asking about Nguyet and implying that I would like to meet her. I'm sure that Nguyet saw all those letters and knew that I wanted to meet her. In the isolated woods, of course, a letter must be shared with everyone. A few years went by, and my sister moved to Hanoi to attend college. Then the war against the Americans broke out. I had already been discharged from the army, but I reenlisted. Right away, the enemy bombed and destroyed many roads in the Mekong Delta and the central highlands. I had never married, but I'd long ago forgotten Tinh's letters and her friend Nguyet. Eventually, as the war continued,

Tinh left school and returned to the Mekong to help the construction teams near the Blue Stone Bridge. Again she wrote to me, talking this time about the enemy's constant bombing of the bridge and about the transportation units that were trying to protect the roads. These weren't new stories to me. But the most interesting part of those letters was this: Nguyet, she said, still thought about me. She was waiting for me, Tinh said. Over the years several men had proposed to her, but she'd always said no. Tinh said that Nguyet worked in the underground tunnels, a very dangerous assignment. But they still saw each other often. Nguyet was now a grown woman, more mature and courageous, and apparently even prettier than before.

As I read Tinh's letter, I felt moved and overwhelmed. It seemed hard to believe that after so many years living in the middle of constant bombing and destruction, a woman could still treasure in her heart the image of a man she had never even met. Deep in her heart a tiny sparkling thread had remained intact, despite the passage of time. Thinking about this made me happy, and I felt like I was indebted to Nguyet. I knew that I had to meet her, so I decided to write my sister and ask her to arrange a meeting on my day off. After completing my delivery run, I'd hide my truck in the Sang-Le woods and then make my way to Tinh's unit. Tinh would take me to see Nguyet, and I would stay for the day as a guest of the female transportation platoon.

That's where I was going that night I found the hitchhiker in the back of my truck. That particular night was quiet and peaceful. My truck ran smoothly on the road. As I gripped the steering wheel, I pictured myself laughing and having fun among the playful group of women. I knew that Nguyet would probably talk only a little, but that didn't matter. The women were all friends to us drivers. They were brave, sincere, and hospitable people.

I'd driven about ten kilometers when I ran into an artillery convoy descending the hill and had to pull over and stop.

Holding my flashlight, I slipped underneath the truck to check a light bulb. As I was unscrewing the bulb I heard a voice ask, "Is it an apple- or watermelon-sized bulb?"

"Who's there?" I called out.

"It's me."

Ah, it was the hitchhiker. She was standing in front of the truck. The beam from the flashlight illuminated the clean pink skin of her feet, her clean rubber sandals, and the hem of the black pants around her ankles. She can't be a construction worker, I thought. I got up and wiped my eyes with the backs of my hands.

"Hello there," I said, coming out from underneath the truck. "If I stop again, please don't get off like this."

"But I can't stand the awful smell of rubber in the truck. I just wanted to get some fresh air."

It was then that I noticed her beauty, there on the side of the road, in the beam of the headlights from the passing artillery trucks. Her beauty was simple and fresh—it made me think of mist-covered mountains. Most of the female construction workers were short and stout, but she wasn't like that at all. Her shirt hugged her slim waist perfectly and her thick hair was woven into two long braids. At her side she carried a bamboo bag and a white hat.

"Do you work at the Blue Stone Bridge tunnels," I asked, "or are you visiting someone there?"

"I work there," she replied. I could tell from her face that she was shy.

"Ah, I forgot to ask your name," I said.

"I am Nguyet," she said.

"Oh . . ." I said, pretending not to react to this information. I gave her a glance and then quickly turned away and opened the door to the cab of the truck.

"The smell of rubber is awful in the back," I said, holding the door open and inviting her in. "Please join me here in the cab."

The artillery convoy was so weighed down with stocks of ammunition that it made the roads and the mountains around us tremble noisily. I felt my heart leap into my chest. She purposely sat very close to the door, holding her bamboo bag neatly in her lap, leaving a big empty gap between us. I have to admit that I'd never sat next to a woman in the cab of the truck in all my driving career. But this was a special situation. I reached up and switched on the cabin light. I could see her looking around to examine my little cabin in a curious but hesitant way.

"Over where you work there must be many people named Nguyet, right?" I asked, trying to make my tone as polite and casual as possible.

"How did you know that?" She seemed shocked for a moment, then continued. "My unit has three Nguyets. One died, so there are only two of us left now. Another worker and me."

"When did the other Nguyet die?" I asked hurriedly, with a feeling as if someone else were asking this question.

"About three or four months ago, when the enemy bombed the Blue Stone Bridge. She fought very heroically and was a great person. Everyone grieved for her."

"Was she married?"

"No. But I think she had a lover."

I tightened my grip on the steering wheel. The ground underneath the truck seemed to be shuddering violently. I drove more slowly and cautiously.

"What about the second Nguyet?" I asked.

"She has four children. We tease her sometimes and call her Grandma Nguyet—she's older than the rest of us. Why are you so curious?"

I said something jokingly; I can't remember what exactly. Deep in my heart I felt extremely confused. Should I ask if she knew my sister Tinh? If I asked, everything would be clear. But I didn't want to seem too nosey about personal matters, especially on a trip like this. But still the thought kept running through my mind: between two women, one young and beautiful and sitting right next to me at this very moment in the cab of the truck and the other who had died heroically, which was the woman who had apparently harbored that tiny sparkling thread of love in her heart for over ten years? I felt this question tormenting my mind, like a red-hot rod painfully piercing my temple.

The truck gained speed as we rumbled down a hill. The enemy's bombs had practically destroyed the road ahead of us. Soil, rocks, and clumps of grass flew up onto the windshield as we drove. My instincts told me to slow down. Up ahead was a weak blue light . . .

"I don't hear any planes," I said, listening. "Where's that blue light coming from?"

The hitchhiker was sitting with her elbows against the door looking out the window. She turned toward me. "It's the moonlight," she said.

She was correct—it was the moon. Today was the first day of the month. I had been driving under this strangely haunting blue moonlight all night long without noticing it.

She seemed comfortable enough in her seat, staring out the window, watching the passing countryside. I struck a match to light a cigarette and switched gears to speed up. I felt suddenly embarrassed. I was an experienced truck driver who had been in many dangerous situations—how was I unable to distinguish between moonlight and artillery fire?

Through the windshield the moon looked gray and dim behind layers of clouds. Whenever the truck hit a pothole, the moon seemed to move back and forth; sometimes it disappeared, as if it had fallen into the dark of the woods. Around midnight, the northwestern winds blew the clouds apart until they dissipated altogether. The wind rustled the leaves that camouflaged the truck, making strange sounds. The sky above us seemed infinitely high and clear. In the darkness I could hear the vague sound of a bird singing. Then a thick fog descended on the road, blanketing everything around us so that it was all we could see. Every now and then we spotted the peak of a black hill or a mountain standing all by itself in the distance.

Our truck traveled through waves of fog. Out on the horizon, the silver crescent moon stood still, as if it had been frozen in time. Moonlight lit up the hitchhiker's seat. I'm not sure why exactly, but I felt extremely happy. In that moment, I believed sincerely that the woman sitting next to me was Nguyet, the same person my sister had always talked about. Every now and then, I'd secretly stare at her and her thick, sweet-smelling hair.

Suddenly she turned toward me and asked something, which I couldn't make out because I was so absorbed in looking at her. The moonlight made Nguyet's face look even more beautiful. I tried to stay focused on the road, which was full of potholes and illuminated up ahead in the moonlight.

"Is it true that drivers like you know a lot of people?" Nguyet said, repeating her question.

"Drivers like me are like migratory birds who live temporarily in different forests," I said. "Our friends are the roads and the moon."

I had no clue how I was able to be so poetic all of a sudden.

It was well after midnight by the time we reached the Blue Stone Bridge. By this time the moon had disappeared. We stopped chatting. I turned on the light and said, "From here on the enemy's planes are often on patrol."

"Don't worry," Nguyet replied. "I know this road well."

She showed me the way to the underground tunnels. The road was muddy and zigzagging, especially since I had to swerve the truck to avoid bomb craters. I paid close attention and drove carefully. I could feel the truck leaving huge, muddy tracks in the road. A few times the front wheels got stuck in a ditch off to the side, and Nguyet had to get out and help guide me back to the road. I put the truck in high gear and slammed my foot on the accelerator; the cab became heated and the front wheels spun frantically and gave off a burning smell as they slammed against the rocks.

Nguyet looked at the road and said, "The enemy keeps bombing this area. The road is still in very bad condition even though we keep filling the bomb craters with rocks."

I squeezed my hat in my hand and wiped the sweat from my face. I thought about having to say good-bye to Nguyet.

"Let me know where you want me to stop for you to get off," I said finally.

She could have gotten off at the first security checkpoint, but she wanted to accompany me until I crossed the river. She laughed. "It's very kind of you to give me a ride. How could I leave when you still need my help?"

I tried to make my tone serious as I responded, "Even if you had gotten off at the security checkpoint, I would never think you were the type of person to abandon your friends in a difficult situation."

"How do you know?"

"I just do."

We continued on. Soon I noticed water up ahead. A few days earlier, torrential rains had flooded the Blue Stone Bridge area; the water was over a meter high. I could hear water bubbling up into the truck's exhaust pipes. The truck rocked violently back and forth like an aggressive buffalo bathing in a river. The headlights shone on the water in front of us. Then the truck stopped moving altogether. We were stuck.

Suddenly, Nguyet jumped down from the cab.

"What?" I asked, confused. "Is it enemy planes?"

"Let me listen for a second," Nguyet said. Then she told me to turn off the lights. "The enemy can see the reflections of the lights on the water, even from far away."

It was dark all around us. I could hear the sounds of water sloshing against the sides of the truck. I tried to drive forward, but the truck just rocked back and forth and the steering wheel locked in place. I noticed then that my clothes were wet. It was an extremely cold night.

Nguyet, meanwhile, waded through the water carrying a rope from the truck, which she tied around the trunk of a tree. After struggling for a while, I was finally able to drive the truck up out of the water and onto a rocky part of the road. We were both out of breath as we stood side by side, coiling the rope.

Then suddenly the enemy planes arrived. They emerged from behind the steep mountains in the distance, giving off a roaring sound. I dropped the rope and ran for the truck, but Nguyet pulled me back and pushed me down into a ditch.

"They are carrying out coordinate bombing," she said calmly, studying the sky.

A sound like thunder rippled through the air. The ground trembled. In the few seconds of stillness we could hear the gentle sounds of a cricket batting its wings. Then pieces of earth—soil, rocks, plants, branches—began to fall all around us. In the distance, I saw the enemy parachuting from the planes. I tried to pull Nguyet toward me.

"If you get injured," she said, brushing me off, "you will lose the truck anyway. Just stay here."

But without hesitation I ran toward the truck. The sound of gunfire was everywhere. My truck was still intact, but the tires were burning. I put out the flames, then started the engine and saw Nguyet come running.

"Get the truck out of here quick," she said. "They will continue bombing this place."

"Okay," I said.

Nguyet had started to cough from all the smoke. I pulled her up into the cab of the truck and closed the door. I kept the headlights turned off and drove on with her help in navigating the dark, cratered roads. It seemed like the enemy was constantly above us, incessantly bombing and shooting. Nguyet continued to give me instructions: "Turn left . . . There is a crater up ahead . . . There is a hill and a turn . . ." When the road descended into total darkness, Nguyet got out and I drove slowly behind her, following her small, bright shadow. After a little while, I stopped the truck and parked it at the base of a tall cliff. I switched on the cabin light, and that's when I noticed blood on Nguyet's shoulder. Blood had dripped down onto her blue shirt. She was injured, though I wasn't sure exactly when she had been hurt. I could feel it intensely at that moment—I loved and admired her dearly. She looked down at her wound and smiled. She was beautiful, though her skin looked pale and she was soaking wet from head to toe. I pulled out a handkerchief stained with engine oil and covered her wound.

I wanted to take her back to her unit, but she said, "No, this is where I'm stationed. Go ahead—leave before sunrise, and don't worry about me. This is just a minor wound. I am perfectly fine." Wild roosters crowed somewhere around us. I still had to fulfill my assigned delivery duty, so we said good-bye. I held her bloody hands and promised, "Tomorrow I will come see you."

I got back in the truck and drove extremely fast to my outpost. I felt excited and happy, but still I worried about Nguyet. The image was burned in my memory—Nguyet in her blue shirt with a wounded shoulder, carrying her bamboo bag and walking away from the truck. Sometimes I pictured her looking back at me and smiling beautifully.

"So what happened next?" asked one of the comrades who was listening to the driver's story. "You went to visit her the next day, didn't you?"

The audience in the bamboo hut was still listening attentively, though it was already two o'clock in the morning. There were roosters crowing and birds chirping in the woods.

I drove very fast that night after saying good-bye to Nguyet, and when I arrived at the base and completed my delivery it was almost dawn. It was too late to drive the truck back to the Sang Le woods, so I hid it where it was and camouflaged it with leaves.

The next night, my commander assigned me another drive to the same outpost near the Blue Stone Bridge. This time, I was able to stop by my sister's unit for a short visit. The female construction workers' huts were located in a beautiful area. The women were always neat and took care of things better than the men; their huts were well kept and neatly organized. When I arrived, my sister Tinh and some other women gave me a warm welcome. These women liked to tease and joke around, but I wasn't in the mood. I looked at my sister Tinh. For the past two days, I'd been fairly confident that I'd already met the woman I'd heard about all those years before. But I also thought about the Nguyet who had died heroically three or four months ago.

Tinh took me inside the hut and asked, "Why didn't you come here yesterday? Nguyet took the day off to come here—she waited for you all day, but you didn't show up, so she went back to the headquarters."

"Why did she have to return to the headquarters?" I asked.

"She is attending a class for new Party members," Tinh replied.

While we were talking, a chubby woman carrying bamboo shoots entered.

"So, this must be your brother, Lam," she said. "He should have come and said hello to me. You're kind of cute. Are you a driver? You know you messed up, right?"

My sister Tinh laughed. I didn't know what she was talking about. Later I learned that she was the head cook of the unit and her name was Elderly Nguyet, my sister's close friend.

"You should have told her if you were interested or not," Elderly Nguyet said, blaming me for making the young Nguyet wait. "She was here yesterday. A soldier gave her a ride. She was injured during the drive here." Elderly Nguyet paused for a moment then asked, "You haven't seen her, right?"

She pulled me toward a far corner of the hut where a photo of my beloved Nguyet was hanging on the wall. I could tell that the photo was from several years earlier—Nguyet looked no older than a teenager. In the photo, she stood on a cliff holding a drill balanced on one shoulder, gazing off into the distance. The photo reminded me of the phase of the war when it seemed like all we did was build bridges. There were hundreds of female construction workers back then; they used to tie leather ropes around their waists and then bravely climb the cliffs in order to choose the best spots for anchoring the bridges. I remembered that the beautiful Blue Stone Bridge took almost two years to complete. It was only a few months later that American bombing completely destroyed the bridge.

Later that afternoon, my sister Tinh and Elderly Nguyet saw me off at the riverbank. Teasing, Elderly Nguyet said, "Lots of soldiers want to marry Nguyet, but she loyally waits for you. I should really help set you two up."

Hurriedly I slipped an envelope into the pocket of her apron. I had spent the entire afternoon writing a letter to my beloved Nguyet.

When I reached the Sang Le woods, I walked toward the remnants of the Blue Stone Bridge. I could see the mountain reflected in the river water below. Fresh grass had grown tall around the old bomb craters. The bridge had been cut in half. Blue rocks that had been used to build the bridge had long ago fallen into the river. Only the columns were still standing and intact.

After so many years of living with bombing and destruction, I thought, Nguyet still hadn't forgotten me. Bombs can destroy man-made bridges, but nothing could destroy her strong spirit and optimism about life. . . .

The storyteller stopped suddenly, as if something had crept up into his throat from the bottom of his heart. The other soldiers didn't say a word. Nobody asked him to finish his story. It was almost sunrise. The birds had stopped chirping, probably because they had already found their mates. A bright light appeared in the sky to the west. The moon rose high over the woods. Leaves scattered on the roof of the hut sparkled like pieces of silver. Moonlight illuminated the bamboo hut and the crater-filled road winding from it.

The storyteller looked up and saw the moon. Then he returned to his corner of the hut and lay back down.

"Let's get some sleep," he said. "We have to get back on the road in the morning."

6 / MS. THOAI

HANH LE

H anh Le (1966–2006) is the pseudonym of Nguyen Xuan Hoang. He was born in Pleiku and lived most of his life in the central city of Hue, the former imperial capital of Vietnam. He was a member of the Thua Thien Hue Association for Literature and Arts and the editor-in-chief of *Perfume River Magazine*, a local literary arts publication founded in 1983. He published one collection of short stories and poetry, in addition to five books of nonfiction about topics ranging from memories of his relationship with his mother to Buddhist-inspired philosophizing on life and nature. Hanh Le died in 2006, at the age of forty, from a heart attack. The story "Ms. Thoai" is notable for its depiction of the wide-ranging impact of the war, how lives were sometimes destroyed on the home front as well as the battlefield. Hanh Le depicts Thoai as a long-suffering but fiercely loyal woman who never gives in to bitterness or cynicism, despite the fact that her life has been violently upended through no fault of her own. Ms. Thoai, Hanh Le seems to suggest, is another innocent victim of the war.

"Try to come home early this afternoon so we can visit Mr. Phuong's grave," my mother-in-law said as I took the motorbike outside. "Yes, Mom," I said, nodding. It was a Friday morning. Every
year, on the anniversary of Mr. Phuong's death, we visited his grave
and burned incense. My mother-in-law said that when he was alive,
Mr. Phuong's favorite food was sticky rice wrapped in an areca leaf,
so she always brought this dish to the grave site. She also brought
an old diary, the pages stained and yellowed, that usually sat on
the altar in our home. My mother-in-law said that Mr. Phuong had
treasured the diary more than gold. He'd even risked his life because
of it—one time, he lost the diary during a fierce battle near Doc
Mieu, then later returned to the battlefield all by himself to find
it. Phuong knew that he shouldn't have taken a risk like that, especially as a leader in his unit, but his life would have been meaningless without the diary. My mother-in-law said that Phuong's life had
been full of sorrow. For a long time, he considered his military unit
his home, and fighting the enemy was his only pleasure and a way
for him to conceal his private feelings and wounded pride.

⁂ ⁂ ⁂

The story started back in 1956. Everyone in Co Lieu village talked
excitedly about Phuong's wedding. They said it would be the biggest and most beautiful wedding the village had ever seen. The
bride, Thoai, was secretary of the village's local youth union.
The groom had graduated from the Infantry Academy and wore
the shoulder stripes of a second lieutenant on his uniform. He
had a tall, lean body; his nose was straight; and his forehead and
face were square. In wartime, weddings usually were not extravagant, but they were still beautiful. The ceremony was like a huge
festival, full of people. Phuong and Thoai walked side by side,
behind their relatives. The bride wore an aqua-colored *ao dai* and
a silver necklace; her hair was untied and flowed naturally down
her back. The groom wore a brand-new military uniform. His

shiny black shoes stood out against the green, grass-covered ground of the rice paddies. The bride was shy; she stood shoulder height to the groom. The young men and young girls of the village whispered among themselves. They all wished to be like this happy couple.

It was a sunny afternoon, and the rice stalks out in the fields were still young and green. More herons than usual flew above the rice paddy, turning the sky white. Phuong looked serious. He seemed nervous; tiny drops of sweat appeared on his bronze skin. As they walked, Thoai stumbled a few times, nervous herself. The back of her *ao dai* was decorated with light-pink touch-me-not flowers. Occasionally she glanced at Phuong walking by her side and imagined that this was all a dream. She was delighted by the thought that Phuong was hers now. As they walked, Thoai sensed a group of young men, water buffalo herders, teasing her. Among the familiar faces she recognized Lo, son of the Bongs. Children lined up along the wedding procession path and chanted together, "A husband and wife! A husband and wife!" Thoai's face felt hot; she glanced at Phuong and noticed that he was anxious too. Thoai felt as if she were flying. Gently she took Phuong's hand and noticed that he was trembling slightly.

Those were Phuong and Thoai's happiest days. Their wedding room was full of co co, a flower that grew only along the rice paddies in Co Lieu village. It was the season of the full moon, and every night during the first week of their marriage, Phuong took Thoai out to the rice paddies where, under the bright yellow moonlight, the land seemed to be drowning in fog. In the distance they could hear herons making panicky, screeching noises. Awkwardly, Phuong searched for the buttons of Thoai's shirt. The sweet, earthy smell of wildflowers coming from her hair mesmerized him.

He asked her, "Thoai, what are you thinking about?"

Leaning against her husband's shoulder, Thoai replied, "I'm dreaming about having a son."

"And what if your son joined the military and never returned?" Phuong asked.

Thoai covered Phuong's mouth with her hand.

"Don't talk like that," she said. "I know that next year we'll have a son."

Their happy days together went by quickly, as if in a dream. Then eventually it was time for Phuong to return to his army unit. The day she said good-bye to her husband, Thoai made two new shirts for him and prepared some sticky rice for Phuong to take to his unit. They walked together through the rice paddy. The bright red early morning sunlight looked like blood. It seemed as if the pink touch-me-nots lining the rice paddies were still asleep. Phuong and Thoai were both quiet, lost in their own thoughts as they walked along the same path as their wedding day, only now they were heading in the opposite direction, away from the village. At the edge of the rice paddies, they finally parted. Thoai began to cry as if her heart were already broken, as if she were experiencing a premonition that after saying good-bye she would lose Phuong forever. When they kissed, Phuong was affectionate, but his mouth was twisted out of shape. Thoai's tears tasted salty on his lips.

Thoai didn't remember which way she'd taken back to her home after that. She ran as if she were being chased by a ghost, and her body was completely numb. A terrifying emptiness occupied her heart. Days of longing accompanied this feeling. The wedding room she'd shared with Phuong seemed to grow bigger and bigger. Every night, Thoai cried as she fell asleep holding Phuong's pillow. A month after the wedding, when Thoai still got her period, she cried even more than usual. Her dream hadn't come true.

Every afternoon, after finishing her work in the rice paddies, Thoai would stop by the office of the People's Committee to ask the mailman, Mr. Ta, if she'd received any mail. For months, Mr. Ta would simply shake his head and offer some encouraging words.

"Your letters will probably be here in a few days," he would say. "I heard that the fighting right now is very intense."

Thoai finally received her first letter from Phuong on a rainy day. Her heart beat fast as she tore it open. The letter must have been transferred among several different people; it felt soft and was covered in sweat stains. She read it voraciously, as if she were starving for Phuong's words. The letter wasn't dated, but immediately she recognized his handwriting: *I'm doing well and take part enthusiastically in the battles. But after each battle, I miss you even more than before. I wish we'd spent more nights together, sleeping side by side in the same bed. . . .*

The next few paragraphs were illegible. But Thoai could read the closing lines of the letter clearly: *Do you have any good news?* Phuong wrote, which was his own shy way, Thoai knew, of asking if she was pregnant. *Don't worry. I'll be home soon. Take care of Mother for me. Sending you thousands of kisses, my wonderful wife.*

After that, letters from Phuong were even more rare. Thoai longed for them desperately. She tried to distract herself by being more social and found, to her surprise, that she was actually quite good at it. Local organizations and unions asked her to speak at their meetings. Thoai was considered a young cadre with a lot of potential and regularly attended evening meetings. My mother-in-law often would accompany her. She told me later that Thoai's mother had asked her to do this in order to keep an eye on Thoai while Phuong was away. But my mother-in-law always fell asleep during the meetings. When they were over, Ms. Thoai shook her by the shoulder and said, "Dung, let's go home."

Thoai seemed to become even more attractive while her husband was away. She was as beautiful as a wild field flower. Young men in the village would stop and flirt with her as she walked along the road running out to the rice paddies. The boldest one was Lo. It seemed like he'd grown from a rambunctious buffalo-herding kid into a big, tall man in only a few months. He called out crudely to

Thoai, "Hey, let me cop a feel!" Thoai responded, "Don't be such a child." Lo just laughed and wagged his rear end as she walked away.

Thoai's life changed suddenly on the day she was selected to attend an exemplary cadre meeting in Hanoi. It was the first time she'd ever ridden in a car. Everything in the city looked unfamiliar. As a young woman from the countryside, Thoai found Hanoi big and beautiful. She felt so small among the elegant and sophisticated city people. At the banquet that evening, she drank a small glass of wine. She had no idea what kind of wine it was; all she knew was that it tasted kind of bitter and sour. There was a rainstorm that night, and water poured down from the gutters into the streets of the city. Back in her room, Thoai felt unusually hot and strangely uneasy. Against the sounds of heavy rain outside she heard a knock on the door, and as she hesitantly unlatched the lock she saw a man's face in the dim light from a sudden flash of lightning. It took her moment to recognize the head of the delegation.

She couldn't remember exactly what happened after that. Her mind went blank, her arms and legs felt numb. As his big, dark shadow enveloped her, Thoai felt her body take flight—she was flying above the road back in her village; it was her wedding day and she was wearing an aqua-colored *ao dai* decorated with light pink touch-me-not flowers. Below, she could see that Phuong was walking along the road, crying and calling her name. But he didn't look up, even as Thoai heard a group of buffalo-herding boys chanting, "A husband and wife! A husband and wife!"

Once the man had finally left her room, Thoai wept all night long.

Two days after she returned from the meeting, Thoai received some news about her husband. Phuong had asked a friend to write to her on his behalf. The letter said that Phuong had gone up North and was now hospitalized in Infirmary E3. Immediately, Thoai packed a bag to go visit him. She woke up at midnight and went to the garden to pick a fresh areca leaf to prepare Phuong's favorite food—sticky rice wrapped in areca leaf—but as she sat staring at the cooking fire, tears began streaming down her face. She felt empty inside and was tormented by a feeling of shame. Vaguely, her thoughts turned to death. Death would put an end to everything. But she was too scared for that option.

My mother-in-law said that Thoai was about twenty-six years old back then. Her hair was long and silky black, and her skin was as white as a freshly peeled hard-boiled egg. About two weeks after Thoai visited her husband in the hospital, she started feeling dizzy and nauseated and knew immediately that she was pregnant. The news cheered up her family. Her father went straight to the garden and began cutting bamboo to make a cradle for the baby, and her mother bought special pregnancy foods at the market. Then suddenly Thoai began to bleed as if she were having a miscarriage. In the middle of the night, her father ran to get a nurse while her mother sat by her bed. The entire family was worried about Thoai—they thought she might die, or at least lose the baby. My mother-in-law was the only one who knew the real cause of the bleeding. That morning, she'd seen Thoai climb to the roof of her family's house and fling herself to the ground like a bird that had been shot. At the time, my mother-in-law didn't understand what Thoai was doing. She just screamed and put Thoai in bed, where she continued to bleed.

Once Phuong was released from the military hospital, he was allowed to return to the village to visit his family. He spent his leave caring for his wife. Again their wedding room was full of co co flowers. Phuong sat by his wife's bed all day long. Thoai's face was pale, and Phuong could see the protruding blue veins running up and down her delicate neck. All she was able to eat was a little plain rice porridge.

Phuong rarely spoke during his leave. On the last day, he went to town and bought some fabric and silk at the market for Thoai to make clothes for the baby. As he packed up his things, he tucked their wedding photo into his rucksack. The moon was full again, like on the nights after their wedding day. The village felt calm and full of white light. In the distance, Phuong could hear the laughter of young men and women echoing from the rice paddies. His throat felt sore. For the past few days he'd been trying to swallow an invisible, bitter thing. It was time for him to speak up.

"How many months along are you?" he asked Thoai finally.

"Three," Thoai replied.

"And who's the father?" Phuong asked.

Thoai began to cry. Her face looked fuller under the bright moonlight.

"Just tell me the truth and I'll forgive you," Phuong said. His voice sounded melancholy, like the sad, desperate song of a lone heron lost above the rice paddies.

"Please forgive me!" Thoai said in a choked voice. "I beg you a thousand times! Please . . ."

A few months later, Thoai gave birth to a son. When Phuong heard the news, he sent Thoai a long letter, along with a request for a divorce in which he informed his family that he was not the father of Thoai's child. The entire Co Lieu village talked about what had happened. Some people said Phuong hadn't been a faithful husband. Others gossiped about Thoai's supposed "night trips." No one knew for sure what the truth was. After the divorce, Thoai's party membership was revoked and all of her cadre titles and positions were terminated. Thoai and her son eventually moved back in with her mother, and the villagers saw her less and less.

My mother-in-law said that Ms. Thoai's life went downhill after that. Sometimes she'd see Thoai carrying firewood on her back; she looked so skinny and wasted away that it took her a while even to recognize that it was Thoai. Ms. Thoai would often pull my mother-in-law aside and ask her about Phuong.

"Dung," she'd say, "does Phuong still send letters home?"

"Yes, but not very often."

"How is he doing?"

"He's doing fine."

Thoai asked a lot of questions; my mother-in-law didn't remember all of them. But always at the end of these conversations, Ms. Thoai's eyes would turn red and she would start to cry. She'd talk about how her life was over and about how she felt sorry for Phuong because his life wasn't complete. My mother-in-law said that whenever Mr. Phuong came home on leave, Ms. Thoai would crane her neck dangerously far outside her window to try to catch a glimpse of him.

Ms. Thoai was remarried the following year, unfortunately to Lo, who was often drunk and a jealous man by nature. He was in the habit of beating Thoai brutally. He would tie her hair to the leg of their bamboo bed, strip off her clothes, and beat and berate her: "You're a whore! Do you hear me? You're lucky that I even married you."

Phuong was very sad when he heard about Thoai's situation. One time, when he was on leave back in the village, he went to the market to look for Thoai, who was selling vegetables there. When she saw Phuong, Thoai's face turned red and her heart started beating fast, like the time she'd received his first letter after he left for the military.

Phuong asked her, "How's your son doing? I have a gift for him." He handed Thoai a package. Then he was silent for a while.

"You shouldn't argue with Lo, otherwise he will keep beating you," Phuong said finally, sighing.

They were standing in the middle of the market. Tears began to stream down Thoai's cheeks.

That was all Phuong said. Then he left.

That night, when she left the house, my mother-in-law found Thoai hiding behind the hedge of a Chinese tea tree. Thoai immediately came running toward her. She was holding a package.

"Dung, please give this to Phuong for me," she said, her voice desperate. "Is he leaving tomorrow?"

"Yes," my mother-in-law replied. "I heard that he's leaving very early tomorrow morning."

"You don't need to cook anything," Thoai said. "I'll prepare some rice."

Thoai stayed up all night preparing Phuong's favorite dish, sticky rice wrapped in areca leaf. The moon was full and bright again in the night sky. It illuminated the verandah of Thoai's house with a sparkling light as she cooked. It was the same intensely bright moonlight as the season when she and Phuong had gotten married, but the light felt empty and bland to Thoai now, as if it had lost its sparkling magic. It had been ten years. Crouched on her verandah in the bright moonlight, Thoai stared at the dancing blue flame of the cooking fire. She thought of the morning after their wedding day. It had been a beautiful morning. Phuong had teased her because Thoai had put on her shirt inside out. She wanted to hear his laughter again after so many years of living in sadness. She pictured Phuong's laughter like an arc of light that illuminated some hidden part of her consciousness and then vanished suddenly.

Once the rice was done cooking, Thoai went to the garden and cut a fresh areca leaf with her pocketknife, and neatly wrapped the sticky rice inside. Then she used a handkerchief to clean the outside of the leaf. The handkerchief was a keepsake Phuong had given to her when they first started dating. Seeing a few stray pieces of rice stuck to the handkerchief, Thoai began to sob.

My mother-in-law said that the following morning, when it was still dark out and a light rain had started to fall, she saw Thoai outside in a raincoat, standing again next to the Chinese tea tree. She looked frail and pitiable. My mother-in-law was surprised to see her there and said to Thoai, "I thought you knew—a car came to pick him up at midnight. Last night, he said he was going to go visit you . . ."

Ms. Thoai's voice, when she spoke, sounded broken. "Oh, really . . . really . . . ?" she said. It seemed like she might suddenly collapse there in the rain. Trembling, Thoai handed my mother-in-law the package. "Dung," she said, "please give this to Phuong as soon as possible."

"Come inside for a minute to get out of the rain," my mother-in-law pleaded with her.

"No, thank you," Thoai replied. "I've got to go home now. If Lo found out, he would beat me."

Eventually, Thoai and Lo got a divorce. Thoai ended up remarrying three more times, but she wasn't ever happy with any of her husbands. Her last husband was paralyzed and had a dozen children from his previous marriages. Every day, Thoai worked long hours in the rice paddies. Her skin became darker and her body frail and bony, and her hair turned gray. But her eyes stayed the same—black and deep, and extremely intense when trained on someone, like two burning fires.

The South was liberated in 1975. Phuong, who had been a second lieutenant, was promoted to major. He was still single, and immediately after the war ended he returned to the battlefield and the headquarters of his unit. His only joy came from being with his fellow soldiers. The younger soldiers called him "Dad," jokingly. Mr. Phuong loved a young private named Son the most. Son's real father wasn't around and his mother was still young and beautiful, so sometimes, when Son would notice that Phuong seemed melancholy, he'd say, only half serious, "Dad, why don't you just move in and live with my mom? You know, she used to be a beauty queen. And she can cook sticky rice better than anyone."

One day, Son and his mother surprised Phuong with a visit. Mr. Phuong's heart jumped into his throat when he saw Son's mother. She looked so similar to Thoai, the way she walked, her oval face, and her deep, intense eyes when she smiled. It seemed like it had been so long since Mr. Phuong had had a genuinely happy day.

But nothing happened between Phuong and the young soldier's mother. Looking at the woman's neatly braided hair and her full shoulders, Phuong knew that he could never forget Thoai. She was all he'd ever had and all he'd ever wanted in life.

Mr. Phuong died in 1984 at his unit's outpost near Battlefield K. He'd been ill for several months. A few weeks later, my mother-in-law received a package back in Co Lieu village that included a diary, a wedding photo, a savings account booklet, and a letter. In the letter, Phuong wrote: "Dearest Dung, I know I won't live much longer because of my illness, so I am writing you this letter. The diary I'm sending contains the record of my entire life. I cannot take it with me, so please keep it in a safe place for me. The savings account contains the money I was able to save from my military salary. It is not a lot, but is still a big sum of money in our village. Please do me a favor: give this savings account to Ms. Thoai so she doesn't have to live a hard life as she gets older. Send my greetings to Thuan and your children. P.S.: I almost forgot. Please keep the wedding photo and don't give it to Thoai. I don't want her to get in trouble. The savings account should already be in her name."

Mr. Phuong's diary was very thick. It seemed like extra pages had been added and that it had been meticulously rebound several times. I turned to the first page, which had a hand-drawn picture of a flying dove. On the subsequent pages, Phuong had written:

> I'd just returned from patrol when I received Thoai's letter. Even though I was exhausted, I read it right away. Thoai says she is not expecting. This news upset me a bit, but I know we can do nothing about it. Some of my comrades stole the letter from me and read it in secret. I know they laugh about our private business. Dear Thoai, please be patient. I miss you so very much.

> It's been raining constantly here. Everybody is homesick; their faces look drained of color. I wonder what you're doing right at

this moment, Thoai. It must be the harvest season now back in the village.

Meanwhile here we lost three soldiers this afternoon. When will I see you again? I can't be sure if I'll ever get the chance.

Why did you do such a shameful thing, Thoai? You have disgraced me. You have killed a part of me forever. Why did you do that? Whose baby is it? If you tell me honestly, I think I will be able to forgive you. But . . .

Do you feel better after taking your anger out on her? Now you're a free, single man. If you are still alive after the war, you will return to normal society and be a popular, desirable bachelor. You can just do what everyone else does. . . .

Did Thoai really do something wrong? Why am I making her suffer like this? Did I make my decision too quickly? Was getting a divorce the only solution? Thoai, I worry that I've ruined your life. My selfishness has ruined everything. . . .

I turned to the final page of the diary, dated March 22, 1984—two days before Mr. Phuong died:

The older I get, the more I realize that the most precious thing in life is the ability to forgive. Knowing that you've been so miserable fills me with tremendous regret. Yesterday the doctor told me that I would recover soon, but I don't believe him. I wish I could see you again before I die. As I face death, I've come to accept an inevitable truth—that making mistakes is only human. The biggest regret of my life is that I was unable to forgive you. I failed to enjoy the short-lived happiness that we had together. Instead I abandoned you. Please forgive me, Thoai. You're my only love in this life. Thinking of you is my greatest happiness. I know that for a long time you've been living unhappily, and this breaks my heart. I know that it's too late now. Please forgive me, Thoai. Sending you thousands of kisses, my wonderful wife.

% % %

In the winter of 1999, I returned to Co Lieu village for my brother-in-law Hai's wedding. My mother-in-law had moved away from the village by then. But before I left, she pulled me aside and said, "You should visit Ms. Thoai while you're there. Tell her I say hello. And give her this diary. I think it's time for her to have it."

I went to meet Ms. Thoai on Hai's wedding day. She was still beautiful, though she looked gaunt and bony. All through the night, she talked with me about Mr. Phuong and the details of their story, occasionally pausing to wipe away her tears with the corner of her shirt sleeve. She said that Phuong had been the best man in her life and she had lost him. I gave her Phuong's diary, which she held in her trembling hands.

"I begged your mother-in-law to let me see this diary," Ms. Thoai said, "but she always said it was not a good time for me to read it."

She ran her fingers over the worn plastic cover of the diary.

"Did you read it?" she asked. "Did he really hate me?"

I smiled. "Why don't you read it and find out?"

Soon the sun started to rise. A thick December fog covered the rice paddies on the outskirts of the village. A stiff wind blew through the banana tree gardens, making a sound like a long sigh. Up in the endless sky, the winter moon looked dull and colorless, like a human face drained of blood.

7 / THE CORPORAL

NGUYEN TRONG LUAN

Nguyen Trong Luan was born in 1952 in Phu Tho and currently lives in Hanoi. He joined the army while he was a mechanical engineering student and served through the end of the war. He has written short stories, essays, and novels about the war, and is the recipient of awards from *Military Literature Magazine* and the magazine *Cua Viet*. His 2016 novel, *Hungry Forest (Rung doi)*, was well received in Vietnam, and is currently being adapted into a play and a film. In "The Corporal," Nguyen Trong Luan pays homage to the hundreds of thousands of female soldiers who served in the North Vietnamese Army. His portrait of Xuan, the poor rural young woman who returns to her village hardened by years of war, highlights the challenges many of these women faced in a patriarchal postwar society still clinging to traditional gender roles. Despite her heroism as a soldier, Xuan's postwar life is ignominious, characterized by an unhappy arranged marriage, hard physical labor, and crushing poverty. Despite victory in 1975 and the reunification of the country, Xuan is doomed to live a "miserable life."

Mr. Buong died the day I returned to my hometown from Hanoi. The entire village was in shock. He hadn't been sick that long, but now suddenly he was no longer with us. My mother just said that he'd had a cold for two days and had stopped speaking. The funeral was simple. I felt sorry for Mr. Buong. My family's house was at the top of a hill while his home was at the bottom. Funeral trumpets blew their mournful sounds that echoed off the hillsides surrounding our village. My mother was the chairwoman of the village's Association of Elderly Citizens, so she kept busy attending to the funeral guests and spent her evenings at Mr. Buong's house, down below. In our house up on the hill, I couldn't sleep.

When I was a kid, I used to tend to a water buffalo very early every morning. My father said I should join Mr. Buong so I'd learn to be braver around the animal. Mr. Buong showed me how to climb onto a buffalo's back, how to guide them to the river so they could bathe, and how to remove leeches from their hooves. Usually, I'd ride on the back of my buffalo, while Mr. Buong walked behind me, leading his own animal with a stick. All my knowledge of how to take care of buffaloes came from Mr. Buong. This experience figures very prominently in my memories of childhood. Mr. Buong always called me cu and never used my real name, Luan. He said the fact that I was a fast learner was a blessing to the family, and that my intelligence was worth more even than many acres of tea trees.

His family was poor, even though Mr. Buong was strong and worked very hard. He'd go into the woods to dig up bamboo shoots and sweet potatoes, then diligently carry them to the market, where he was able to earn just enough money to buy a jar of fermented shrimp paste and a small bottle of rice wine.

My grandfather said to him one time, "Buong, you work too hard. A person who does too much physical labor won't enjoy life!"

To which Mr. Buong laughed and replied, "That's my fate, sir."

"You were born in the Year of the Monkey," my grandfather continued. "So if you want to be successful, you must have specific plans."

"Yes, sir. I know," Mr. Buong said.

But his family remained penniless. Mr. Buong's wife was a small-framed woman who knew only how dig up wild forest plants and sell them at the market. Together the couple toiled tirelessly in the woods, digging up whatever they could find, but their life didn't get any better. Still, Mr. Buong never complained or asked his neighbors for anything.

I knew that my father loved Mr. Buong. Sometimes when my father caught fish, he'd ask my brother to invite Mr. Buong over to eat and drink with him. Mr. Buong usually drank in silence. But one night, he took a drink, then sighed and told my father, "I am worried about my daughter, Xuan. She dropped out of school and now has to take care of the buffaloes. She's not as good-looking as the other girls, so in the future . . ."

My father interrupted. "You're thinking too far ahead. She's a good, hardworking girl."

Xuan was Buong's oldest daughter. She was two years younger than I, but we treated each other as peers. Xuan looked like a typical peasant, with a scrawny neck and dirty black feet. But she was unusually strong and hardworking. I couldn't even pull her bundle of firewood. In school she studied poorly, so she always sat in the last row, and every month she was named the worst student in her class.

From our house, we could hear Buong's wife shouting, "Oh, Xuan! Xuan! I pay the tuition and contribute rice to the school every month, but you always get the lowest grades. You're a big girl now, but you're still studying with the little kids."

Xuan was embarrassed and went to cry by herself underneath a palm tree outside. She didn't dare enter the house. I stood in my family's manioc garden, listening to Buong's wife berate her daughter, and felt sorry for Xuan.

Eventually I went off to college and only came back to my hometown twice a year to visit my family. When I came back, I noticed that Xuan had grown up—she was taller, and now we called each other *anh* and *em*, "brother" and "little sister." She had become a youth officer, and I heard that she was doing a good job.

A few years later I joined the military. At the end of 1975, I returned to the village. On the day I got back from the South, my mother asked me, "Did you see Xuan, Mr. Buong's daughter? She sent me a letter saying that she'd gone to Gia Lai to look for you last May." There were stories that women who went to the highlands became infertile, that the malaria fevers they might contract could wreak havoc on their bodies and cause baldness. I had seen it myself.

In 1979 Xuan returned to the village. She carried a huge rucksack on her back, but she walked with perfectly straight, upright posture. She spent all of her money to buy her mother a cotton blanket, because she said that her mother had never slept under one. At the age of twenty-five she'd lost most of her hair, and her skin was much darker now. She'd stayed in the highlands after the war to help cultivate land for rubber plantations in Doc Co, Le Thanh, and Chu Pa. Several people had died, Xuan said, from the remaining bombs and land mines hidden in the earth. She'd asked for permission to come home finally because she missed her family. So she was allowed to come back, and she eventually returned to the work of tending to the buffaloes.

Xuan was still single when she turned thirty. Because she had no formal education or experience, she was not qualified for a comfortable position in the local government. She worked on her family's farm for a few years, but there was still no marriage proposal, and Xuan was extremely sad.

"Do you want to be a single woman forever, Xuan?" her mother asked.

"I will get married, Mom. I'll even marry a crazy man with cracked lips and a belly button that sticks out," Xuan replied bitterly.

But eventually this prediction came true. A dull, slow-witted man with a limp was introduced to Xuan by the man's family. Xuan didn't look at anyone; she just nodded in agreement and the wedding was arranged. The man's family offered five chickens, twenty kilograms of rice, a bundle of areca fruit, and several bottles of manioc wine in exchange for Xuan's hand in marriage. During the wedding, Mr. Buong sat hugging his knees and watched the neighborhood children eating around a tray of food laid on a bed of banana leaves. He sighed to himself. He loved his daughter Xuan a lot. It was unfortunate that this had to be her fate.

Xuan and her husband didn't have their own house, so after the wedding, Xuan said to her father, "Dad, please build a hut for me on a hillside and I will live there." Mr. Buong spent ten days building a hut on a remote, abandoned manioc farm. On the day Xuan moved into her new home, my mother gave her a hand. Xuan carried two baskets balanced on a bamboo pole. The baskets were filled with everything she needed—pots and pans, bowls and dishes, clothes. Lowering her head, Xuan muttered a farewell to her parents as tears began to fall from her eyes. Her mother's shadow became as small as a clay sauce jar under a palm tree.

Xuan's hut was isolated in the woods. Occasionally local kids looking for their lost water buffaloes would stop by and ask for a glass of water, but those were the only visitors she had. Next to the hut, Xuan farmed a piece of land given to her as a favor by the village so she wouldn't have to travel somewhere else to work. Once a month she went to the market to buy food. After two or three years of this life, Xuan began to walk unsteadily. And she remained childless. People said that her husband was impotent. Xuan worked hard on her farm, digging holes to plant manioc and banana trees. She said she would keep burying manioc roots until she was buried herself. She planted only banana trees because she didn't know how long she would live. Trees like jackfruit and plum needed a long time to grow.

I lived far away from the village, so I only heard about Xuan second hand. I heard that she'd had a bad experience with her husband's family. Her brothers-in-law had come to the farm and taken all the good, ripe bananas. They even pulled up the young maniocs and taro roots to make a sweet soup. Meanwhile, Xuan's dimwitted husband was sick all the time. Xuan, of course, wasn't allowed to get sick, otherwise both of them would starve to death in the woods.

The kids who tended to the buffaloes said that in her hut there was a military medal in a glass frame. The framed medal hung high up on a pillar where Xuan had tied the frame so it wouldn't fall and break. The medal was for the rank of corporal; after nearly a decade in the military, that was the highest rank she'd been allowed to attain. She was Corporal Xuan of our village.

At Mr. Buong's funeral, Xuan wore an old soldier's uniform and a white mourning cloth tied around her head. Later that evening, I talked to my mother. "I forgot to tell you," she said. "The day Xuan moved out, she had no clothes or blankets to take with her, so I gave her the two sets of uniforms that you brought home and left here. When I gave them to her she started crying and said, 'So then, I'll wear the clothes of a soldier from the central highlands again.'"

Mr. Buong died, and his daughter continued to live a miserable life. He must have known about her fate. That was why, when he stopped breathing, his eyes were still open.

8 / RED APPLES

VUONG TAM

V uong Tam was born in 1946 in Hanoi. He studied at Hanoi University of Science and Technology and has published both poetry and fiction. He is a member of the Vietnam Writers' Association and works as a reporter for the newspaper *New Hanoi*. His story "Red Apples" first appeared in 2008 and was included in the short-story anthology *The Female Faces of War* (*Chien tranh cung mang guong mat dan ba*). The story is unique in that it features a character from the *van cong*, the North Vietnamese Army military unit composed of singers and performers tasked with traveling the country during the war to provide uplifting, nationalistic entertainment to both military and civilian audiences. For the pianist at the center of the story, the injuries she sustained as part of the *van cong* make it difficult for her to leave the house and establish an independent life in postwar Hanoi. She is similar, in this sense, to other female veterans in Vietnamese war fiction—stoic yet traumatized and scarred by the war, and unable to easily transition to the traditional roles of wife and mother.

I glanced at the piece of paper in my hands. It contained the address of a girl I wanted to get to know. A newspaper dating agency called "Looking for Friends" had sent me the address. Obviously I was nervous because the information about her couldn't really help me imagine how she might actually be. She was apparently 1 meter and 58 centimeters tall and "healthy," which made it hard to say whether she was chubby or skinny. Her hobby was interesting. In that category she'd written only two words: "sad music."

It was chilly outside, and the alley seemed quiet and empty. I stood near the entrance and looked for someone to ask about Miss Hanh An's house. From somewhere in the distance I heard the sweet singing voices of a children's choir and the sounds of a piano slowly accompanying the singing. "Mother's eyes are gentle," the voices sang. "We listen to her lullaby . . ."

As I stood there listening to the slow rhythm of the music, a boy came running toward me. I stopped him and asked for directions.

"Over there, where you hear the singing," he said, pointing immediately to the end of the alley. "That's Miss Hanh An's house."

I started to get more nervous as I walked closer to where the boy had been pointing. Then, all of a sudden, the children opened the iron gate of the house and came rushing out into the alley.

"Good-bye, Miss Hanh An!" they called out.

"I'll see you tomorrow," a voice replied.

Hesitantly I walked to the gate and saw a young woman wearing a pair of glasses with dark lenses.

"Excuse me, are you Miss Hanh An?" I asked.

"Yes, that's me," the young woman replied. "Are you Cuong? I received a note from the newspaper that said you'd be coming today. Please come in."

At that moment an elderly woman hurriedly ran out from the house, greeted me with a nod, and closed the iron gate. Then she held Hanh An's hand and led her up the steps to the house. I followed behind them.

"Do you like Chopin?" Hanh An asked cheerfully. To the elderly woman she said, "Nanny, please take Cuong to the living room." She turned to me and smiled. "Give me a few minutes."

Hanh An went into the adjacent room and I followed the old nanny into the living room.

"Please have a seat," she said. "Every morning, Hanh An teaches music here. You've come at a good time."

A cold wind blew in through the open window, scattering sheets of music all over the floor. The nanny began picking them up, and I went to help her collect the scattered music from the marble tiles. One of the sheets of music, I noticed suddenly, had been written by hand. It contained a handwritten note across the top of the page: "For you, Hanh An. This is a song written in a combat trench, a memory of the days we fought side by side. Composer Doan Thanh."

Gently I placed the handwritten song on the piano and sat down quietly in my chair. There was a photo hanging on the wall above me; I could clearly make out Hanh An's oval face and sad eyes as she leaned against a young soldier. She must have joined the war as an entertainment performer, I figured, adjusting my collar so I looked as proper as a soldier. I was fully aware that making conversation with a musician was not a simple proposition. Maybe I had no hesitation when crossing a combat trench, a gun in my hands, the sounds of trumpets and marching chants urging us forward, but I felt that in this moment it would be difficult for me to express my feelings accurately to Hanh An. Before coming here, I had arranged logically all my ideas about what I would say to her, but now my mind had suddenly gone blank.

Well, whatever happens, happens, I thought, taking a deep breath. *As long as I am honest. . . .*

At that moment, Hanh An entered the living room carrying a big plate of apples. They were red apples and smelled very good.

I noticed now that Hanh An's body had a nice symmetry to it and she was actually taller than I had previously realized. The old nanny seemed upset when she noticed me staring at Hanh An's dark glasses.

"Cuong, please have some apples."

"Thank you, Hanh An."

Nanny hurriedly stepped forward and said, "Let me peel the apples for you."

"You don't need to, Nanny. I can do it myself," Hanh An said. "Look, they are big apples."

I felt uneasy because the old nanny seemed perplexed.

Meanwhile, Hanh An seemed to be staring at me attentively as she peeled the first apple.

"Hanh An," I asked, "do you often play sad music by Chopin?"

"Yes. Almost every day."

"Why?"

"Why?" she repeated. Then suddenly she flinched. "Ouch!"

"Oh no! I told you. Now you've cut yourself," said the nanny. "Here's a bandage."

She must have known this was going to happen; that was why she'd placed some gauze bandages in her pocket.

A drop of red blood ran down the white flesh of the apple. I hurried over to Hanh An and helped her tighten the bandage around her index finger. Nanny took the plate of apples away and left the room.

Hanh An's arms were trembling. I tried to comfort her.

"That's nothing! It's just a minor cut. Soldiers aren't afraid of a little blood."

"Blood?" Hanh An screamed. "Is there blood?"

Her face turned pale. It seemed like she had suddenly descended into some sort of bad dream. As I finished tightening the bandage around her finger, she held my hand and whispered, almost babbling, "I see blood on his forehead, where the bullet hit . . ."

My heart was beating fast at seeing Hanh An so terrified. All of a sudden, the old nanny re-entered the room and said, "Please don't scare your guest."

I was speechless and didn't know what to do. But Hanh An stood up suddenly.

"Get up from your seat and run away like everyone else," she said. "Yes, I am blind. Look . . ."

Hanh An removed her dark glasses. Her eyes looked soulless and cold. They stared directly at me.

"You are afraid, so please leave," she said.

"Please don't say that. I beg you," said the nanny to Hanh An.

She hurriedly ran to Hanh An and slid the dark glasses back over her eyes. The nanny then told me that Hanh An had been blinded by an exploding artillery shell while performing for a military unit that was on the verge of launching a large offensive attack. Hanh An stood there silently while her old nanny spoke. In a croaking voice the old woman concluded her story by adding, "It was after this incident that she learned of her boyfriend's heroic death on the battlefield."

Regaining my composure, I walked toward Hanh An and held her hands.

"I am a soldier as well," I said calmly. "Don't think that I'm scared. I will peel the apples and eat all of them. You'll see. I'm not leaving."

The nanny pulled Hanh An to a chair and gave me a small knife. I began peeling an apple.

"Hanh An," I asked, "will you let me join your music class with the children?"

I waited for her to answer, but she remained silent.

Slyly, the nanny said, "We've never met anyone as kind as Mr. Cuong, have we?"

I smiled at the nanny and felt suddenly very close to this household.

"Hanh An," I said, "I'd like to hear you play the piano."

Hanh An was quiet. Her face remained bewildered, like a silent wall. The nanny went over to her slowly and said, "Please play the piano," then began gently pulling her by the wrists.

After a little while, Hanh An seemed to regain her composure.

"Cuong, I apologize," she said. "It has been twenty years, but it's difficult for me to forget the battlefield."

Hanh An stood up and walked briskly over to her old piano. The nanny motioned for me to stay seated. From the piano bench, Hanh An turned toward me and said, "Let's get to know each other."

Then she began to play. The sound of cheerful piano music filled the room. I recognized the tunes she played—the melodies, the rhythms—as marching songs used in the war. These must have been songs about soldiers—and could one of these songs have even been composed by Doan Thanh, for Hanh An herself?

Her fingers glided effortlessly over the keyboard, producing sounds that reminded me of rolling ocean waves. In that moment, sitting there listening to the music, I recalled the time I'd stood on top of an artillery cannon and raised a flag to signal the order to attack; then from far away an American plane suddenly appeared in the sky, and I pointed the muzzle of the cannon directly at it. There was an extremely loud explosive noise, and I collapsed as a piece of shrapnel pierced my thigh. I watched the plane, off in the distance, making loud noises before crashing into a field and then bursting into flames like a torch.

"Please sit down," the nanny said to me.

This startled me, since I didn't know how long I'd been standing. Hanh An stopped playing the piano.

"So, do you remember the smell of gunpowder?" she asked.

I forced myself to calm down and walked toward her.

"I heard an explosion," I said, "and saw a red flag with a yellow star flapping in the wind."

Hanh An smiled. She said, "Only those who have fought in the war can imagine such things. On which front did you fight?"

She stood up from the piano and went to sit next to the nanny. I held up the plate of sliced apples, offering them to her.

"My first battle was in the highlands," I said.

"That's impressive," Hanh An said. "You're a true Hanoian soldier."

She had a charming and cheerful smile.

"So," I said, "when can I hear you play Chopin's sad music?"

But the nanny suddenly stood up and said, "Let's just talk and eat the apples. Sad music another time. What do you think?"

Hanh An laughed and I did the same. I didn't know, really, why I was laughing so happily—probably from some sudden, unexpected joy.

Then the doorbell rang and the nanny ran outside.

I placed a piece of apple in Hanh An's hand. Surprisingly, she took my hand and held it.

"This apple tastes really good, doesn't it?" she whispered.

The old nanny came back into the living room.

"Mr. Thai who came here a month ago is here to see you again," she announced.

Hanh An was silent for a moment. She turned toward me and took off her glasses. I couldn't control my emotions when I looked directly into her dead, soulless eyes. I held her hands firmly. At this very moment, I felt as if I were back next to my comrades in the trenches years earlier, and the female soldier standing in front of me was someone I could rely on for the rest of my life.

I took Hanh An's warm hands and placed them on my shoulders. Hanh An smiled and turned toward the door.

"Nanny, please tell him that I am not taking new students for my music class."

I laughed again. What she'd said was funny. But the old nanny understood and quickly returned to the gate to deliver the news.

Hanh An and I enjoyed the sweet, crispy red apples.

9 / THE MOST BEAUTIFUL GIRL
IN THE VILLAGE

TA DUY ANH

Ta Duy Anh was born in 1959 and studied at the Nguyen Du Creative Writing School in Hanoi, where he taught from 1994 through 2000. Since 2000, he has worked as an editor at the Vietnam Writers' Association. He has published several novels and short stories, often writing about politically sensitive or taboo topics, like corruption. As a result, several of his most recent books have been banned in Vietnam. "The Most Beautiful Girl in the Village," on the contrary, is among his most widely read and celebrated stories in Vietnam. Set in a *lang que Bac bo*—a northern pastoral countryside, where life is considered simpler and more idyllic than in the city—the story centers around Tuc, a young woman who is depicted as almost unrealistically perfect. "You are indeed Tam, with hundreds of magical talents. You're not a flesh-and-bone being," the character Hao tells her at one point, invoking Tam, the most famous female character from Vietnamese folklore, often compared to Cinderella in her pure innocence and stoic suffering. The irony is that, for Tuc, this suffering does not prove redemptive; she ends up a tragic figure by the end of the story, and largely as a result of her moral purity.

Tuc, back then, was as beautiful as a flower. She concealed her young, supple body and firm shoulders under a light brown blouse. At the age of eighteen she was irresistible; men could not keep their eyes off her, and many couldn't help but express their feelings for her.

"Will you please stop for a second?"

It was the voice of one of the men in the village, imploring Tuc to stop in a desperate, frantic voice, as if he'd been suppressing his feelings for a long time.

Slowly Tuc turned around. She opened her lips and smiled gently. Her eyes were like two pieces of elegantly cut areca nut. She was beautiful, but not stuck up. She blinked as she looked away from the man at the ground, waiting for him to speak. But the man seemed intimidated by her beauty. So he just stood there, speechless, until finally Tuc continued walking.

In the afternoons, Tuc usually went to the village well to collect water. In general, well-behaved girls were taught not to stare at themselves in the mirror. As she bent down to pull the bucket of water out of the well, Tuc avoided her reflection in the water. But it seemed like the rippling surface of the water was flirting with her, tempting her to look. Instead, she pulled her head up quickly and laughed. Her laughter was innocent. As she walked away from the well, carrying two buckets of water balanced on a bamboo pole, her bare white feet calmly padded against the dirt path. Wherever she walked, someone would always call out to her, and Tuc would simply tilt her head slightly as a reply.

Eventually the village men started joining the military. The war reached out and snatched eighteen-year-old kids for the battlefield. Each time Tuc said good-bye to the young recruits, she cried until her eyes became dry.

% % %

I did not know exactly where the military units that came to our village were from. They usually stayed for a few months—enough time, at least, for us to miss their presence once they finally left, which they always did. Sometimes we'd wake up in the morning and they would already have disappeared, as if by magic.

One time, I found my mother reading a letter while wiping away tears. She said it was from Mr. Kieu, one of the soldiers who had stayed with us before. When she wasn't around, I found the letter and read it in secret. Then I read it out loud to some of the village children as they listened, wide-eyed.

"After we left Quang Tri, our battalion had only a few dozen soldiers left. The enemy was very cruel. A huge stretch of land was destroyed over and over again. Now the earth there is the color of gunpowder."

At the end of his letter—after he wrote, "Farewell to you and your children"—Mr. Kieu added, "Oh, I forgot. Please send my greetings to Ms. Tuc."

Back then, we could not fathom the cruelty of war depicted in those lines. War to us was like a ghost that we were scared of but still wanted to tease and play with.

The next day, my mother gave the letter to Tuc. She lay on the bed reading it over and over again, repeatedly turning it from front to back as if she were searching for something hidden between the lines of writing. When she returned the letter to my mother, Tuc looked somewhat listless. But just like us, the younger kids, she had no time really to ponder whatever was bothering her about Mr. Kieu's letter. The entire village once again started busily preparing to welcome a new battalion.

Soldiers who were around Tuc's age came to my house to play chess, but it was just an excuse. Whenever Tuc stepped into the house, the chessboard immediately belonged to me and the rest of the kids, and we could do whatever we wanted with it. We put the chariots and cannons and horse pieces into our pockets and played with the pieces like they were our toys.

After a few months the soldiers disappeared, as usual. The village was quiet again, and everyone missed the soldiers tremendously, especially the young kids like me. There'd be some commotion whenever the village would receive a letter from one of the soldiers. We'd gather in small groups and listen as someone read the letter out loud.

But Tuc received a letter addressed directly to her, with her name scribbled on the envelope. That night she came to talk to my mother. My mother was only five years older, but Tuc still called her co, auntie. Tuc's face looked serious. The glow of the winter moon outside flickered through our house. Tuc was quiet for a while; then she clumsily pulled a folded envelope from a fold in her shirt where she had been carrying it nestled against her chest.

I could feel her looking in my direction as she whispered to my mother, "Is he asleep?"

"He played all day," my mother responded, "so he fell asleep as soon as he lay down."

"I want to tell you something," Tuc said, her voice trembling.

I peeked through my half-closed eyes and saw my mother snatch the letter from Tuc's hands. My mother brought the lamp closer to her, examining the letter front and back. Then she gave it back to Tuc.

"Read it to me. It's just the two of us here. Don't worry."

"Promise me you won't share this with anyone," Tuc insisted.

"Listen to you," my mother said. "Such a child!"

Tuc breathed deeply and then started to read: "Dear my love . . ."

"Who wrote you this letter?" my mother asked suddenly.

Tuc pretended that she didn't hear the question and continued to read in an uneasy voice:

Probably very soon, I will not exist anymore. The bombing this afternoon killed twenty soldiers in my unit. War is a cruel game in which you can either gain or lose everything. I feel that I still have time to prepare for death, no matter how unpredictable it may be. Tonight the moon has risen bright in the sky. Strangely, I have the feeling that everything is peaceful, as if the war has been permanently delayed, just an echo of what it was before. And I am waiting—waiting for you to step from the bright, risen moon and bandage our wounds and cool the scarred, battle-torn ground. . . .

Tuc could not bear to read any further, so my mother had to finish the rest of the letter, reading quietly to herself. I don't know what the rest of the letter said, but after she was done reading, my mother and Tuc sat in silence.

Suddenly my mother sighed and said, "My god! When will this war be over?" She turned to Tuc. "Is this letter from the commander?"

"Yes," Tuc replied. "It's from him."

"I can tell," my mother said. "He's a tall, good-looking man. No wonder . . ." she trailed off, then added, "I feel so sorry for both of you."

Tuc started to cry. "The night we said good-bye," she stammered through her tears, "he asked me to let him hold my hands, but I didn't let him. He must have been extremely sad."

"Don't worry," my mother said, coming over to where I was pretending to be asleep. "He will love you more if . . ."

But she couldn't finish the sentence. As my mother bent down, pretending to adjust the blanket over my shoulders, I saw her quickly wipe away tears with her shirt sleeve.

※ ※ ※

Tuc organized all the letters she received according to the dates they were written. Some had been written in the summer, but they didn't get to our village until many months later, in the winter.

Some had been written deep in a forest along the northernmost border. Sometimes the letters had gotten lost, transferred from postal station to postal station, with people writing on the back of the envelope "Urgent." At another postal station, one of the workers might write "Censored and deliverable," or even "Love in wartime must be urgently delivered. Send my northern countrymen millions of kisses." That last must have been written by a soldier.

Among the hundreds of letters she received, there were only about ten Tuc was able to reply to. The rest of the letters had no return address, which made Tuc feel anxious. Only my mother knew how much this upset her.

Mr. Kieu, the commander, did not write to Tuc after that first letter. At the time, the fighting on the B1 front was at its cruel peak.

※ ※ ※

In our village, Tuc was head of the local government group called "The Unit for Prevention of Spying and Protection of Army Secrets." The group had the right to stop and interrogate any stranger who passed by the village after 7:00 p.m. The war had also spread to the North—spies could be anywhere, trying to gain access to sensitive information. Tuc's group had already caught a spy in our village who had disguised himself as a street beggar.

But mostly the village seemed quiet. In the still night sky, the moon was bright. Out in the fields, on the outskirts of the village, the group who had night rice-harvesting duty sang folk songs that sounded both harsh and romantic. They were all women, loud and tough, outspoken and often careless with their words. Tuc was afraid of them. Once, some of the younger girls from the group had surrounded Tuc and tried to coerce her to reveal her lover's name and age. Cornered, Tuc admitted that she loved "a soldier." She thought her answer was enough, but they kept questioning her.

"Did you guys *kiss*?"

Tuc looked as if she were about to faint. One of the younger girls replied on her behalf: "Yes they did! I knew it!"

"How did it feel?"

"Like an electric shock!" one of the other girls shouted, before finally Tuc managed to break free and run away.

The group's singing echoed through the village at night, depending on where the wind was blowing. Tuc felt as if each lyric to the outlandish songs was coming toward her like a wave. The wind also carried the scent of rice stalks. Tuc shouldered her rifle and looked out at the sea of fog covering the fields.

There was the sound of footsteps on grass. In the moonlight, Tuc saw the shadow of a big man coming toward her. When it got close, the shadow stopped and just stood there. Tuc adjusted the rifle on her shoulder. She was trembling. Still, in a stern voice she asked,

"Who's there?"

"It's me."

"Who are you?"

"I am a lonely man."

"Be more specific or I will shoot you," Tuc said, readjusting the rifle against her shoulder. "What are you doing here?"

"Tuc, you 'shoot' me every day. Isn't that enough?"

His answer sounded sad and sentimental, but it was obvious that he knew her. Then suddenly she recognized him. It was Hao, son of the vice-chairman, Doc, one of the most powerful and well-connected villagers. Hao was something of a dandy, his long hair always neatly combed as he used to follow her around during the yearly rice-cooking contest. Although they were the same age and lived in the same village, Tuc rarely saw Hao because he didn't hang around the other young men. When it was time to enlist, Hao had excused himself, saying that he had to follow in his father's career path, and disappeared.

Then suddenly he'd shown up a few weeks earlier at the rice-cooking contest, all well groomed like an urban intellectual. He wouldn't leave Tuc alone, which bothered her. Still, she won the first round of the contest. When the lid to Tuc's pot was removed, the smell of her cooked rice filled the air. Tuc cooked the rice so well that each grain was perfectly fluffy and tender. The bowl filled with her rice looked like a bowl of cotton. Even though the judges were experienced and picky older villagers, they ranked her at the top.

Round two of the contest involved cooking rice on water. The contestants were given a bundle of sugarcane stalks, a pot, and a box of matches. The sugarcane had to be chewed first to extract the liquid inside so the stalk would be flammable. The contestants had to cleverly calculate how many sugarcane stalks to use so that the rice cooked in a timely manner.

Tuc knew that thousands of eyes were watching as she tried to cook the rice in the melon-shaped bamboo basket that kept dancing on the water.

But she won first prize, and continued on to round three—perhaps the strangest round of all. This time, the contestants were meant to play the role of mother. They would again have to cook a pot of rice using sugarcane stalks as fuel out on the open water, only this time each contestant would also receive a mischievous child, and if he cried while the rice was cooking, the contestant would lose.

Who in the past had come up with this ridiculous challenge? Tuc thought, blushing. But she was by nature a kind and gentle woman, so throughout round three her assigned child only held onto Tuc's neck and waved cheerfully at the crowd while she finished cooking the rice. Her pot gave off a nice smell, the steam pushing the lid off.

When they announced Tuc as winner of the contest, the crowd roared as loud as thunder, which almost made her and the child fall into the water.

"You are indeed Tam, with hundreds of magical talents. You're not a flesh-and-bone being."

It was Hao who said this. As Tuc made her way through the crowd, he followed a few feet behind. The way he moved seemed sluggish and full of sorrow, as though he were an abandoned person. Tuc felt somewhat sorry for him. But why hadn't he joined the military? Back then, this was a dangerous question for any young man who had been "left behind." Was he afraid of death? Or was he ill or disabled?

Now, out in the middle of the deserted rice paddy, under the bright moon, Tuc felt nervous and annoyed that Hao had surprised her.

"Why did you follow me?" Tuc asked, lowering her voice.

"Finally my patience is rewarded," Hao said.

"Nobody is forcing you to be patient and stay in one place, just waiting," Tuc said gently.

Hao picked up immediately on what she meant. He replied quickly, "Don't think that I am afraid of death. Tomorrow morning I will put on my rucksack and go to the battlefield. Only tonight . . ."

A cold shudder ran up Tuc's back. Hao moved toward her.

"The moon is so lovely tonight," Hao said, inching even closer. "But why is your soul as cold as ice?"

"Watch your mouth, or I will take you to the village authorities," Tuc said.

"Tuc, why won't you give me a chance? Do you know why I haven't left yet? Because I love you."

"Don't be ridiculous!" Tuc said. "Aren't you ashamed to talk like that?"

"I'm not going anywhere before you tell me that you've never loved anyone," Hao said, suddenly insistent.

"I would appreciate it if you only cared for me as a friend," Tuc said, still trying to be gentle but also firm now.

"Why are you so cruel? You know very well that I love you and cannot live without you. You know that my life would be meaningless if I didn't include you in everything I do. Go ahead and curse me, scold me like a dog, but please don't be cruel to me."

As a woman, Tuc suddenly felt sorry for Hao. She could see that he was indeed a very lonely man. He was an attractive, elegant person who could get a wife easily, especially when all the other men were gone. She pitied him.

"I need to be honest with you," Tuc said. "My heart is already devoted to someone else. There is no room for your affection, though I believe it is sincere."

"Don't lie to me!" Hao screamed, acting all of a sudden like a petulant child. "I beg you! Tell me that you love me, and tomorrow I can leave for the battlefield with no regrets. I will make great contributions, I will . . ."

Hao stopped talking when he noticed the distant stare that had come over Tuc's eyes. He did not understand it. He did not know that there was only one person, and that person wished to see her holding a bunch of flowers tied with a blue silk ribbon as she stepped out from the moon. Hao was merely someone who evoked this other person's image.

Tuc's eyes grew even more distant. It seemed like she was contemplating the very mystery of the universe.

Then all of a sudden she felt a sensation of falling, as if she were tumbling down into a dark abyss. The starry night sky spun around her uncontrollably and she heard the sound of grass crunching under heavy footsteps. She was on the verge of screaming out, but Hao's hand already covered her mouth. Like a giant reptile, he crawled over her body, his hands clawing wherever they could. Tuc felt like she was suffocating. She wanted to throw up. She felt her body curling up into itself like a piece of dried fruit left too long out in the sun. She felt the moon in the sky above breaking apart and starting to bleed. But in that moment, she gained a kind of power she'd never known before. Righting herself underneath Hao's weight, she managed to pull back and then kicked him with all her strength. Hao screamed like a beaten dog. Tuc grabbed her rifle and stood up.

"Is that how you express your love to me?" she demanded, her voice like fire.

Hao held his stomach, where she had kicked him, and rolled on the ground in agony.

"You avoid death just so you can do more terrible things!"

"All I wanted was to show you my love," Hao said pitifully.

"It's an evil kind of love." Tuc raised the rifle to her shoulder and pointed it at Hao. "Get lost before I pull back the bolt."

Hao stood up clumsily. His clothes were all disheveled. With his head bent, he walked past the barrel of the rifle. Then he stopped and said, "You're just playing hard to get," before running off into the night.

Tuc bit her lip and followed Hao's black shadow with her rifle. She aimed directly at his back and closed her eyes.

No, she thought finally, her hands loosening their grip. *Let him live. People like him suffer more in life than in death.*

※ ※ ※

I don't remember exactly how many military units stayed in our village during the war. Probably at least a couple dozen. The young soldiers always promised that they'd return one day. The war back then was at the height of its cruelty, and that "one day" seemed very uncertain. As the years went by, we didn't see any of them return.

But our village did receive letters from the soldiers. Some were from the North, which meant the sender was already dead. Other letters were only a few scribbled lines, as if these were their last words before death. Tuc was the person who received the most letters. Many of these soldiers probably died in a jungle somewhere before they received her kind reply.

Tuc turned thirty-five the year the war finally ended and millions of people were smiling and crying out of happiness. Whenever they saw each other, my mother and Tuc would embrace tightly and lie on the bed together crying. They cried joyfully because of the glory of victory, but they also shed unhappy, miserable tears. When she regained her composure, Tuc would go to the post office to look for letters sent from the South. For over a month she looked for letters at the post office but didn't find any sign of the soldiers who had once visited our village and promised to return. Had the war killed them all?

Meanwhile, people started to gossip. The village women thought each person had a responsibility, and Tuc's responsibility was to marry someone, whoever was available, in order to fulfill her female duty prescribed by heaven. What was she waiting for? And what did she think she'd eventually get? Was it simply her karma to be a tired, lonely woman?

Then one day Tuc left the village quietly, like a lost bird. As usual, rumors were ubiquitous. One claimed that Tuc had left in search of men to satisfy her libido. Another said that Tuc couldn't stand the sound of firecrackers during the wedding season. The weather then was cold and unpleasant from the northern winds. It must have been hard out there, wherever she was, for a thirty-five-year-old woman all by herself.

After Tuc had been gone several months, Hao suddenly returned to the village. Everyone had assumed that he'd been killed in the war, and his return was an important event in our village. Hao wore the stripes of a major on his uniform and rode a black '67 Honda motorbike that kicked up lots of dust. The village dogs chased after him, barking loudly, and children rushed out to greet him. On the back of Hao's motorbike was a large, modern-looking suitcase. Physically, Hao looked strong and healthy, which made the war seem like only a wholesome game. He talked and laughed loudly and pinched the girls' cheeks. Vice-Chairman Doc's house became a site of attraction and curiosity. People came by on the pretext of "village solidarity" to smoke Ruby cigarettes that smelled like burnt dog hair and to touch the Japanese blinking-eye dolls that Hao had brought from the South. "Is it true," people asked, "that in the South valuable goods are discarded like trash in the North?" Everyone was curious how Hao had managed to accumulate such wealth. And of course, they also congratulated Mr. Doc on his son's promotion to the rank of major.

In the village, Hao became something of an idol. "Look at Hao," people said. "Not only is he successful, but he also brings back these pilfered treasures for his father." Hao's words had an even greater impact on the people of the village. He talked about the spoils of war like market women talked about haggling for a good price. Abandoned French wineries where you could take as much wine as you wanted. A storage manager who handed out silver watches to whomever he liked. Apparently the black '67 Honda motorbike Hao drove was nothing extravagant, because every family in the South had four or five motorbikes that they used to take their children to school. Hao talked about these things with great excitement, as if the sacrifice of millions of lives was simply a personal opportunity for him to collect valuables from wealthy aristocrats and landlords.

Once the parade of villagers coming to Mr. Doc's house slowed, strangers from out of town started to arrive. They entered quietly, using eye contact to communicate, and left only when Mr. Doc's guards standing at the gate indicated that it was safe. Mr. Doc quit his chiseling job, and on Saturdays he carried a small purselike bag with him. Nobody knew exactly where he went. Nothing escaped the scrutinizing eyes of the villagers, who figured that Mr. Doc must be making a lot of money selling the goods his son had brought back from the South. It was a mystery exactly how Hao had reached the rank of major in the military, since everyone knew he had no basic knowledge of how to shoot a gun.

Nobody, including Mr. Doc, understood why Hao was still delaying the decision to find a wife and get married. The reason, of course, was that Hao was waiting for Tuc. He still resented her for what had happened that night out in the rice fields. But he couldn't forget her beautiful, angelic face, which seemed like a challenge to him and dominated his burning desire. If necessary, he would kneel down in front of her and beg as he had done before.

Hao had already overstayed his leave by three days when Tuc suddenly returned to the village. Within ten minutes, the topic of Tuc replaced that of Hao and his pilfered goods among the village gossips. Almost immediately, Hao put on his uniform with the major's stripes and bright red chiffon scarf and went to find her. He was sweating from head to toe. It was strange to hear the villagers refer to *co* Tuc, but it made sense, Hao realized, since she was now almost forty years old. How had he forgotten this fact? Hao waited for Tuc out in the rice fields, near the spot where she had once aimed her rifle at his back before sparing his life. Because he was afraid that he wouldn't be able to recognize her, he hired a young boy and paid him a Ruby cigarette to help him. When the boy cried out, "There she is!" Hao felt his heart leap up and begin beating frantically. Was that Tuc? A pale, droopy-faced woman walked directly toward him. He had the urge suddenly to run away, but there was no time. Hao sighed with relief as the woman quietly passed him; then he made his way back to his father's house.

Hao didn't know that Tuc had glanced behind her, seen his chubby face, and been unmoved.

Hao left the village very early the next morning, when the roosters were crowing. Village dogs chased after his motorbike all the way to the rice fields on the outskirts. The road was full of potholes from the heavy footprints of water buffaloes, so the motorbike jostled and bounced as it sped away. Hao never looked back.

※ ※ ※

From Tuc's diary:

I have gone through huge stacks of letters at the Hanoi post office. The postal staff was very kind. Every day they have to satisfy the requests of various customers, as well as my particular request. I still haven't found him. I pick up another letter that might be the one. Which Kieu is this? If it is the Mr. Kieu that I used to know, then maybe I can find out some information about him. My heart beats like mad. I feel a little sick and disoriented. What's going on? Nervously, I turn the envelope over in my hands. Damn it! It's Mrs. Kieu, not Mr.

There are other people also searching through the stacks of letters. Sometimes one of them screams and runs frantically out of the post office. When will it be my turn?

It has been two days since I left the village. I wonder what people think about me now. Maybe that I'm a crazy woman? Who cares anyway? I find myself thinking instead about my friend Le. I love her so much. She has suffered tremendously. Le has been married for seven years but is still childless, so she has to put up with all the village rumors. Her father-in-law is an evil person, a devil camouflaged in human form. He's the one who convinced his son to turn the bed upside down and throw Le out of the house on a stormy night. But of course the father-in-law is always the first person to come to the village shrine. Le has not admitted it to me, but I can see it written on her face: she took revenge by giving her body to him. She wants them all to be imprisoned in an incestuous maze so that their family will one day be extinct.

The village is very different now. People have started to become indifferent to everything.

. . .

I can't find him anywhere. There are forty people named Kieu, but none is the one I know. Maybe he wants me to go to the afterlife to find him. How unfortunate! If he is still alive, I believe he will return.

The moon is blue this season.

. . .

A disabled veteran was sitting alone on a stone bench, oblivious to the noisy world around him. Why did he look so sad? I could see that he'd lost a leg and an arm and had several scars on his face. His eyes looked full of sorrow, quietly lost in the twilight. He stared off into the distance, not looking at anything specific. Who, besides me, even noticed him? A few feet from where he was sitting there was a couple, cuddling and caressing each other like a pair of cats. My god! How could they do that in public when it's wasn't even dark yet? I felt like running away, because there was nothing more gruesome and cruel than this scene. Gruesome because . . . (Because I envied them, perhaps?) They were cruel. They should at least have known that there was a person who had lost almost everything sitting right next to them. But how strange! Even that scene didn't affect him at all. He was still sitting there quietly and looking up at the evening sky. He looked like a shadow in a black-and-white painting.

Suddenly he looked at me. (Why did he do that?) I had trouble handling how sad his eyes looked. Now it was my turn to sit still. The modern couple had finished what they wanted to do. Now they were tired and bored. They would probably go to a restaurant to try to relieve this burden. It looked like they, in fact, were the lonely people.

"It's getting dark already."

I was startled and looked at him fearfully.

"Yes, it's getting dark," I replied mechanically. "Who are you waiting for?"

"No one. I just wanted to be alone."

"Every day?" I asked.

But he didn't respond. Instead he stood up and started walking away, his wooden leg clopping against the ground.

Maybe Kieu is disabled just like that veteran. Maybe he imagines that I married long ago and have lots of children. Is he tormented by memories of the past?

No—I will keep looking for you and slap you in the face before I shed tears against your chest.

. . .

I have visited eighteen military hospitals where seriously wounded veterans are being treated, but he is not there. All the other veterans say, "He is probably dead," when I ask about him. Why do they say that about their comrade? Maybe they are talking about themselves. They're trying to test me. He must be alive, and probably suffering—maybe in the final military hospital, which I have yet to visit.

"But how do you know how many military hospitals there are in this country?" I hear him saying to me.

I don't like this question at all.

. . .

I don't know what inspired me to visit the war museum. Life is such a cruel game! All the personal belongings on display—reminders of the thousands of people who died for our country. I stopped in front of an old photo of a young female guerrilla. But wait! My god—I recognized my own image in the photo! I must have been mistaken. The photo was so warped and blurred that the image looked like it was composed of decaying leaves. But why—why did I want to run immediately from the eyes staring back at me from this photo?

Suddenly I heard the voice of the museum guide behind me.

"This is one of the most treasured mementos from the war," he said. "It was found on the body of a fallen soldier on the outskirts of Saigon."

I couldn't take my eyes from the picture.

"Perhaps he carried this photo with him during the entire war," the guide continued. "A visitor from the country that lost the war offered a million dollars to buy this photo and take it with him back to the United States, but we refused to sell it."

I left finally, because I didn't want to let myself be deceived. It must have been a different woman. Because if it were me . . .

No, it's impossible! He is still alive and in the military hospital that I haven't visited yet.

But that mole under the lower lip of the woman in the photo . . .

How have I never noticed that mole before? I want to smash the deceitful mirror!

. . .

For three months I've been wandering around desperately with this sorrow.

I returned to the stone bench outside the military hospital. The same veteran from before was sitting there again. I had the sense that he had been alone for a long time. Where the cuddling couple sat before, someone had left a flower, a purple flower that looked like spilled blood.

"It's getting dark."

"Yes, it is," I said.

"What are you looking for here?"

"Nothing. I just wanted to come back."

"I knew that," he said.

"What did you know?"

"I knew that you would come back."

"How strange," I said.

"Yes, it is strange. But why else should I have survived being crushed by a heavy piece of metal shrapnel? I knew there would be someone out there looking . . ."

"The person I am looking for is dead," I said all of a sudden, surprising even myself. "Sometimes I think he is just like you. Have you ever imagined that there might be a woman like me waiting for you?"

"No," he said, hurriedly. "Both of us are liars. You're looking for something that is already lost, and therefore irreplaceable, and I am waiting for someone who doesn't even exist."

He stood up unsteadily.

"I was eighteen when I joined the war," he said. "I didn't have a fiancée, which was a fortunate thing. Nobody was tormented when I left."

He looked at me more seriously.

"Please leave this place immediately," he said. "You shouldn't live in your dreams. Let it pass." As he started to walk away he added, "I probably won't live much longer."

I felt my heart beating wildly as the sound of his wooden leg against the ground gradually grew distant.

. . .

Days later, I heard him return, the same determined clomp of his wooden leg against the ground.

"I knew you would be back," I said.

"Really?" he said.

"You wouldn't leave me here all by myself when it's dark."

He looked deeply into my eyes, and for a moment his face brightened like that of a child.

I'm not sure why I cried so much when I gave myself to him. He cried as well. In that moment, I think I honestly believed that if my tears and his ran together, something divine would happen.

. . .

I have never seen a man's face that is as strange as his. There is anger in his eyes, and something like sorrow on his lips.

"Are you sure?" he asked.

"It's been a month," I replied.

He sat there quietly, touching the small veins on my hands. I wondered if he could hear what I was hearing: sounds from some distant world, the beating of two immortal hearts.

"You're serious," he said, looking for confirmation.

"Yes, I am serious."

He stood suddenly and began shouting like a maniac.

"Yes! Oh, yes!"

His wooden leg beat the ground in a way that sounded musical.

Three days later he died from a recurring illness.

※ ※ ※

Anyone who visited the village and asked about Tuc would hear the story of her out-of-wedlock pregnancy. She had been lovesick and gone crazy and left the village, the gossips would explain. When she finally returned, she had a child and lived the rest of her life like a mute, reclusive woman. But her child was beautiful, as if he'd stepped out of a painting.

Well, ill fate was always associated with beauty, the gossips would say, sighing. If only Tuc had not been too picky and married Hao, she would've had a great life. In my entire village, only Hao was wealthy. He joined the military but never shot a gun or fought in a battle, and still he was promoted to the rank of major. Though his wife was eccentric and unattractive, she came from a powerful and rich family. Hao needed only to rely on his father-in-law for his own upward mobility. Who else from our village could've done better than he?

Nobody remembered that Tuc had once been the most beautiful girl in the village.

10 / BROTHER, WHEN WILL YOU COME HOME?

TRUONG VAN NGOC

Truong Van Ngoc was born in 1973 in Hung Yen and currently lives in Hanoi. He is a high school teacher and an emerging author whose short fiction has been well received in Vietnam. Every summer, he devotes his time to searching for the remains of soldiers who died in the war with America. Over 300,000 Vietnamese soldiers are still missing, a staggering statistic that impacts hundreds of thousands of families, mostly in northern Vietnam. The trip to Dien Bien in "Brother, When Will You Come Home?" is typical of the privately funded search missions organized by the families of the missing. These private search trips were enabled mostly by improved economic conditions in the wake of the market reforms of the early 2000s; families suddenly had the financial means to actually go look for their loved ones. These searches continue today and, like the trip in the story, often employ a mix of spiritual and logistical methods for tracking down a missing soldier.

There were six of us crammed into the white Toyota SUV as it bounced violently along the road. The mountain road from Hanoi to the northwest was full of twists and turns, ups and downs.

National Highway 6 was under construction, so all the vehicles moved slowly, like languid cows.

Quan was tired and looked out the window. This was his third trip up to Dien Bien. The first two times he hadn't accomplished what he wanted. This time, though, with meticulous planning and preparation, he was convinced that he would accomplish his mission.

Mr. Hung sat next to Quan in the bouncing Toyota. He was a veteran who had fought in the same unit as Binh, Quan's brother, whose body we had come to this place to look for. Other people in the car included the driver, Quan's younger sister Lan, her husband, and myself.

Quan was an atheist and didn't believe in fortune-tellers or ghosts. He had faith only in friendship, witnesses, and hard evidence. The Province Military Headquarters had drawn a detailed map marking the location of his brother's grave and given it to the family. Our trip relied upon it.

Around noon, we arrived at the peak of Pha Din Mountain. Thick fog covered the mountains, and some local people had set up shops along the side of the road selling wild game that smelled really good. Looking back down at the road we had just traveled, winding back and forth through the layers of fog, I recalled some lines in a poem by To Huu: "At Pha Din, she carries things on her shoulders, he transports goods by bicycle / At Lung Lo Pass, he chants, she sings." The poem talked about the nation's heroic years and the difficult time Quan's brother and Mr. Hung had experienced. Now that our country was unified and socio-economic conditions were starting to improve, we needed to look for the bodies of fallen soldiers—it was the duty not only of their families but also of the entire society. Finding his brother's body was Quan's most important wish. He knew it would make his elderly parents happy, and it would give him peace of mind because he would finally be able to pay respects to his brother.

Quan and I worked together at the same company in Hanoi. We were colleagues. But unlike Quan, I myself was spiritual. I believed that, in the afterlife, the dead had the same kind of lives as the living. The dead had wishes and desires, just like the living. After all, our ancestors had always said, "The earthly life and the afterlife are similar." I had already participated in finding and exhuming nearly twenty graves, of both civilians who had been killed in the war and fallen soldiers. Quan had asked me to accompany him because he believed that I would be able to help him with his mission.

Before we left, I had told Quan to prepare himself for dealing with the spiritual world on this trip. But he had insisted, "As long as I am sincere, I will be able to bring my brother's remains back. Plus, this time we're going with one of his old war friends, and we have the map of the grave."

※ ※ ※

The area of the woods where Nguyen Thanh Binh, Quan's brother, was apparently buried was located on a steep hillside. Beneath the hill was a creek that ran all the way to the border with Laos.

Quan stood quietly, studying the map and looking at the area in front of us. The forest here was thick, dense with green, leafy trees and vines. It would be difficult to find the grave.

Mr. Hung walked back and forth, measuring and doing mental calculations. Then he paused for a moment. His face looked agitated.

"Everything has changed," he said finally. "This path"—he pointed at a thin sliver of dirt running up the hillside—"I don't know if it's the same path. There was a cement factory on that side of the lake before, but everything is gone now. This map won't be much help. What should we do?"

I tried to stay calm and recalled my previous experiences with exhumation.

I told Quan, "Maybe we should go into the village and ask around. Maybe someone will know something."

Quan seemed excited and agreed to my suggestion.

We met Ut, an older man who was one of the village leaders. Ut told us that back during the war, Company C3 had been stationed right next to the Na Hai Mountain village. There was a young soldier who went with his unit into the forest to collect bamboo for building huts, but he was swept away when Pam Not Creek flooded. Three days later, the other soldiers in the unit found his body and buried him on a hillside, which contained an old Montagnard cemetery, just as indicated on our map.

Quan was extremely happy about this information. Right away, he and his sister hired a group of strong laborers who had all the necessary tools to begin the work of digging up the grave site. They dug for a whole day and cleared away a section of the forest. By the end, everybody was exhausted. Quan and Mr. Hung ran back and forth anxiously.

Elderly Ut said, "It must've been in this area, because up there is the old Montagnard cemetery." As is customary among the Montagnards, the earth directly above the graves had been flattened and no incense had been burned, so trees had grown everywhere.

It was already late in the afternoon at this point. Dim sunlight pierced the forest leaves, making everybody's face look pale. I thought of a spiritual explanation for our failure: something hadn't been done right on the trip up here in the white Toyota SUV, and that was why the gods and maybe even the spirit of Quan's brother were not happy. That was why we found nothing.

I had certainly witnessed plenty of incredible incidents on trips like this before. For example, I'd seen the relatives of one fallen soldier who chose to stay at a luxury hotel, spent money extravagantly, and displayed no patience; they'd looked for the grave several times but always failed to find anything.

Perhaps Binh was testing us.

The next day the laborers continued digging. The morning went by quickly. We'd erected a temporary prayer altar at the location of the grave—the location that was marked on the map—and after lunch I requested that everyone sit in meditation. Then I lit some incense and began to pray:

"I bow down to the earth and forest gods, to all local spirits, and to the spirit of fallen soldier Nguyen Thanh Binh. Please protect and guide us, Binh, so we can find your grave quickly and bring your remains to reunite you with your ancestors."

Once the incense had burned down all the way, everybody stood up, clearly tired and disheartened. Quan again asked the village leader Ut about the details of the burial years ago, during the war.

"The people here are very honest," he insisted. "The soldier was buried here. I'm not lying. Trust me."

Suddenly one of the laborers spoke up. "Well, if he was buried several years ago," the laborer said, leaning on his shovel, "we won't find the grave here. Everything sank. We should look over there instead. Look for a low spot in the ground that has the shape of a coffin. I should know, I used to dig graves on this hill."

Everyone dispersed and went back to work. Only a few minutes later, one of the laborers shouted, "Here it is!"

Quan was overwhelmed and came running over to the fresh hole on the side of the hill.

The next steps were done very quickly. I personally washed and wiped each bone carefully and arranged them in a wooden urn. The dead had no material possessions left except his shoe heels, which were believed to belong to a pair of standard-issue soldier's shoes, and a damp, curled ID card, though the words printed on it were illegible.

"Did ID cards exist back when Binh died?" I asked.

"Yes," Mr. Hung replied, without hesitating. "ID cards were issued starting in 1972."

"I told you!" Ut the village leader said excitedly. "That's him! A soldier. He was the only one buried here." Ut turned to address the bones I'd cleaned and placed in the urn. "Return to your hometown now. We'll have a prayer ceremony for you."

Everybody was delighted and forgot immediately about how exhausted they were. Quan was so happy that he cried. He would finally be able to bring his brother back to his family and back to their ancestors so Binh could rest in peace.

Back in Hanoi there was a party at Quan's house. The whole family got together. People cried and laughed. Quan's elderly parents trembled as they held the wooden urn that contained the bones and had been covered with the national flag. They cried, "My son, why did you leave us for so long?"

The usually calm residential street suddenly filled with excitement. Neighbors and other veterans stopped by to congratulate the family. Anyone walking past would have easily mistaken the party for a wedding.

"Let's drink to our accomplishment," said Quan's uncle, who fashioned himself leader of the family.

It was late winter. Outside, the air was cold and the winds blew violently.

※ ※ ※

This would not be an easy mistake to fix.

While everyone was celebrating and eating cheerfully, I suddenly remembered the ID card found with the remains. It was still in the pocket of my jacket. After so many hours, and probably because of my body heat, the ID card had dried so that the words were now clearly legible: "Full name: Lo Van Thang. Born in 1917. Birthplace: Muong Phang, Tuan Giao, Lai Chau. Registered residence: Sam Mun, Dien Bien. Issued on May 28, 1988."

After reading the information on the card, I told Quan about it right away. His face turned dark as he examined the ID card himself. He read and reread each word. Then he picked up the phone and called the village leader Ut in Dien Bien. After hearing the name on the card, Mr. Ut confirmed that the remains belonged to his brother-in-law, who had died in 1990.

The next day, Quan called an emergency family meeting. His parents, after hearing the news, were speechless. They leaned against a wall of the house, both of them shocked and in a daze. The most important thing was to keep this news confidential. And it was necessary to return Thang's remains to his original grave as soon as possible.

※ ※ ※

Once again, the white Toyota SUV bounced along the windy mountain road from Hanoi to Dien Bien. In the car this time we were joined by Ms. Hoa, a psychic. Quan had finally taken my advice and decided to seek the help of a medium.

Quan was quiet during the whole trip and rarely talked. He looked pensive. At work he was a firm and determined manager. Under his leadership our company had won the highest government recognition several years in a row. But when dealing with things like this he could hardly hide his confusion and sadness.

We arrived at Sam Mun late in the afternoon, and everybody went to work immediately looking for a place to bury the urn. The village leader Ut brought a boiled chicken and a raw egg. He walked back and forth, throwing the egg up in the air, but each time it fell to the ground without breaking. He explained that if the spirit liked a specific spot, the egg would break. Ut continued for several minutes until finally the egg broke—the spirit had chosen its spot—and everybody started to pray.

The atmosphere was so still it made us shudder. I opened my eyes for a moment and saw in front of me, hovering in the smoke from the burning incense, the image of a hunchbacked old man grinning cheerfully, showing his shiny black teeth. Then the image vanished almost immediately into the tufts of smoke.

The next morning we returned to the area very early. Ms. Hoa, the medium, quickly set up a small shrine. I stretched out a piece of canvas to cover the ground, and everyone sat in meditation. She prayed for a while and waited for the incense to burn down completely. Then she gave us an order:

"Everybody close your eyes," she said. We were all still sitting on the piece of canvas in meditation. "Relax your arms and legs. Do not get distracted, and concentrate your thoughts on the dead."

Then Ms. Hoa continued her prayer:

"I bow down to the forest and earth gods and to all local spirits. Today is December 22, according to the lunar calendar. On behalf of Nguyen Hong Quan and his relatives, I summon the soul of the fallen soldier Nguyen Thanh Binh, who was buried near Ha Nai Mountain, Sam Mun, Dien Bien. I respectfully request that you guide your relatives to your lost grave so they can reunite you with your ancestors."

Ms. Hoa paused for a while and observed the rest of us burning incense. The hillside was extremely quiet. Incense smoke was everywhere.

She continued:

"Spirit, we respectfully summon you. We miss you. We invite you to come here and sit wherever you like. You are a sacred spirit. Please show us the way. Do you live down by the creek or up in the mountains? Please show us the way. I bow down to you. Sit wherever you like. . . ."

After a little while the medium turned to Lan, Quan's sister.

"I summon you, spirit," Ms. Hoa said, lowering her voice. "Please enter her body a bit further and show your family the way."

Lan was shaking. Binh's spirit, I assumed, must have occupied Lan's body. Everybody gathered around her now.

Quan spoke first, in a trembling voice.

"Hello, Binh. Is that you? This is Quan."

Mr. Hung said, "Brother Binh. I am Hung C3. Do you recognize me?"

Lan's body was still shaking.

I said, "Hello, Binh. I am your brother's friend. If you have arrived, please say something."

Suddenly Lan let out a loud shriek, then began to cry. Tears covered her face.

Ms. Hoa said, "Spirit, if you are unhappy or unsatisfied with anything, please let your family know. We are ignorant earthly people."

Then finally Lan spoke. She spoke on behalf of the spirit. In general, the spirit missed and loved his parents and every day protected all members of his family.

"Please, spirit," Ms. Hoa said, "we respectfully request that you show us the way to your grave."

Lan stopped crying for a moment. She wiped the tears from her cheek with the back of her hand.

"That's my house," she said, pointing to the area directly in front of where she was seated. Then she added that the spirit had just apologized to Mr. Thang's spirit because of the mistaken exhumation.

Quan and everyone else seemed thrilled and began to enthusiastically dig and clear trees. Yet another area of the hillside was eventually cleared and dug up. Occasionally someone would shout out, "Oh!" as if they'd found something, but it would only be a mound of dirt built by termites.

It was late afternoon, and a light rain had started to fall. Cold winds blew across the now barren and ripped-up hillside, making us shiver. The air was full of incense smoke, which drifted off into the dark, quiet woods.

The medium, Ms. Hoa, continued her job. She burned more incense and kept repeating mantras.

"I summon you, the spirit of the dead," she said, sitting in meditation again, her eyes closed. "We miss you. We invite you to come here and be seated wherever you like. You are a sacred spirit. Please show us the way. . . ."

I listened as her praying continued.

Someone off down the hillside let out a long, weary sigh. It seemed like there was no real borderline out here in the dark woods between the living and the dead. It began to rain more heavily. Out on the horizon I saw the day ending, the bright aura of the sun glowing as if it were trying to say good-bye.

Quan's cell phone rang and he answered. It was the voice of his uncle back in Hanoi.

"What are you guys doing there?" Quan's uncle said, his voice ringing out through the phone. "It sounds like soldiers marching!"

Quan seemed astonished and looked around. Everything was quiet. On the far side of the hill, down near the creek bed, a group of blue birds swooped down and landed on the ground near where the laborers were continuing to dig. It seemed like they never stopped digging. The holes became bigger and deeper.

Suddenly one of the laborers shouted, "I found a piece of green cloth, and a belt . . . !"

Everybody rushed over to the hole. We all stood around anxiously staring down into the dark, upturned earth.

Quan paced back and forth. He looked haggard. I noticed for the first time that there were some gray spots in his hair. His voice, when he spoke finally, sounded like a sob.

"Tomorrow is December 23rd of the lunar calendar, almost Tet," Quan said. "Brother, when will you come home?"

11 / WAR

THAI BA TAN

T hai Ba Tan was born in 1949 in Nghe An and lives in Hanoi. He is a writer, poet, translator, and English teacher. He earned his BA in English at Moscow State University of Foreign Languages in 1974, and has been active in Vietnamese literary circles ever since. For years, he was vice chairman of the International Literature Department at the Vietnam Writers' Association. More recently he has earned the ire of several high-ranking Communist Party officials by using his Facebook account to publicly criticize the Vietnamese government; as a result, he is now considered a controversial figure in Vietnam. In "War," Thai Ba Tan turns his attention to a domestic conflict that emerges between a young married couple after the husband returns from battle. This "new war," the narrator says, "required something more complicated and subtle" than simple battlefield endurance—"compassion and forgiveness." The story highlights a common theme and concern shared by writers of this generation: for the Vietnamese people, the war did not really end in 1975.

Imagine a story that happened like this:

There was a young couple who were in love. A few days after their wedding, the husband left for the battlefield, leaving his young wife at home all alone. She worked and waited wearily for him to come back. It wasn't only one or two years—she waited for ten years. And during those long ten years she never received any news about her husband. Nobody knew why, exactly, or what had happened to him. Then the war ended and the husband came home. He was very moved to see that his wife had waited faithfully for him all this time. But when they lay in bed together that first night, he put his hand on her belly and suddenly sat up.

"Are you pregnant?"

"Yes," said the wife.

Silence.

"Who were you with?"

"With you, of course," she replied calmly. "How could I be with anyone else besides you?"

The husband said nothing and crawled quietly out of the mosquito net. He put on his clothes and sat at the kitchen table, smoking for one hour, two hours, probably longer. Then, because there was only one bed in the house, he pulled out a piece of plastic, spread it out on the floor, and lay down.

It all started that night, the night that ended ten long years of longing caused by a cruel war, the night that presented new challenges and the declaration of a new war these two people now had to fight. Unlike the war they had just won, this new war was without weapons.

It was hard to tell if they would be victorious in this new conflict. There were new challenges in peace time that didn't necessarily require extraordinary endurance or sacrifice, but required something bigger, something more complicated and subtle: compassion and forgiveness.

Dear readers, the scene I described above did not derive from my imagination. It was a true story that happened in my village.

The husband was named Nam, and his wife was Xuyen. They didn't say anything else to each other that night, though neither of them could fall asleep. The next morning, Nam took a walk around the village. He wanted to ask people about his wife during the time he'd been away. He was surprised, and a little confused, when everyone reported positive things about Xuyen: that she was hardworking, well mannered, and respectful in all her relationships.

Maybe she hid it so cleverly that nobody knows, Nam thought.

And as soon as he got home he asked his wife again, "Who were you with?"

"You," she replied gently.

"Me? How could that be true?" Nam yelled. "Explain this to me!"

Xuyen looked up at her husband. Her eyes were wet with tears and her face had turned red with embarrassment.

"Go ahead, tell me!" Nam said, getting angrier now.

"Nam, please don't yell at me like that," Xuyen said. "I didn't do anything wrong. I love you. I've always loved you and been faithful to you. I wish you could know, even just a little, how I've lived the past ten years in misery and fear. Why am I pregnant? It's simple. Every night when you were away I slept with your pillow next to mine. Sometimes I imagined I could feel you sleeping next to me. Then one night, a few months ago, I imagined you came home and got into bed like everything was normal. I could even feel the warmth coming from your body. I felt much closer to you on this night than the nights before. When I woke up, I was still alone, like all the other times. But I knew you had just been with me. I could still feel the warmth from your body on your side of the bed, and the blankets were even crumpled. . . ."

"Do you expect me to believe you?" Nam said. "Do *you* actually believe such nonsense?"

"Please don't talk like that. I didn't . . ."

Nam walked out of the house.

He thought about what Xuyen had said. He could certainly empathize with her—he used to dream about lying next to his wife all the time. But how could this actually explain her pregnancy? *No! It's impossible!* he said to himself, though he wanted desperately to trust her words. He tried quoting the theory of telepathy that everyone seemed to be talking about recently, but it was no use. He concluded sadly that Xuyen had not been faithful to him and must have slept with another man. He could not bear this fact. It was an obstacle that he failed to overcome, though he'd always loved her. But there was no other way for him—he was the kind of man who could not hold a woman in his arms who had been held by another man.

Nam, Xuyen, and the newborn baby all lived together in the same tiny house. Nobody ever heard them argue. Nam was a strong and healthy man who loved farming. He was able to provide his family with enough food and even had some extra rice left over to sell to the state. Within a short period of time he furnished their house with all the necessities. He didn't talk much, especially to his wife. He worked hard during the day. When he finished his work, he'd sit quietly, often staring attentively at something in front of him for hours on end. At night he slept by himself, not on the piece of plastic on the floor but on a small, newly purchased bed placed next to the window.

Xuyen was a small woman, and after giving birth she became even smaller. She moved around the house quietly, like a shadow. She wanted desperately to share with Nam the burden of the thoughts that tormented him, but he had such a cold and cruel attitude that her attempts failed. So in general she tried to avoid him and often sat by herself in a corner of the house farthest from her husband.

Strangely, the baby looked just like Nam. For a moment, this fact made Nam reconsider Xuyen's illogical explanation. The baby was beautiful. Nam harbored no resentment against the child whose existence had become the wall between him and his wife. In fact, to his surprise, Nam found that he loved the baby as much as he loved Xuyen, and he felt miserable when he had to conceal this love. Sometimes, if he was in a particularly good mood and Xuyen was busy, he would hold the baby and help wash the cloth diapers. Nam's internal psychological debate raged on, but the prejudice within him always triumphed. He refused to let the baby inherit his last name and insisted that the child call him "Uncle," not "Dad." At night, when Nam heard his wife crying while she held the baby in her arms, he wanted to come to her, to caress and comfort her, and do something kind to make her feel better, but he decided not to. Lying quietly in his small bed underneath the window, he'd just stare up at the ceiling, or he'd go outside and walk and smoke until the morning. In moments like this, sometimes he'd get angry. He was frustrated with Xuyen, with the baby, and most of all with himself. The situation seemed hopeless. It was his personality, and nothing could be done about it.

One day, Nam stopped by my house for a visit.

"You have a few days off to visit your hometown, so why are you just sitting at home?" he asked loudly as soon as I opened the front gate. "Writing again?"

"Yes," I replied. "That's my job." I motioned for him to sit. "Please have a seat."

The baby was older now, running around the village with the other children, but his family remained the same. People said that several times the local authorities had advised Nam to reconcile with his wife, but he refused to listen. We all knew that Nam was a reasonable man, but once a thought entered his mind, it was not easy to get rid of it.

"So Nam," I asked, "are you still 'at war'?"

Nam said nothing. From his facial expression I could tell that he was sad. After a while, he said, "Look, what can I do?"

"Why can't you just have 'peace' with her?" I said gently. "You must know how much you're making Xuyen suffer."

"Don't you think I also suffer?"

"That's why you should let this whole thing go."

Nam sat in silence. Then suddenly he said, "Let me ask you something."

"Go ahead."

"Do you believe Xuyen's story? I mean, the story of how she got pregnant?"

"Yes, I do," I replied.

"Well, I don't." He stood up. He seemed furious all of a sudden. "No! Never!"

"But at the end of the day that isn't even important," I said, getting angry myself. "What's most important is that she waited for you all those years and she still loves you."

"Mr. Author, you talk like it's an easy thing," Nam said sarcastically, his lips barely parted. "Everything is so simple to you guys."

He said nothing else and left.

You see, a person who had spent fifteen years on the battlefield, who had done extraordinary acts of heroism, who had overcome thousands of dangerous challenges, had nonetheless failed to overcome a relatively minor obstacle to end suffering for himself and his beloved woman. This seemed unfair and extremely depressing. How were we supposed to convince him?

In February 1979, when the border war with China occurred in the North, Nam volunteered to rejoin the military. Xuyen didn't oppose this decision and only said, "You're leaving again, and I will wait for you, no matter how long."

"And every night, will you dream of me coming to visit you?" Nam asked, derisively. "Will you be pregnant again when I come back?"

"Yes," Xuyen said, ignoring his tone of scorn. "But please believe me. I've always loved you and only you. If I get pregnant again, the baby is yours."

Nam said nothing and left quietly. He never returned.

※ ※ ※

Several years have passed, and Mrs. Xuyen has become Mrs. Elderly Xuyen. She has aged and become frail. She is still waiting for her husband, like she did during the war. And like before, she never receives a letter from Mr. Nam, who has become Mr. Elderly Nam.

This was their personal story. At first I had no intention to write about it, but after considering various factors, I decided to go ahead and write all this down. I imitated the French author Andre Maurois, who wrote *The Return of the Prisoner,* and published this story in a local newspaper with a tiny hope that if Mr. Nam reads it, he will change his mind. Mr. Nam, Mrs. Xuyen, and I are all from the same village. I think none of us has the right, therefore, to be indifferent to the fate of others.

12 / THE CHAU RIVER PIER

SUONG NGUYET MINH

S uong Nguyet Minh was born in 1958 in Ninh Binh and currently works at *Military Literature Magazine* in Hanoi. He
joined the army in the 1970s and was among the Vietnamese
troops who liberated Cambodia from the genocidal Pol Pot regime.
He writes mostly about war and its effects on the Vietnamese countryside and its people, and has published one novel and many short
stories. Like other female veterans found in Vietnamese fiction, the
character of May in "The Chau River Pier" is portrayed as a heroic
but damaged and somewhat lost figure. May has been changed by
the war in a way that comes into stark relief when she returns to her
village on the evening of her former fiancé's wedding to a younger
woman. It is painfully clear that May, a seasoned battlefield medic
now missing a leg, cannot pick up her life where she left off before
joining the army. Still, she manages to become a mother by the end
of the story, fulfilling that traditional gender role even against the
slim odds offered by the harsh realities of her postwar life.

San got married the same day Aunt May returned to the village.
The water in the Chau River was red. Waves lapped against the lone

remaining column of a collapsed pier; the column had been standing there all alone since the Americans had bombed the area. Thick
dark clouds hovered in the sky. The water in the river began to rise
and flow more quickly. The guests attending San's wedding said,
"The flood from the mountains is coming."

Mai didn't want to think of Aunt May on this day, so tried to
force the thought from her mind. She had been tasked with helping
her grandfather transport guests to the wedding in his boat. San
was getting married to Thanh, a schoolteacher from the village of
Bai located on the other side of the river. San was still unemployed
and had only recently returned from an apprenticeship abroad.
He wore a shirt and tie and stood at the front of the boat. The
young women, in shirts with lotus leaf-shaped collars, sat along the
sides of the boat, chatting among themselves, while the elderly
wedding guests wore simple brown outfits and sat down in the
cabin, silently chewing betel nut. San looked happy; he smiled,
showing a set of shiny teeth.

Whenever Mai's thoughts turned to Aunt May, she had the sudden urge to sink the boat. An evil thought! But mostly she just felt
extremely anxious.

Mai lifted her head and, not trying to hide the disrespect in her
voice, said to San, "It seems like there are many guests attending
your wedding. You should have rented a dragon boat."

San frowned. "Don't say that. We don't want to upset your
grandpa."

Mai looked at her grandfather rowing slowly and steadily. He
seemed to be sulking, with his chin held in the air and his long
gray beard flapping in the wind. He had been given a peculiar job
on this particular day: transporting his daughter's former fiancé
to the house of his new bride. But the old man revealed neither joy
nor sadness as he sat there rowing the wedding party across the
river. If you looked into his eyes it seemed like waves were gently
lapping against his pupils. It wasn't until the last wedding guest

had debarked from the boat that he finally wiped away his tears with the sleeve of his shirt. Then he went to lie down in his hut while Mai anchored the boat to the pier.

※ ※ ※

Aunt May arrived at the village after the wedding ceremony had begun. She wore a faded old army uniform and had a soldier's rucksack slung over one shoulder. She stood on the Bai side of the river and called to her father. Amid the sounds of lapping waves and the blowing wind, she heard some buffalo boys nearby saying to her, "Ma'am, you missed the boat."

In the hut, Mai thought she was dreaming. When she got up from the bed, she saw that Grandpa had untied the boat and was already rowing across the middle of the river.

On the bank, Aunt May stepped onto the pier as she saw her father rowing toward her. He had started rowing faster. He was teary-eyed. His boat bounced on the waves as it reached the pier. When he finally embraced May, his shoulders trembled as he muttered in a broken voice, "Oh, May! Why has it taken you so long to come back? My dear child . . . I thought . . ."

Mai stood there speechless, watching this scene. Tears rolled down her cheeks. The boat floated freely down the river. The old man and his daughter held each other tightly. Their shadows were reflected in the red water of the river. Mai ran along the riverbank calling their names.

※ ※ ※

It was getting dark and the wind had picked up. The leaves on the banana trees behind the hut flapped violently in the wind. The river continued to flow off into the distance and a few parrots, returning from their late-day search for food, made strange noises.

Mai secured the boat to the pier while Aunt May limped behind her father toward the house where Mai's family lived. Mai's younger sisters didn't know Aunt May, so they looked at her with wide eyes. Grandpa took down the black-and-white picture of May and the family's "The Country Is Grateful for Your Sacrifice" certificate and stored them in a closet. Aunt May meanwhile stood in front of her mother's altar, leaned her head against a bowl of incense, and began to sob.

"Mom, Mom! When I left for the war, you said you would pray for me. You said you wanted to see me return with a husband, that you wanted to hold your grandchild."

Grandpa lit three incense sticks and placed them in May's hands. He stood next to her, muttering quietly to the dead.

Soon Mai's father and then her mother came home, and they were both shocked to find Aunt May in the hut. Mai's father stared at his sister-in-law in disbelief. While Mai's mother assumed that May was a ghost.

"I beg you, little sister," she mumbled. "You are a sacred spirit. Please don't haunt my children. Dad and I have never forgotten your death anniversary."

Aunt May stood up and approached her sister. The lights from the altar flickered behind her and incense smoke enveloped her body.

"It's me!" May said. "Your sister."

Mai's mother seemed to snap out of it. She and May embraced each other tightly. The older sister looked May up and down as if examining her body, and when she realized that May had lost a leg, she began to sob.

"I grieved for you until my tears ran dry," Mai's mother said. "It is thanks to the blessing of our ancestors that we are able to be reunited today. But you scared me, standing there like a statue surrounded by incense smoke. I thought . . ."

Mai's father interrupted. "That's enough," he said. "Let her get some rest."

Aunt May went and sat on the porch in front of the house. San's house was right next door—the properties were separated only by a row of hibiscus shrubs—and the wedding party was still going on. A banner with words in silver that read "Double Happiness" hung over the door of San's home. Every now and then May would peer over the row of hibiscus at the party. The guests were talking and laughing and cheerfully congratulating the new couple.

Thanh, the bride, wore a pair of elegant silk pants and a white blouse. She walked from table to table offering the guests more food. Mr. Quang, San's father, was obviously very pleased with his well-mannered daughter-in-law.

"Lam, where are you?" Mr. Quang said, calling out to a young relative.

"Yes?"

"Mr. Truong's table needs more wine."

"Yes, sir," Lam replied and then busied himself with bringing more food and liquor to the guests.

Mr. Truong pointed at the bride and drunkenly droned on, "You…you…you're lucky to join this family.…If we hadn't heard about May's death, this marriage never would've never happened.… Try to have a son soon."

An older woman named Ba spoke up, raising her voice to be heard over the music coming from an old cassette player.

"You're just drunk and don't know what you're talking about. Thanh and San are very compatible. Look at those hips, and that butt! She'll have plenty of children!"

Everybody at the party laughed.

Mr. Truong angrily slammed his wine glass down on the table.

"What are you laughing at?" he yelled, reprimanding Ba. "You think you can lecture me, huh? Go home and lecture your bastard son instead."

Mr. Quang stood up and ran toward Mr. Truong.

"Please, Mr. Truong," he begged obsequiously. "Today is my son's happy wedding day."

"But she was rude," Mr. Truong said.

"She realizes her mistake," Mr. Quang said. "Lam, turn up the music."

The music was already quite loud. Ba quietly moved to an isolated corner of the party and began to cry. Three years after her husband had died, Ba had given birth to a son named Cun. When the villagers asked who the father was, Ba had remained silent. Stoically she'd accepted the consequences. It was said that the benefits she'd been receiving for being the widow of a fallen soldier were cut off.

Nobody at the wedding party knew that May had returned. On the porch now, Grandpa asked her about things from long ago when she was a child. Mai's father commented that May was lucky to have survived the war at all. Their conversation was neither particularly sad nor particularly happy. Mai's mother was the only one who seemed especially nervous; she broke anything her hands touched. Mai's heart was beating fast as she observed all this. Every now and then Mai's father would ask May another question, but it was obvious that her mind was occupied with thoughts of what was happening next door at the wedding party in San's home.

May hated herself for feeling lonely and resentful. She had fought in the Truong Son Mountains hoping for the day she would be reunited with her fiancé. But now he was completely oblivious to the fact that she had returned, and he was enjoying his newfound happiness and laughing. May shut her eyes. The light from the wedding party next door was like a thousand needles piercing her bleeding heart. She opened her eyes and, with great sadness, looked down at her amputated leg.

"My poor sister!" Mai's mother called out, pointing toward San's house. "Look! They're holding hands! I can't stand this scene any longer! May, how can you just sit here while this is going on?"

"What else can she do?" Mai's father asked. "She can't stand here screaming. Besides, before he got married, San's family came and talked with us very politely."

Mai's mother cried out, "My gosh, my gosh! They're happy while my sister is suffering!"

Mai's father ground his teeth.

"Will you just shut up, please? She's lucky enough to have come home alive. What else do you want?"

⁂ ⁂ ⁂

A shout from San's house brought the music to a sudden halt. Ba was standing over San, whispering something in his ear. San slumped down into a chair and held his head in his hands. The noise from the wedding party had stopped. All one could hear now were the sounds of people cleaning up the tables.

Then, without hesitating another minute, San got up and walked through the hibiscus hedge to the house next door. He was covered with vines and leaves as he emerged onto the porch in front of Mai's family. Mai's father held his knees and turned his face away. Mai's mother grunted a perfunctory greeting. Grandpa added tobacco to his pipe and began puffing away incessantly.

San apologized for his intrusion and said he wished to speak with May.

May swallowed her tears. "We have nothing to talk about," she said. "Please leave."

She stood up and walked with her crutches to the gate. San followed her.

"Please, let me explain," he said.

"You don't need to explain anything," May said.

"Please, May."

May breathed heavily and leaned against a pomelo tree.

"It's my fault," San said, beating his fist against the pomelo tree. "I'm a bad person. May, I want you to curse me."

"I didn't know that the day we said good-bye was the day we broke up," May said bitterly.

They were both silent and said nothing else. The pomelo tree gave off a pleasant citrusy smell.

On the day they had said good-bye, years ago, the river pier had been covered with fallen red petals from the surrounding hibiscus shrubs. In the distance, they could hear the sounds of American bombing and the firing of anti-aircraft artillery. Plumes of gray and black smoke floated up into the blue sky. May was rowing the boat as San sat watching her. She was dropping him off because he was going abroad. The boat bounced gently against the waves of the river. Planes streaked through the sky above them. May let go of the oars and leaned her head against San's chest. The boat drifted freely on the river as the couple held each other, trying to forget about the war and their impending separation.

San looked at May now underneath the pomelo tree in the family's front yard.

"When I was abroad," he said, "I thought about that day on the river every night."

"When I was in Truong Son," May said, "I wrote your name on every page of my diary."

They had had very different experiences during their separation. May had lived through bombings deep in a mountain military outpost, and San had enjoyed the peaceful beauty of falling snowflakes in a foreign country. But love and longing seemed to shorten the passage of time and narrow the space between them. Their love for each other was still there. They felt it suddenly rekindle for a moment.

San ground his fist into a branch of the pomelo tree and said, "May, we can start from the beginning."

"Why are you saying that?"

"I'll give up everything. We'll live together."

May was speechless. Overcome, she suddenly fell to the ground. San helped her get up and then sit down on a stack of firewood.

On the other side of the hibiscus hedge, Thanh, San's new bride, was pacing back and forth, occasionally plucking a hibiscus leaf, which she wrapped nervously around her fingers.

What would happen next? Mai wondered anxiously. There was no wind blowing, no clouds flying in the sky. The trees in the garden were still. The air felt stale and suffocating.

"No," May said, her voice breaking the quiet. She stood up and started toward the house, using her crutches. San ran after her. He took her hand. May stopped. She seemed out of breath.

"It's going to be okay," she said. "It's too late now. Please leave."

San seemed like he wanted to say something, but he didn't speak.

"Don't worry about me," May said, sighing. "Everything has already been set and done. You should try to live a happy life with her."

From the other side of the hibiscus hedge, Thanh called out, "Thank you, May! We're very grateful!"

May said nothing and turned away from San. She headed into the house, threw her crutches on the ground, and began to sob like she had never sobbed before. Mai's mother, who was also sobbing, helped her sister to the bed. May lay with her face turned to the wall.

%. %. %.

The night felt endless.

Rats chased each other noisily on the roof of the house. One could hear the screeching sound of two bamboo trees twisting around each other in the wind. May sighed as she sat up against a wall, holding her knee. For a long time she sat awake next to a dim oil lamp. A blond-haired doll rolled out of her rucksack, a present she'd planned to give her nieces. She looked at the doll, then held it in her arms for a while, like a baby. When she got bored of this, she pulled out her diary and began flipping through it. San's name was on every page. She brought the diary with her as she limped into the kitchen, then struck a match and began to burn the yellow-stained pages. Her face looked soulless. She sat like a statue in front of the flickering fire.

※ ※ ※

News of May's return spread throughout Trai village, and soon people were stopping by the house to pay her a visit. May greeted them shyly. Around mid-morning, once the parade of guests had stopped, May took her rucksack and went to sit by the bank of the river. Mai went and sat next to her.

Quietly, Mai said, "Auntie, our family is very happy that you've come back. The most important thing is that you survived."

May seemed lost in her thoughts, like she hadn't heard what Mai had said. Her voice, when she spoke finally, sounded like a whisper.

"A long time ago, San and I used to sit in this same spot. The day we said good-bye, the pier was covered with red flower petals, like it is today."

May sighed and looked off into the distance.

Mai's father approached the riverbank. He seemed upset.

"May, please," he said. "You can't just sit here like this. The rest of the village will laugh at us."

He angrily threw the oars into his boat and began to push off from the pier to go pick up some passengers on the other side of the river.

"Mai," he said, before rowing off. "You can stay here with Auntie, but don't swim in the river. There are unexploded bombs in the water."

Mai said, "Dad, you worry too much. People drag their fishing nets through the water every day. Yesterday Ba was catching crabs and pulled up a piece of bomb shrapnel in her net. But it was okay, nobody was killed."

※ ※ ※

Mai's mother brought pomelo tree leaves out to the riverbank so she and May could wash each other's hair. May's hair was now thin and brittle, but before she'd joined the military it had been long and silky. Back then, she would often ask Mai to bring her a stool to stand on while she combed and washed her hair. Afterward, May would swirl her hair around so it would dry, and minuscule drops of water would spatter Mai's face. San often hid behind the hibiscus hedge to spy on May washing her hair, and sometimes they would catch him and he'd be startled and embarrassed.

When it was lily season, May often took her niece to play along the riverbank. As they chased each other, May's long hair floated like clouds in the wind. Mai had wished that she could have beautiful hair like her aunt when she grew up.

Her mother and Aunt May were very close, Mai knew. They talked a lot, though Mai wasn't sure exactly what they talked about. Sometimes her mother seemed sad after they talked and would sigh a lot. She'd say things like, "Mai, you should study hard and help Grandpa and Auntie. Don't go and play and leave them here all by themselves."

It seemed like May was always sad, living with her father in the hut on the riverbank. She'd sit staring wistfully out over the water of the river, or up at the sky. She tried to busy herself with the cooking, but when Mai wasn't around it was only May and Grandpa who ate the meals and they had trouble enjoying the food. Grandpa loved May so much and would try to swallow what she cooked, but his eyes would still be full of tears. Occasionally May didn't even eat at all. The daytime was easier for her, because she could walk around the village and try to forget everything that was occupying her mind. But at night she had trouble sleeping, and thus lay in bed listening to newborn babies crying in the village medical aid station.

Sometimes May helped Grandpa row passengers across the river. She'd remove her artificial leg and painstakingly step onto the boat with her crutches. May always refused to charge her niece's classmates for rides along the river.

"You never take our money," the kids would say. "We feel bad."

May smiled and said, "It's okay. You can pay me back when you're older and get a job."

"We'll save up and give it to you as a wedding present!" the kids cried out. Then they saw that this had made May sad, so they changed the subject. They really loved May, and often gave her fruit and cakes. Some even handed her lilies to place at the foot of her bamboo bed in the hut. Mai's friends were like a flock of sparrows that brought excitement to the pier when they descended, but then left a melancholy silence when they eventually flew away.

A few months after her return to the village, May's hair had grown back and she started to look healthier. On bright moonlit nights she would let her hair down and bathe in the river with Mai. The water felt calm and cool. Mai could clearly see her aunt's bare shoulders, full breasts, white neck, and sparkling eyes. She remembered that her mother used to say May had been the most beautiful girl in the village and that the local boys would sneak up to the riverbank to spy on her while she bathed.

"Auntie, you're still very young," Mai said one night when they were in the river water together.

May smiled. "I will be old soon. But look at you! Every year I get older your body becomes more beautiful."

Mai blushed and glanced down at her own breasts. Her aunt's body sparkled in the silvery water as she swam in circles.

One day the head physician at the medical aid station quit, and the village chairman asked May—a former medic—to take over her position. She spent her nights now hobbling over the poorly kept village roads to visit sick patients.

"You should learn to ride a bicycle," the village chairman suggested, "and I'll pay to fix the roads."

"Save the money for the medicine we need for the aid station, there isn't enough," May replied. "Anyway, the walking is good exercise for me."

A few months went by. On rainy days the roads were full of her footprints.

※ ※ ※

It was raining again the night that San's wife, Thanh, went into labor prematurely. Ba, who worked as a midwife, tried her best to help deliver the baby, but there wasn't much she could do. Thanh screamed out, "Ba, I can't stand it! I feel like I'm dying. It's so painful!"

Thanh was exhausted and still hadn't managed to push out the baby. It was too far to travel from their house to the town hospital. There was no other option—they had to call May for help.

May put on her raincoat and made her way to San's house. When she got there, she found Ba outside with her son, Cun. Ba pulled May aside.

"We don't have enough time to transfer her to the hospital, and anyway, surgery might kill her. Plus San is still unemployed. All the money he earned abroad is gone. There's nothing left to buy medicine." Ba paused for a moment. She scolded her son, who was restless at her side. "Maybe it's better if you don't get involved," she said finally to May.

But May didn't seem to care what Ba said. She entered the house and immediately gave Thanh a few injections and then began performing a procedure. She told Thanh to push harder.

"Please!" Thanh begged. "I can't!"

"Try harder," May said. "Think of your baby. Come on . . ."

Thanh bit her lip and called upon her last reserves of strength.

Mai, who had followed her Aunt May to the house and was watching all this, suddenly got scared and ran outside. A few minutes later Mai heard the sound of a newborn crying and Aunt May's voice telling Thanh to put a bandage around the baby's belly button. It was already dawn and the rain had stopped.

San began jumping up and down excitedly.

"My daughter!" he cried. "She's alive!"

As she packed up her supplies, May began to cry. San noticed and felt immediately uncomfortable.

"It's okay," Ba said, ushering San toward his wife and newborn child. "Let May cry. Go be with your wife and baby."

Under the silvery sky, the river looked white. It began to drizzle again. In the light early morning rain, May hobbled away toward the pier.

※ ※ ※

San eventually named the baby May.

Ba shook her head. "It was terrifying! I've been a midwife for twenty years, and I have never seen such a difficult birth before." To May she said, "You're very talented. If we had taken her to the hospital, they would have cut her belly up into pieces."

A few days later, May returned to San's house. She kissed the baby's cute lips. Thanh was in tears.

"My family is indebted to you forever," she said to May.

May gave Thanh some money as a gift for the newborn. When she refused to accept the gift, May explained, "This is for your daughter, not for you. Please take it."

San meanwhile stood quietly in the corner. Nobody knew exactly what he was thinking about.

When Mai's father heard about May delivering the baby, he didn't try to hide his disapproval.

"You do people a favor without thinking of the consequences," he said. "You're so naïve. What if they thought you were trying to get some kind of revenge? You could've ended up in a nasty fight or thrown in jail!"

Ba, who had suppressed her bitterness and anger for a long time, suddenly burst out, "I'm glad you said that, because it only proves that you're a hypocrite! Don't try to hide the truth: you pretended to be sick so you could stay home in comfort and peace while your younger brother—my husband—had to join the military in your place!"

Mai's father seemed taken aback.

"Please don't say that," he said to Ba. "He was your husband, but my own flesh-and-blood brother. Since his death, I've tried to take care of the family as best I can."

"Oh, bullshit!" Ba screamed. "In Party meetings you voted to approve the committee's disciplinary decision on my case. You know perfectly well that Cun is your son. Here—take him and raise him as your own!"

Although Ba had said this, she still clung to Cun as if she feared someone would actually try to take him away from her. She began to sob. "Son, I'm a terrible woman . . ."

Mai's father seemed shocked. "Ba must be crazy," he said uncomfortably. Then he got on his motorbike and drove away.

May went to comfort Ba. "All women suffer," she said. "We just need to put up with this fate. We must find a way to show only the good and hide the bad."

"It's all my fault," Ba continued, still sobbing. "I'm not a good person." She wiped away her tears only when she noticed Mai watching them.

"Go away," Ba said to Mai. "Children shouldn't eavesdrop on adult conversations."

Mai sprinted home as if she were being chased by a ghost. She didn't understand exactly what had just happened among Ba, May, and her father, but tears were running down her face. She felt angry with her father for acting so impulsively.

She had a vivid memory of something that had happened a few days after Aunt May's return. Grandpa wanted to give the family's "The Country Is Grateful for Your Sacrifice" certificate back to the local authorities. While he was dusting the frame, Mai's father had asked, "Will they also take back the war pension we've been getting?" Grandpa had gotten suddenly furious. He'd thrown the feather duster down on the ground, put the framed certificate in a bag, and headed right away for the community hall. Mai's mother had cried.

※ ※ ※

March arrived in the village. Hibiscus flowers covered the path to the river. Grandpa had grown physically weak and begun to cough regularly. On the far side of the river were piles of construction materials. Mai's father said, "They're going to build a bridge over the river, and then there will be no need for boats to transport people across."

Mai felt suddenly sad as she realized Grandpa would have to give up his job. She knew he was getting older and weaker. She wondered to herself whom Aunt May would live with if Grandpa died.

"Whatever you're thinking about," Mai's father shouted, "I hope it doesn't have to do with those construction workers. Stay away from the construction area. If you get a crush on one of them, you'll get pregnant and bring us shame."

She didn't understand why her father had such negative thoughts. It seemed like he was always skeptical of everyone and constantly on the alert, as if anticipating an attack.

One day Mr. Ninh, the commander of the construction battalion, came to discuss logistics with Mai's father, who was in charge of the local militia. They negotiated an agreement: Mai's father would ask the militia to help secure the area around the river while the construction battalion cleared unexploded bombs from the water.

"But you will be responsible for providing our militia members with something to eat," Mai's father insisted.

They were talking inside the family's house. Suddenly, Mr. Ninh noticed the photo of May hanging on the wall and seemed startled. He stared at the photo closely, as if he recognized the female soldier pictured in it wearing a combat helmet.

"That's my sister-in-law," Mai's father said. "They told us she had died shortly before the liberation of the South, but it turns out she survived."

Mr. Ninh blinked his eyes, stunned. Then he got up and left.

The construction workers searched for bombs in the river all day. Their skin turned dark from being in the sun and mud. Mai's classmates often teased them. One day, while Mai was at home studying, her mother came running into the house. She looked terrified.

"You're a sacred spirit . . ." her mother mumbled, as if in a daze.

"What's going on?" Mai's father yelled. "Tell me, don't just stand there crying!"

"It's Ba," her mother started. "They said while she was out catching crabs she stepped on a cluster bomb."

Mai ran with her father to the river. A big crowd had gathered. They stepped aside to let Mai's father through as he approached. Aunt May was sitting quietly next to Ba on the ground. May's hair was untied, and her eyes looked soulless as they stared off into the distance. Ba was dead. Her body had been torn apart by bits of bomb shrapnel. Blood ran from her chest and limbs. A fishing net floated out on the water of the river.

After Ba's funeral, Mai's father started to lose weight and look haggard. At night he would wander restlessly around the garden. One morning he said to May, "I know that Ba wanted you to take care of her son, Cun. I'm not sure if this is appropriate, but why don't you let him live with me?"

But May rejected this suggestion. "Let me raise him. We can discuss the details later."

"Okay," Mai's father said. "I appreciate that."

※ ※ ※

The weather turned chilly at the end of autumn. In the gray sky, flocks of cranes flew in v-shaped formations to escape the coming cold of winter. People in the village started knitting sweaters. Grandpa now put on warm clothes when he went to the river pier. The construction workers had almost completed the bridge. They gossiped about how their project was almost over and the commander still hadn't won May's heart.

By now the people in the village had heard the story: back in the Truong Son Mountains, May had lost her leg guarding a tunnel where a group of soldiers were recovering from malaria. Mr. Ninh had been one of those soldiers. He owed his life to May and her sacrifice. The construction workers knew that Mr. Ninh had walked up and down the length of the Chau riverbank looking for the Truong Son girl who had saved his life.

"Maybe May will get married soon," the villagers gossiped.

May was living now with Cun in a new house near the river. She often sang lullabies at night to put him to sleep.

Nobody knew exactly what had happened between May and Mr. Ninh. It was possible that the construction workers exaggerated the romance and turned it into a legend. But there was at least one undeniable truth: at night, if the workers didn't hear May's singing to Cun coming from the newly built house, they couldn't fall asleep.

※ ※ ※

At night, the Chau River turned a silvery color. Nature seemed to be in perfect harmony. Millions of shining stars illuminated the sky and the ground. Exhausted, the villagers fell into a deep sleep. The air smelled of grass mixed with wet mud. The Chau River seemed restless—waves lapped against the shore.

Through the night, one could hear May singing a lullaby to put Cun to sleep. Her sweet voice echoed across the river. The construction workers stopped welding and listened. Her voice was deep and melancholic and bitter. It touched their hearts. The singing flowed into the nocturnal sounds of the river and the smells of nature.

13 / STORMS

NGUYEN THI MAI PHUONG

Nguyen Thi Mai Phuong was born in 1977 in Bac Giang in Northern Vietnam and is a member of the Bac Giang Province Association of Literature and Arts. She is the author of three collections of short fiction. Although she was born after the war, many of her short stories are about veterans in the postwar period, works inspired by the stories of her father and his friends who fought. "Storms" deals with one of the most insidious and persistent legacies of America's involvement in Vietnam: dioxin poisoning. During the war, the U.S. military used chemical defoliants like Agent Orange to shear back thousands of acres of the jungle foliage that covers much of the Vietnamese countryside. The dioxins contained in the defoliant mixture are known to cause severe health problems in humans, including cancers and birth defects in the children of those exposed even decades earlier. An estimated three million Vietnamese have experienced health issues related to dioxin poisoning, and the cleanup of certain "hot spot" toxic zones continues to this day.

———————————

Her name was Hoa Binh, "Peace." Her frail legs seemed to drag along the ground as she walked. Seventeen was usually an age associated with strength, an age when one was capable of snapping off the horn of a water buffalo. But Hoa Binh was thin and weak, like a cabbage leaf that had been left too long in boiling water. Her skin was pale and her nipples protruded underneath her shirt, physical traits that suggested she was still just a young girl.

As for her face, the villagers said, "People with Down syndrome all look alike." But Hoa Binh was not a person with Down syndrome. When she was born, she seemed normal like everyone else, but as she got older she became scrawny and frail. Fortunately her mind remained sharp. Although the village children laughed at her skinny bamboo-stalk legs under her silk pajama pants, she paid them no attention. She forced herself to get used to people's judgmental stares and tried to forget the tormenting pain of her body.

It was said that every family had one unlucky person who bore all the bad karma for everyone else.

Hoa Binh eventually had learned to live with her constant discomfort and endless anxiety. But in the past few days she'd started to have the feeling that a new storm was approaching.

One night, she dreamed that a group of villagers had tied her to a wattle tree at the entrance of the village and cut off her long, silky hair. She screamed as chunks of her hair fell to the ground. When she woke up she had an anxious feeling that something horrible was about to happen. It made her feel extremely sad, like the time she'd tried to catch a praying mantis that was running along the window sill but had stumbled over her stalklike legs and fallen down. Her father eventually had come over and silently picked her up off the ground.

Everything would be okay, Hoa Binh thought, as long as her younger siblings remained healthy. Every morning she got up early and sat by her brother, Tu Do, and her sister, Hanh Phuc, as they slept. She wanted to make sure their legs were still normal. They were only in fifth and ninth grade; there was still a long way ahead, and who knew what would happen? Hoa Binh herself had dropped out of school after eighth grade because of her physical problems and because she wanted to help her mother, a woman who masked her innermost emotions with endless household chores.

Hoa Binh's father was a fastidious and cranky man. For work, he biked around the village delivering letters. He seemed unable to get over his memories of the war. He still heard artillery fire during meals and while he slept. He was suspicious and exacting in everything he did, as if he were still psychologically preparing to fight the enemy. The neighbors called him Crazy Trong. He was obsessively punctual. Whenever his wife complained about this he would yell, "If you acted like that in battle, the enemy would blow your brains out! In order to enjoy what we have today, we need to be disciplined and stick to a strict schedule."

Trong had once told the whole family about a terrible bombing he'd experienced back in Quang Tri. His company was marching through a stretch of mountains where B-52 bombs already had annihilated the platoon that had marched there just minutes earlier. The bombs were so destructive that they didn't even leave a trace of blood. Only flesh and bones stuck to the scorched mountain foliage. Trong was twenty years old back then. When the bombing and shooting started up again, he had jumped into a hole to take cover. Then he had a premonition that this spot wasn't safe, so he moved. A different soldier immediately took his place in the hole. And then, in the blink of an eye, Trong watched this soldier's young body turn to dirt.

Trong had never forgotten the feelings he'd experienced in that moment. They came back to him especially the day he was forced to bury his child in a sprawling cemetery outside of the village. Nobody in Hoa Binh's family had ever forgotten this particular stormy day. Hoa Binh's mother had given birth to another daughter after the birth of her little brother, Tu Do. Her father was delighted with the new baby girl and cooked all kinds of wonderful dishes for the family to celebrate.

Hoa Binh liked to touch her little sister's hands because they were so delicate. But as the days went by, the baby's skin started to turn yellow and her body became emaciated. Hoa Binh's mother carried the baby out into the yard. The sky was full of dark storm clouds and the wind blew violently, stirring up hordes of mosquitoes. Her mother held the baby in her arms and prayed desperately up at the stormy sky. The baby died, shriveled like a dry leaf in her mother's arms. Outside in the yard, Trong sat motionless, holding his chest. Two trails of tears rolled silently down his cheeks. Hoa Binh didn't know what to do. She cried and lit an oil lamp, thinking that the light might somehow help. Her mother's hands were trembling as she asked Uncle Ut to take the baby out to the rice paddies.

Uncle Ut said, "I don't think Trong is going anywhere. Even though it's so windy and dark, he's just sitting there like a rock."

The war had ended years earlier and Trong had named his daughter Hoa Binh, "Peace," but it seemed that peace continued to elude this family.

The day Hoa Binh and her father had gone to the hospital for her health check, Trong was speechless as he held the results in his hands. Hoa Binh sat uneasily on the back of the bicycle and listened to her father's breathing under his sweaty shirt. On the way home they stopped at a bookstore where Trong bought a book called *Never Give Up*. During the war he had lived in the woods under constant bombardment and gunfire; his hair and beard had grown long, his body was soaked in mud, and he'd survived on wild vegetables and creek water. But he had not felt as miserable as he did now.

Back then Trong had been enthusiastic about joining the military. "Our singing drowns out the sounds of bombing!" people chanted. "The road to the battlefield is very beautiful this season!" There was a general excitement about joining the war effort. If people didn't join, they would feel isolated, like an outsider. So Trong didn't hesitate about signing up himself. It was only later, when he was stationed deep in the jungle and woke up one morning to see the soldier sleeping next to him completely covered by a giant swarm of termites, that Trong truly understood the cruelty of life.

Trong's mother assumed he'd died out there in the jungle. She was observing his death anniversary, in fact, the day he finally returned to his hometown. He carried his soldier's rucksack on his back and cried out, "Mom, I'm alive!" Relatives and neighbors gathered at the house, laughing and talking cheerfully. Once she had finished sobbing, his old mother said, "The war is over and you are a hero because you have returned home alive and still strong. If you were dead, there would be nothing left for us to say. . . ."

Trong's unit had wanted to award him the title of hero officially, but he'd refused this recognition. Now he felt that he had only really acted honorably back then, during the war—his life since had been full of deception and nasty tricks. Maybe it was an act of bravery that he continued to have children after Hoa Binh. Thankfully, his son, Tu Do, and daughter Hanh Phuc grew up and developed like other normal children. Still, though they didn't say it out loud, Trong and his wife were anxious on a daily basis.

In her pocket calendar, Hoa Binh marked her siblings' birthdays so she would remember those days. In the morning of their birthday she would get up early and go to the market to buy black beans for a sweet bean soup. For their birthday parties, she peeled and sliced mangoes and pomelos. Tu Do and Hanh Phuc would climb over Hoa Binh's legs and laugh. Hoa Binh shook her billowy silk pants to tease them. Watching this scene, Trong's face would cheer up and he'd actually smile, a smile that seemed to come from someplace very far away but made everyone happy.

%% %% %%

It was another dark day, with storm clouds swirling in the sky above the village. Hoa Binh stumbled clumsily as she carried two baskets balanced on a bamboo pole to collect buffalo manure for her mother to use as fertilizer in the rice paddy.

"Are you collecting dung to eat with rice?" a drunken man in the village asked as Hoa Binh stumbled past. But she didn't reply.

The man's name was Toan. He was known for being obnoxious. He liked to brag to the local children that he was a disabled veteran from the American War. But whenever Trong was around, Toan would lower his head with embarrassment. More than once Trong had said, "He's a reactionary. If I have enough evidence, I will destroy him."

When Hoa Binh arrived back at her family's house that day, she found her father in the yard talking with a town official. She watched as her father opened an old suitcase, removed a stack of papers, and handed them to the official.

"These days they review Agent Orange cases very carefully," the official said, as he smoothed out the papers. "As you know, there are travel costs associated with each case, as well as a waiting period. Plus, no result is ever guaranteed."

"We joined the military and risked our lives for this country, and for people like you to live in peace," Trong said angrily. "Look at my daughter! Is she not eligible?"

The town official seemed embarrassed. He lowered his voice. "No, I just meant you might want to offer money to those who help you. And I can always help with the networking. . . ."

Trong seemed surprised. "You mean I should pay money under the table?"

Hoa Binh's mother, who was listening from inside the house, came outside and said to the town official, "Just please find a way to help us. We'll take care of those other things." To her husband she said, "Give him some money for the 'transportation fee.'"

But Trong was now furious.

"This is ridiculous! I won't pay a bribe to get the benefits we deserve. This should have been taken care of a long time ago, but every time I submit the paperwork it somehow gets lost!" He moved toward the official. "Get out of here! I don't have time for state officials like you."

Once the official's motorbike had completely disappeared in the distance, Hoa Binh watched her father polish and clean his old dagger, one of his most cherished mementos from the war. The whole family was scared. Whenever Trong was angry, he would polish the dagger and then place it in a drawer at the foot of the bed. Then he'd stay up late listening to the radio, taking notes, and making strange phone calls. He seemed so serious.

Sometimes Tu Do and Hanh Phuc would play "war," using sticks as guns that they pointed at each other—"Bang, bang!" Then one of them would pretend to lie dead on the ground.

"Children," Trong said once, after silently watching them pointing the sticks at each other, "stop playing that game, or it will ruin you before you even know it."

Hoa Binh could see the horrifying memory of the war on her father's face as he sat motionless on the bed. Sometimes, when he was asleep, she would sneak up to his bed and watch his cheeks twitching in panic as he slept. One night he woke up suddenly and asked, "Hoa Binh, is that you? Why aren't you in bed? I just had a dream. A big, tall, bloody American fell on me." Her father had sat up in bed and told her about the time his scout team wandered into an ambush and they'd ended up fighting hand-to-hand with the enemy, and Trong had used his knife to stab an American GI through the heart and kill him. Amid the bombardment and gunfire of war, of course, death was common. But Trong hadn't known that after the war ended, death would still haunt him every night.

※ ※ ※

Nobody in the family could stop Trong from taking the trip back to Quang Tri. Mr. Thanh from the neighboring village would go with him. They both carried rucksacks filled with supplies. Mr. Trong also carried his old dagger, freshly cleaned and polished. Hoa Binh didn't understand why they were taking so many things with them, including yellowed old letters with blurred handwriting.

Hoa Binh felt worried while her father was away. One day he called, and over the phone he told her, "I'm not dead, so don't worry." The sky outside the house was dark and gloomy again; it seemed like a storm was coming. Hoa Binh slept all day, skipping lunch. When she woke up finally her mother said, "Your dad came back. He and his friends went to meet someone in the village, I don't know who."

She went to look for her father and walked along the grassy riverbank. When she came to Mr. Toan's house, she heard voices and stopped to take a closer look. There were six men in Mr. Toan's yard, including her father, Mr. Thanh, Mr. Toan, and the village chairman. Mr. Toan seemed to be acting differently than normal. He trembled as he spoke: "I . . . I . . . beg you! Please forgive me!"

Calmly, Thanh said, "Do you feel ashamed of stealing credit from your comrades? Tell us, when were you injured in the war?"

Trong was staring at Toan with fiery eyes.

Toan lowered his head and said, "The truth is I shot myself in the leg. I beg you—please forgive me!"

Later that day, a crowd of men gathered at Hoa Binh's house. They were all veterans who had come to visit after hearing that Trong's old army friends were in town.

"I am by no means a hero," said Vinh, one of Trong's old friends. "It's Trong who gave up the official designation of hero and passed it on to me. He's the one who deserves the recognition." Vinh clapped Trong on the back.

"It was a cruel war," one of the elderly veterans added. "But we survived. In a sense, we're all heroes."

Trong remained silent. It seemed like he didn't want to say anything in this particular moment.

Vinh stayed with Hoa Binh's family for a few days after this. She often saw them marking a map with blue and red dots and cleaning old war mementos. They were preparing to take another trip to look for the graves of fallen soldiers from their unit. Hoa Binh had never seen her father so happy.

Over the radio, she listened to the announcement of another storm approaching, but this time she felt a strange sense of relief. . . .

14 / THEY BECAME MEN

PHAM NGOC TIEN

Pham Ngoc Tien was born in 1956 in Hanoi and graduated with a B.A. in literary studies from Hanoi University. He has been a member of the Vietnam Writers' Association since 1997 and has won several awards for his fiction. His most famous work is a collection of short stories called *They Became Men*. The title story addresses an aspect of the soldier's experience rarely acknowledged in Vietnamese fiction: the fact that many young men were still virgins when they went off to fight and die in the war. By celebrating the female character at the center of the story—a woman who sleeps with multiple young soldiers—Pham Ngoc Tien challenges the traditional Confucian values that had dominated Vietnamese society for thousands of years and dictated how a "virtuous" woman should act.

I

The MC's voice rang out loudly over the speaker system: "Pham Van Ngoc, a junior majoring in literature at University X, will be presenting her research paper titled 'Sacrifice: The Unique Fate of Women in the War to Defend the Country.'"

The morning session of the conference was almost over. The audience of literature majors culled from different universities was getting tired and restless.

"Not war *again*!" some of them cried out.

"This is a forum on literature, it has nothing to do with war!"

"What's the point of digging up some outdated past?"

"What does *she* know about the war, anyway?"

The student, Van Ngoc, hesitated at first as she reached the stage. Then she walked confidently to the podium. Her elegant white *ao dai* and kind face immediately silenced the unruly crowd. Her posture and mannerisms were determined and confident, but her voice trembled slightly as she began to speak.

At first it seemed there was nothing out of the ordinary in her presentation. She shared some of her research findings and several examples. The audience was quiet throughout—a kind of indifferent silence. Her topic was nothing new. Everyone already knew and accepted that women had made tremendous sacrifices during the war. It wasn't until the conclusion of her presentation that Van Ngoc posed a rhetorical question about a specific kind of sacrifice and the role it deserved in any honest accounting of the war, that the audience started to get restless. What was she talking about? Why was she bringing this up?

The audience began to grumble even more vehemently as Van Ngoc finished her presentation. Her usually rosy face went suddenly pale. Their voices were like the sound of gunshots.

"You've turned the entire value of sacrifice upside down!"

"There's no need to talk about this filthy subject!"

"This is crazy!"

"Get her off the stage!"

Van Ngoc's entire body shuddered; then she collapsed suddenly behind the podium. After a few seconds she got up and ran off the stage, then stumbled her way out of the conference hall altogether.

I couldn't bear it any longer and finally ran after her. I found her in the hallway outside, crying. It was like something extremely heavy had overtaken her otherwise innocent face. As she saw me approaching, she wiped away her tears, then said hurriedly,

"You were a soldier and you're a writer. Please help me understand. The war happened not that long ago, so why do people seem to forget so quickly? Why won't they acknowledge the sacrifice those women made? Is it just old-fashioned morality? But it was wartime! Why should they think this is something that somehow blemishes victory? Please answer me!"

I remained silent.

"My father," Van Ngoc continued, "was a soldier who became a man after his experiences with one of these women. She helped him overcome many challenges. You know that, and yet you remained silent back there. This woman helped my father in more ways than anyone can imagine. No matter how much time goes by, we can't let people question her dignity."

Again I said nothing.

"Why won't you help me tell the truth about these women? Why won't you help me fight for their honor?"

I couldn't bring myself to speak. There was nothing really for me to say. So instead I took her hand and held it tightly in my own. But with all of her strength she tore away from me and ran quickly down the hallway.

I stood there all alone for a moment. From the conference hall I heard the speaker announce, "Nguyen Trung Hieu, a senior at University Z, will now be presenting his paper titled, 'Illusive Poetics in the Surreal Poems of Han Mac Tu.'"

II

She was twenty years old and had been in the military for one year. The war against the Americans was at its peak. She was stationed at a small base deep in a section of the jungle where heavy bombing had destroyed most of the dense foliage. After long, grueling marches, different companies of soldiers would stop at the base to rest before going into combat. Female soldiers were rare at this particular jungle base. There were only five females out of the over one hundred soldiers stationed there. And she was the only one from the city. She wasn't particularly beautiful, as she readily admitted, or at least wouldn't have been considered so back in the city. But in the wilderness of the jungle, amid the cruelties of war, her beauty seemed mesmerizing: her smooth, lithe body; long silky hair; and fair skin.

Next to the base was a creek. The water was clear and calm, though it wasn't deep; the reflection of the golden moon often shone off the bottom. She was well educated—she'd been studying literature before dropping out to volunteer for the army—and the other soldiers would criticize her for her bourgeois habit of bathing in the morning, typical among female soldiers from the city.

One morning, as she made her way down to the creek, the air felt unusually chilly. It was like autumn had suddenly arrived overnight. The sun was still low on the horizon and the mist hovering over the water looked silvery. Everything had that pure silver color. She stood still as a statue, enjoying the early morning air. In that moment everything seemed to suddenly disappear. There was no war, no sorrow, no worry.

She touched the water gently, then lowered herself down into it. Behind her, on the bank of the creek, there was a rustling sound. A chicken jumped from a bush and ran off into the jungle. Suddenly she had the sense that someone was watching her. Then she heard two young voices coming from behind a pile of rocks.

"She's gorgeous! Just like the Venus!"

"I don't know about the Venus, but she's more beautiful than all the girls in my hometown."

"Did you spy on them too?"

"No. In my village everyone just bathes together in a local pond. But the girls don't have light skin like hers."

"This is the first time I've seen a girl's body so clearly."

"Same here."

"I should've gotten married before getting sent out here. I should've known to do that."

"Don't be an idiot. You can't marry someone just because you want to take off her clothes." The voice grew quieter all of a sudden. "With my girlfriend, I could've known her body, if I'd wanted to. She wanted to get married but, you know, we don't know when we'll come back. She's in the prime of her youth; I didn't want her to feel tied to me. Who knows what can happen in the middle of all this shooting and bombing? So I refused to get married. The day before I left, we went out together to the fields and sat there until morning. She cried a lot. I felt sorry for her. She said that I didn't have to marry her and all she wanted was to have a child with me. She didn't care how long the war might last or about her reputation. She didn't mind suffering through hardships. She would raise our child and wait for me, no matter how long it took. To be honest, I was really moved by what she said and almost agreed. But in the end I had to control my emotions and make the right decision. I hope she understands. In the future, maybe I can find her again. But what if . . ."

"Shhh! Keep your voice down. You don't want anyone to hear us. I was about to say the same thing. Our country is at war. We don't know what will happen to men like us. It's not fair to ask a woman to wait for us."

"If I died now, I'd still be a boy, not a man. It's sad."

"Let's go collect some water. And don't make too much noise! It would be embarrassing if we got caught."

She didn't miss a single word they said, and her eyes followed the shadows of the two young soldiers as they retreated from behind the rocks. She forgot that they had just been spying on her. Thinking about their conversation, she shivered. Why was the creek water so cold? Her entire body trembled as she steadied herself on a rock and ground her teeth. She tried to understand it: If they died before being with a woman, would their souls wander lost in the afterlife, full of regret and longing?

But no! she told herself. That was ridiculous. *If I died, I would simply die.*

Gathering all of her strength, she stood up from the creek bed. It was so cold that her body felt as if it were being poked by thousands of tiny needles. Somehow she managed to get out of the water, put on her clothes, and stumble back to her unit. On the ground of the main tunnel back at the base she collapsed.

※ ※ ※

A sensation like floating. Her body bouncing gently up and down. What kind of bomb had they dropped on the tunnel this time? Had the tunnel collapsed? No, it couldn't be that. She'd experienced the bombings before, the suffocating feeling, the soil closing in all around, her hands clawing in every direction to dig herself out.

But this was different.

It was completely dark. She wanted to scream but couldn't. To take her mind off the fear she tried thinking of her mother. But she knew that her mother wouldn't be able to bear seeing her in this situation, so forced her from her mind. And her father? He had died at Dien Bien Phu, and she'd never met him. Soldiers are funny like that—they stop home for a short visit, get their wives pregnant, and then leave forever. She could imagine her father shaking his head and saying, "You can't die. You're all we have."

She must think of something else.

My boyfriend.

He'd lost his life in an aerial bombardment. They bombed the tunnel where he was stationed, and his fellow soldiers painstakingly removed his body from the dirt. His hand was still clutching a Truong Son pen, a gift she had given him. Perhaps he'd been killed while working on a novel or a poem.

As this thought occurred to her, the sky suddenly brightened. She closed her eyes and heard voices.

My comrades, she thought, wishing she could scream out the words. *I am alive!*

She felt as if she were on a ride at an amusement park, being carried off somewhere by forces beyond her control. She felt dizzy and scared and called out to her mother. But no, it wasn't her mother. Her mother would never wear a white shirt and white hat like that. Whose voice was that? It sounded totally unfamiliar.

"Forty-four degrees . . . Delirium . . . Get her in the bed over there. . . ."

She felt herself floating even more quickly now. The figure in white faded. In the distance she thought she could see Long Bien Bridge back in Hanoi. The smell of bombing. They had destroyed one of the bridges' pylons again.

Hurry up! someone yelled. *Why are you so slow?*

There was fire everywhere. A rocket had also hit the Phuc Tan neighborhood, a dense working-class part of the city.

Is anyone hurt? she heard herself call out, but she was only answered by the haunting echo of her own voice. She wasn't sure exactly why, but she laughed. How embarrassing if someone could see her laughing like this while their countrymen suffered and died.

He always said she was tactless.

You're mean! she said back.

Go ahead, he teased her. *Find someone more charming.*

They were on the roof of her school, which had been evacuated. Tomorrow he would be sent to the B combat zone; they had only this night together before he left.

Sitting next to him there on the roof, she had the urge to lean against his body, but instead she moved away. That's how girls are supposed to act.

How's school? he asked. But this was a silly question. They'd both gotten caught up in the war effort; there was no sense talking about school now.

I want to kiss you, he said suddenly.

Normally she would have pretended not to like it, but this time she pressed her entire body into his. Still, she broke away first.

You want too much, she said. *I feel suffocated.*

An air-raid siren went off. Then another. Level three. It didn't matter. They were only vaguely aware of things flying in the sky above them. The explosions generated circles of yellow light. He shielded her with his body.

Let's go down, it's dangerous up here, he said.

But she refused. Her lips hungrily found his again.

Are you scared?

No. But I'm worried about you.

I want to be with you forever, she said, and held him so tightly it was as if she was trying to give him everything she had.

Below them, it seemed like the entire city was ablaze. The roof around them had started to turn pink.

Suddenly she stopped herself.

No, no! We shouldn't do this.

I love you.

But it's a sacred thing. I don't want to do it while there are bombs falling all around us.

Sweetheart, I'm leaving tomorrow. When do you think we'll be able to do it?

After we win the war. You'll come back and we'll get married.
But when will we win the war? Ten years? A hundred years?
I don't know.
Are we going to wait for each other forever?
Please don't say that. You need to trust me, and my love for you.
After this she cried for a long time. He apologized.
No, she said. *You didn't do anything wrong.*

Dawn had just begun to break across the sky. She felt that she truly loved him. The city in the early morning was unusually quiet. It seemed like everything that had happened the night before was unreal.

They were both calm as they climbed down from the roof. He kissed her passionately one last time before leaving. It was then that she realized the sorrow of separation had only just begun.

※ ※ ※

She stayed two months in the jungle hospital to recover from the fever. The sickness took a toll on her physically, but slowly she began to get better. During this time she often thought back to the incident at the creek the day she'd first fallen ill. She had the sense that overhearing the two young soldiers who were spying on her had affected her soul tremendously, though in what way exactly she still wasn't sure.

She also thought back to the day she'd received the news of her boyfriend's sacrificial death. She had sobbed without shedding any actual tears; tears don't accompany the most intense agonies.

Darling, I am suffering.

It had only been three months since their last night together on the roof of her school. She couldn't eat and started to become emaciated and weak. If her mother hadn't been there, she would have deteriorated completely. Her mother, of course, had experienced her own sorrow caused by loss and seemed to have endless sympathy for her situation. With her mother's permission, she placed her boyfriend's picture on the household shrine honoring her father. And the next day she volunteered for the army. Soon the cruel war had taken over her life. She hoped that being a good, responsible soldier would somehow alleviate her agony.

But that cold morning at the creek had reopened old, unhealed wounds, causing them to bleed.

Darling, are you also suffering?

If his soul were actually wandering in the afterlife full of regret and longing, she would never be able to forgive herself. Why hadn't she just offered herself to him that night on the roof? Why not? She felt tremendous regret that she hadn't given this to him before he left.

These thoughts tormented her. They became a kind of obsession. The day she was released from the hospital and returned to her unit, she found herself walking alone on a path through the jungle. Suddenly she saw him everywhere. There he was standing behind an old *sang-le* tree. His voice carried to her on the wind: *I love you.* She saw him hanging from a tall tree, dense with leaves. His body was covered in blood. His voice sounded broken: *When will we have peace?*

In the wilderness of the jungle, the thoughts intensified. She was tormented by images of him—his bandaged limbs, his bloody face. His hands dropped pages of a manuscript. She didn't want to read the pages, but the wind blew them toward her.

Please read this, he implored her. *It's my journal. I wrote about you.*

She wasn't afraid and didn't feel lonely. The idea of loneliness had ceased to exist for her the day he died. She cried because she pitied herself. "What have I done wrong?" she asked, but no one answered her.

One day she returned to the creek and found that the water looked unusually clear. She stared at her reflection in the water and was surprised to find that she didn't recognize the woman she saw. The fever seemed to have aged her by ten years. Then she saw his reflection next to hers on the surface of the creek. He looked pensive.

What? she asked. *Are you bored with me now?*

But his reflection vanished suddenly, and he appeared a few seconds later on the other side of the creek.

I will always love you, he said, his voice echoing off the rocks.

Right after he spoke these words, the creek water began to bubble as if it were rising to a boil. The water turned cloudy with mud and began to rise around her feet and ankles. A flash flood. Hurriedly she began to fight her way to higher ground, grabbing at shrubs and vines. Suddenly she was startled by a voice from above:

"Climb up here quick, the creek is flooding!"

It was a young soldier. He pulled her up into the fork of a tree where he'd taken shelter. Together they huddled there as the rain grew heavier.

"You must be from the armory," the young soldier said. "I'm with T10."

But they didn't talk much beyond this because soon the air was filled with the sounds of C130 Hercules planes. The flooded jungle began to tremble as gunfire and explosions rang out all around them.

"Don't worry," the soldier said, covering her with his body so she wouldn't be hit by any shrapnel.

Gunfire tore at the tree, scattering bits of bark all around them. She could feel him pushing against her. His breath felt warm in her hair. She thought back to the feeling she'd had that night on the roof of her school. Without hesitating, she pulled the soldier's head down onto her chest. She had already considered giving her virginity to him when the gunshots started. Actually the thought had occurred to her earlier than that, when she first walked down to the creek that morning.

She didn't hesitate; she knew they could be killed at any second. He was so young.

Silently, she said a kind of prayer: *Please accept this small gesture so that you can become a man and will never have to regret such a simple, unfulfilled desire if you happen to lose your life in this cruel war.*

The soldier seemed a bit confused at first, but then he understood. Tremblingly he pushed his body against hers. He seemed suddenly lost in complete happiness. She held her breath and tried to enjoy the moment as long as possible. She felt it was her responsibility to share in his desire. Pure happiness. The blood ran warm in her body. The rain stopped. The floodwaters subsided. The guns went silent. There were no longer any signs of planes in the sky above them.

Afterward, time seemed to cease to exist. She felt completely satisfied. Later, when she would offer her body to other young soldiers so that they could become men, she would experience the same sense of total satisfaction and happiness as she had during this first encounter.

The young soldier was so moved by what she had done for him that he began to cry. He tried to speak, but she quieted him and gently caressed his hair.

"Please don't cry," she said. "Men don't cry."

"I will never forget you," the soldier said.

"You don't have to remember me," she said. "I'm very happy just like this."

Her satisfaction made her unusually confident. She wasn't bothered by her comrades' criticism of what she did. On the contrary, she felt content. She silently welcomed this unavoidable anger and didn't try to defend herself or justify her actions.

My comrades, this is a decision I have made by myself. I am responsible for everything.

The soldiers left her with little keepsakes—a pen, a photograph that had an address scribbled on the back, the pink flattened petals of a dried flower, a comb made from salvaged airplane metal, and a silver ring that was supposed to prevent her from catching a cold. There was a face behind each item. And who among them had died?

She put her hands against her swollen belly. The baby was kicking.

※ ※ ※

She was going to become a mother. Her breasts had started to become fuller. She felt an unfamiliar warmth all over her body. She felt as if her soul were expanding. Whenever she was alone, she quietly sang lullabies to her baby. She wanted it to be a boy who would look like his father.

As she sat up late one night in the tunnel, stitching clothes for her unborn child, a shadow suddenly appeared in the entryway. It was a man. He aimed his flashlight directly at her. She brought her hands up to her face to block the harsh light. She recognized the man—he was an older soldier in her unit. She knew that he'd been wanting to sleep with her for a long time, but she kept refusing him.

His voice sounded shrill, almost like a shriek, when he spoke.

"Haven't you heard?" he said. "The bombing yesterday killed eight of our comrades. And you're sitting down here stitching clothes for your *baby*? You should be ashamed!"

She stood up immediately. She wouldn't let anyone insult her child.

He ran the flashlight up and down her body. She had the sense that something bad was going to happen and turned away. The older soldier was breathing heavily as he moved toward her.

"Please," she said, as he pressed closer to her. "Don't humiliate my baby. Be respectful of the other soldiers. Some of them have already died. Let their souls rest in peace."

She couldn't find more words. Her voice felt weak, like she was in a daze.

The soldier pushed her against the ground. She fought back as best she could. She sat up and pulled an AK-47 from the wall, but it was no use. He was too strong and pushed her back down again, even more violently this time. She had never experienced pain like this.

It's over now, she thought. *My baby, I'm sorry. Please forgive me.*

She had no real sense of direction as she ran afterward in the dark through the jungle. But finally she arrived at the creek. It was early morning. The water was covered with a silvery mist. It enveloped her body as she stepped into the creek. For a moment she stood motionless like a statue, luxuriating in the happiness she had felt as well as the pain she'd just experienced. Gently she stirred the water, then placed her hands on her belly and quietly began to sing another lullaby to her baby.

III

By the time I joined the army, the story of this woman was all over the front. She had become a legend.

Some people said that the water had carried her the length of the creek and that they'd found her body a week later, so severely bloated that no coffin would fit her; a platoon of combat engineers had to spend an entire day building a special coffin from a large chestnut tree.

Others said that it would have been impossible for her to climb the giant tree where she had hanged herself. The tree was hundreds of meters tall and must have been a thousand years old. It took dozens of people to safely bring her body down. After that there was no bombing, no wind, no rain, no thunder, no lightning. But somehow the tree collapsed; before that it had withstood countless bombings from B52s.

Others claimed that a bomb had hit the creek that morning and her body was blown to pieces. Afterward, the jungle became unusually lush and verdant—flowers bloomed everywhere and birds could be heard chirping from the dense foliage. Bombs and chemical defoliants could no longer destroy this land.

At the army base they listed her as MIA. Nobody knew anything else about her.

※ ※ ※

I didn't know what to say to Van Ngoc after her presentation. But something in her gentle, kind face made me think of this woman. I purposely stayed silent and accepted her accusation that I was a cruel person. All I could do was write this story to somehow pay respect to a true incident that occurred years ago. The reader can make their own judgment.

15 / AN AMERICAN SERVICE HAMLET

NGUYEN THI THU TRAN

Nguyen Thi Thu Tran, who writes under the pseudonym Thu Tran, was born in 1963 in Bien Hoa and currently lives in Ho Chi Minh City. She has published more than twenty books, including collections of short stories, novels, and poetry. "An American Service Hamlet" is based on her experiences growing up among American soldiers stationed in the South. She has said that as a child, she did not understand why everyone hated the Americans and talked about fighting them while most of the GIs she interacted with treated her and the other children kindly. The memory of this paradox inspired her to write this story, one of the few pieces of Vietnamese literature about southern women who worked for or had relationships with the Americans. The story is unique in that the American characters are portrayed as innocent victims of the war as opposed to cruel, bloodthirsty killers, which is how Americans had been previously depicted in most Vietnamese fiction about the war. Here, the tone is one of reconciliation and mutual understanding, of acknowledging the tragedy and suffering on both sides and searching for a way to move on.

Miss Trung didn't shut the door this time as Smith entered her house. Bach stood watching from across the street.

"Bach, go back to the house!" her mother called out to her. "Or are you trying to get a glimpse of the naked American?"

The naked American? Before, when Miss Trung had invited this man into her house and closed the door, Bach had no idea what went on inside. But now the door was left ajar, and inside she could see Smith resting his head against Miss Trung's chest as he sobbed. It seemed strange to see an adult, especially an American, crying like this. Why was he crying? Miss Trung ran her hand over his head as if he were a child and said something that Bach couldn't understand because it was in English. Bach craned her head to get a better look . . .

A sudden pain shot up her back.

"You little slut!" her mother screamed, slapping her with a rattan rod. "Do you want to work for the Americans? Is that what this is about? Get in the house!"

※ ※ ※

Bach was on the verandah in front of the house. She saw four eyes and two tongues poking out from behind a hibiscus shrub.

"Ha ha! Your mom beat you for spying on the naked American. Ha ha!"

It was some neighborhood kids, Li and Anh.

"So what?" Bach said defensively. "How do you even know the American was naked? *You* guys are the ones who want to watch."

Li and Anh continued to stick out their tongues at Bach, but she didn't care. She found herself thinking about Smith; she wondered if he'd stopped crying.

One time, Bach had referred to Smith as *anh* 'Mit, using the typical pronoun for an older male and mispronouncing Smith's name. Mr. Tam, a driver who was cleaning his *tuk-tuk* nearby, had overheard what Bach said and shouted, "You must not call the American GIs *anh*! Call them *no*," the disrespectful pronoun.

Miss Trung happened to be standing nearby. She laughed.

"Call them whatever you want," she said. "In English they're all called '*you*' anyway."

So Bach decided to make it easy: she would call them all *you*— you Tom, you John, you Henry. But Bach's favorite was you Smith. Smith was the nicest one.

Li and Anh left finally and Bach again was alone sitting on the verandah. She thought about Smith and his beautiful smile. She had noticed that he liked to carry Teo, Mrs. Xi's little son, on his shoulders. Smith had blonde hair and blue eyes. He often patted Bach on the head and gave her chocolates. Miss Trung said that Smith had a younger sister who was Bach's age back in America.

From the verandah, Bach looked across the road to Miss Trung's room and saw Smith opening the door as he left. Why was he leaving so soon? Well, maybe because today he had cried and he wasn't as happy as usual, Bach reasoned. Smith began walking along the red dirt road. Bach checked to make sure nobody was looking, then ran after him.

"'Mit, hello! No can do!" Bach said in English, smiling cheerfully, though she had no idea what she had just said.

But Smith seemed to understand that the little girl empathized with him. He patted her on the head and smiled down at her.

"Bye bye for now," he said.

When she returned to the verandah, Bach saw Miss Trung across the hedge that separated their houses, out hanging clothes to dry while talking with someone.

"Well, he was full of sadness today so he left early. His close friend was killed in combat yesterday."

She bent down to pick up more clothes.

"Why are you staring at me like that?" Miss Trung said suddenly. "Go away now. My nipples and your wife's nipples look the same."

It was Mr. Ba Ga she had been talking to, Bach realized now as she saw him walking away down the red dirt road. He was known as the most lustful person in the neighborhood.

Miss Trung continued hanging up the clothes. She sang to herself as she worked:

> We had agreed to meet this afternoon
> But you didn't show up.
> A gentle breeze cools my heart.
> The sky is foggy—
> or is it your burning cigarette that makes
> the air turn smoggy?
> How do you feel about standing me up?
> You promised you would be there,
> but you never showed up.
> Someone wearing a blue shirt
> is walking away into the night. . . .

Bach leaned her chin against her palm and sighed. Miss Trung's singing sounded so melancholy. And Smith's friend had been killed—no wonder he hadn't brought her any candy this time.

※ ※ ※

Bach's village was now called an American Service Hamlet because many of the homes there had rooms for rent. These rooms were usually occupied by young women who worked for the Americans. The biggest American employer was the Bien Hoa Airport, which was nearby. The American soldiers stationed there hired the young women to clean and do their laundry, and some of the women also offered a massage service.

All of the young women who rented rooms in Bach's neighborhood worked as maids in the American offices. This included Miss Trung, Miss Xuan, Miss Hong, and Miss Tuyet. At the end of the day, they each brought home an American man. They'd spend a few intimate hours together behind closed doors; then the Americans drove away in Jeeps, headed back toward the airport. The girls would then joke around among themselves for a while or go outside to wash.

The people who lived in the American Service Hamlet hated the American soldiers and looked down on these girls, though they relied on them for the rent money. There were at least five households in the neighborhood that survived only on income from renting out rooms in their homes. Other people in the neighborhood profited from the girls as well. Mrs. Nam Bong provided a monthly meal service to Miss Trung and her girlfriends, who paid a full month in advance but often didn't eat every meal, so Mrs. Nam Bong was able to make a decent profit. Ms. Xi, who had been a street cleaner before, got a janitorial job in an American office thanks to Miss Trung. She would pick out candy, canned food, newspapers, and books that the Americans had thrown away and sell them on the street to earn money to raise her son Teo, who didn't have a father. And then there was Mr. Tam, the *tuk-tuk* driver, who hated Americans more than anyone else but still didn't refuse his services to the girls who worked for them.

There were thousands of ways to hate the Americans and the girls who associated with them. It was a constant refrain among the older generation in the American Service Hamlet whenever the American soldiers came to look for the girls: "Damn it! They're invading our country and they also get to have fun with our girls." Or, "My gosh! The Americans stink like owls! I can smell them from all the way over here." But the Americans just grinned. They had no idea what these local people were saying.

Meanwhile the children in the hamlet would chase after the soldiers, shouting things like, "Hello, Tom! No can do!" Sometimes the soldiers would give them candy. When the girls who worked for the Americans returned to their rented rooms, mischievous boys hiding up in the trees would use slingshots to shoot "bullets" of wadded paper at their buttocks.

The adults knew about the children's behavior, but nobody yelled at them. Ms. Hai, who made a living selling cigarettes, said, "I have no pity for those girls. The kids are only punishing them for flirting with the Americans." One time Ms. Xi argued back, saying, "But if the girls didn't flirt with the Americans and bring them around, who would buy your cigarettes?" Then the two women got into a fight.

It seemed like the Americans were afraid of the young men who lived in the hamlet, especially the school dropouts, draft dodgers, and members of the local security militia. In the afternoons some of these men would get together to drink, use empty pots and pans as musical instruments, sing war songs, and taunt the American soldiers. Mr. Tinh, a leader of the security militia, said that he would never live under the same sky with the Americans because they had "stolen" Vietnamese girls. One time, Mr. Tinh and some other men from the hamlet beat up Tom and John, who were friends of Miss Hong and Miss Tuyet. The men put sacks over the heads of the two Americans and poured shrimp paste over them. But when Tom and John came back with their guns, the entire group ran away. Not long after that, both Tom and John were called up into combat. Miss Hong and Miss Tuyet soon found new American boyfriends.

Smith was also a target. One day a group of drunken men grabbed Smith and tied him to a fence pole in Mrs. Hai Danh's garden. The pole was crawling with fire ants. Bach's heart beat violently as she ran to tell Miss Trung what had happened. But Miss Trung wasn't at home. Why had Smith come to the hamlet if she wasn't home? Bach wondered.

He was such a kind person. Just the other day he had given Mrs. Sau, an old widow, money to see a doctor. And the day before that everyone had seen Smith visibly grieving when they buried Hoa, who had been killed in combat.

Bach remembered her father saying, "Smith is a fine man, the nicest American among all American men who are dating the girls in the hamlet."

While Bach was worrying about how to help Smith, she ran into Kiet. He was crossing the rusted, flimsy old bridge that connected the houses in the hamlet to the rice paddies. Nobody lived in the paddies; the only structures out there were ramshackle huts for the duck attendants. Kiet ate and slept in one of those huts. Bach knew that he didn't have any parents or relatives. When she saw him now crossing the bridge, he was carrying a sack, which Bach guessed probably contained frogs he planned to sell in the hamlet.

"Kiet!" Bach called out.

"What's going on?" Kiet asked.

"Please! You have to help save Smith!"

"Save an American?" Kiet seemed surprised. "Why? Are you in love with him?"

Tears suddenly flooded Bach's eyes. She didn't think she knew anything about love; she just felt sorry for Smith because he was nice and shouldn't die from ant bites.

Kiet approached Bach and patted her on the head.

"Geez—you cry so easily! Okay, where is Smith?"

Kiet was only about eighteen or nineteen, but the group of drunken men deferred to him because he was articulate and a good drinker. He was decisive and efficient in the things he did, and this earned him respect in the hamlet. Physically, he was tall and lanky with dark skin, and he always wore black *ba-ba* pajamas and an old conical hat. He spent his days in the rice paddies, catching frogs and small fish. The people in the hamlet thought he might be a Viet

Cong infiltrator and avoided him because they didn't want to get in trouble with the South Vietnamese police.

Bach liked Kiet. Sometimes when he was out late catching frogs, he would stop by the house and Bach would ask her mother to give him some leftover rice.

Her mother would grit her teeth and say, "You act so brave, asking me to give him rice. But do you know who he is?"

Her father, meanwhile, was always on Bach's side. "You're overreacting! He's just a kid from the neighborhood." Then her father would load a bowl with rice and even some fish stewed with pepper, oil, and green onions.

Bach wiped away her tears with the hem of her shirt. She took Kiet by the hand and led him to the drunk guys and Smith. Kiet stood in the middle of the group and put his hands on his hips.

"Who tied 'Mit to the pole?" Kiet asked.

"Why do you want to know?" someone asked. "Is the American your grandfather?"

"He isn't my grandfather," Kiet replied, "but he *is* a human being."

The crowd began talking boisterously among themselves.

"I did see him cry a lot at Hoa's funeral."

"Nonsense. He was crying because he's afraid of dying in combat."

"Well, that's still better than a cowardly draft dodger."

"Motherfucker! What did you say?"

The drunken men had suddenly turned on each other.

Kiet intervened: "I think you guys should let 'Mit go," he said firmly. "Anyway, you'll get in trouble if the MPs show up."

"The *American* police? We're not scared of them! And you can go tell them that! You're a Viet Cong and you come here to defend Americans?"

"Let's not talk about Viet Cong or Americans right now," Kiet said. "We're in wartime. If you are real men, you'll save the fighting for the battlefield."

And with that Kiet began to leave the circle of drunks. They seemed much more subdued now.

"Hey, wait a minute," one of them said, grabbing Kiet's arm. "How about maybe a little something to bail out the American?"

Kiet handed over his sack. "Here—it's full of fish and frogs. Go ahead and eat all of them, but don't mess with the American anymore."

"You gonna drink with us?"

"No," Kiet said. "I'm going home."

*% *% *%*

Tom and John were never seen again in the hamlet. Miss Trung told Bach that she'd heard they had both been wounded in combat and had returned to their country.

Miss Hong and Miss Tuyet changed boyfriends like they changed clothes. They always seemed sloppy and disheveled. Once while they were eating rice-noodle soup at Miss Bong's shop, Miss Trung asked loudly,

"Where are your bras? You girls let your breasts hang down like that, it's embarrassing!"

Miss Tuyet dipped a piece of tofu into a bowl of shrimp paste and gave a fatalistic smile. Her breath smelled of alcohol when she spoke.

"The Americans are about to return to the United States," she said. "They have already been defeated. Haven't you been listening to the news on the radio?"

"Oh, but what does the Americans' withdrawal have to do with you girls?" Miss Trung said dismissively, putting a piece of crab meat into Bach's bowl.

"Well, it's different for you," Miss Tuyet said. "'Mit really loves you, so you're not worried."

"If the Americans leave," Miss Trung said, ignoring this last, "then you girls should think about turning over a new leaf."

"Turning over a new leaf?" Miss Hong said. "Can't you see that everyone in this hamlet looks down on us?"

"Let's stop arguing." It was Miss Xuan, eating rice cake rolls one stall over. Her voice sounded tired and sad. "You girls stay here and try to be happy. Tomorrow I'm going back to my hometown."

"Why?" Miss Tuyet asked, genuinely surprised.

"Henry is dead," Miss Xuan replied.

Miss Trung kicked Tuyet under the table. "Stop asking questions," she whispered. "Yesterday she found out that he died in a battle."

Bach didn't understand all of the conversation, topics like fighting and death and pain. But she was aware of one thing: not many Americans came to the hamlet anymore, and the girls who used to work for them had started to move out of their rented rooms. Mr. Tam, the *tuk-tuk* driver, no longer had many customers; with no work, every morning he lay in a hammock singing folk songs. Mrs. Nam Bong stopped her monthly meal service and started selling *banh mi* sandwiches at the entrance to the hamlet. And Ms. Xi took her son with her back to her hometown where they stayed for good, working in the rice fields that belonged to her parents.

※ ※ ※

Eventually, Miss Trung was the only one left out of all the girls who had moved to the hamlet to rent rooms and work for the Americans. She quit her job at the American office and waited for the day when Smith would take her with him back to America. Everyone realized that theirs was a sincere love, so the older generation would stop bad-mouthing the Americans when Smith was around, riding his bicycle through the hamlet in the afternoons.

One afternoon, after a particularly heavy rainstorm, the people in the hamlet heard the sound of gunfire coming from a prison on the other side of the creek. Mr. Tam said that it was just business as usual. The guards must have fallen asleep and some Viet Cong had broken into the prison to steal guns and grenades.

Everyone knew that soon the authorities would come to their homes and they'd be asked to show their papers. The men in the hamlet would be interrogated and Kiet would probably be a primary suspect. Indeed, business as usual.

But then, a little while after the gunfire had died down, the people in the hamlet suddenly heard a cry of "Help!" coming from the creek, which had overflowed with dangerous rushing water after the heavy rain. It was widely known that drowning had claimed almost as many lives in the hamlet as the war. Everyone, including Smith, rushed to the creek. In the crowd, Bach stood on her tiptoes to catch a glimpse of the black spot struggling in the churning waters. Then all of a sudden Smith jumped into the creek. Five, ten, fifteen minutes passed, before Smith finally was able to drag the drowning person up onto the shore. Everyone was shocked to see that it was Kiet.

"But Kiet is a good swimmer," someone commented. How could he drown?"

Smith and Miss Trung began to give Kiet CPR. Finally Kiet began to breathe again, though he was still very weak. He'd hardly been conscious for a few minutes when everyone heard the distinct sound of police cars approaching. The police ordered everyone to stand back and began to search Kiet's body. Bach watched as the police turned and flipped Kiet's body in every direction, as if they were cooking a rice cake. But they found nothing and eventually departed, leaving behind them a trail of thick smoke and the smell of gasoline.

"Damn it," cursed Mrs. Nam Bong. "They're worthless. All they ever do is make a big scene with their noisy vehicles!"

The sand on the shore of the creek was covered with heavy boot marks. Kiet stretched and lay on the ground, exhausted as if he'd just almost drowned a second time. Smith and Miss Trung built a fire to help him get warm.

※ ※ ※

It was more than thirty years later when Miss Trung and Smith returned to Vietnam for the first time since the end of the war. At sixty years old, they still seemed like a happy couple. They returned for a visit to the old hamlet, which had now become the Hung Phu district of Ho Chi Minh City. Bach still lived there, in a new three-story house. In fact, many of the residents of the old hamlet now lived in bigger, more comfortable homes. Life was much better than before.

Smith seemed to recognize Bach immediately, as if she were the same little girl with the friendly smile and crooked teeth.

"Hello, Bach!" Smith called out in Vietnamese. "How have you been?"

Bach was shocked—Smith could speak Vietnamese! Mrs. Trung said that when she'd taught her two children the language Smith had joined her lessons.

So they had two children together, Bach thought. The war had in fact created something beautiful.

After catching up with Bach, Smith asked about Kiet. Bach explained that he now held an important position in the local government. Smith said that he would like to meet Kiet, if possible, and Bach promised she would help arrange it. Then Mrs. Trung and Smith went around saying hello to Mrs. Trung's old neighbors. Mrs. Nam Bong, her former landlady, invited them over for lunch, and they stayed there talking with her all afternoon.

※ ※ ※

A few days later, Kiet invited Bach and Smith and Mrs. Trung to dine with him at a local restaurant. Kiet seemed to be in a particularly cheerful mood, talking and laughing. He was especially interested in having a conversation with Smith in Vietnamese. Before the food arrived, Kiet filled two glasses with wine and said,

"Smith, here is a drink that I've been saving for you for over thirty years. I want to thank you."

"I should be the one thanking *you*," Smith said.

"Why do you have to thank me?" Kiet asked.

"Without you and Bach, I would have been killed by those fire ants."

Kiet laughed so loud that his shoulders began to shake.

"When I helped you that day," Kiet said, "I was really angry with that group of guys." He paused for a moment, then continued. "They were correct, you know, in suspecting that I was a Viet Cong infiltrator. I was serving back then as a spy for a unit stationed deep in the jungle. Fortunately, you and the American boyfriends of the girls in the hamlet were never on our radar."

"Well," Smith said, sighing, "it was wartime back then. Anyway, you don't need to thank me." Smith slapped Kiet on the back. "When I jumped in the creek I had no idea I would be saving a would-be very important state official!"

Mrs. Trung clapped her hands and said, "Bach and I congratulate both of you on this reunion!"

They spent two delightful hours eating and drinking together. Everybody talked about the past. Bach felt so happy sitting with these older people whom she still saw as adults, though she herself was a schoolteacher now with two children of her own. She felt that she still had permission to lean on Mrs. Trung's shoulder and smell her sweet-scented hair. She didn't care what the adults were saying. She closed her eyes and remembered the day before Smith was scheduled to return to America.

Bach had cried when she'd said good-bye to Miss Trung and Smith. That night she couldn't sleep; she felt that she loved them and was scared about the possibility that they would never return. Finally at the break of dawn she drifted off into sleep and had a strange dream in which she ran into Smith and Kiet out walking along the railroad tracks behind her house. Both men were walking very fast, as if soaring along the iron tracks. They picked Bach up and the three of them flew toward the lights of an oncoming train. Both men were laughing, while Bach screamed and cried, absolutely terrified.

In the morning, Bach went to Miss Trung's house to look for her and Smith, but they had already left for the airport. She felt a sudden emptiness that filled her with a fear of being lonely, so she walked across the bridge to the rice paddies to look for Kiet in his duck hut. But the hut was empty.

She had no idea where he had gone. But later, once Uncle Ho's forces had liberated the city, she heard that people had seen Kiet sitting on one of the tanks leading the convoy.

※ ※ ※

The reunion at the restaurant eventually had to end. A car came to pick up Smith and Mrs. Trung and take them to the airport. Although everyone promised to get together again at some point, nobody wanted to leave. Mrs. Trung eventually had to pull Smith away from the table.

"We have to go," she said to her husband. "And you should give Kiet's stuff back to him before we leave."

"What stuff?" Kiet seemed surprised.

Smith pulled a bag out from underneath the table.

"These are the weapons I found in your pockets when you were drowning in the creek," Smith said, placing the bag on the table for everyone to see. "I knew that if I left them there you would have gotten in trouble. And I was right, because the police came to search you right away."

"You've been keeping them all these years?" Kiet asked, astonished.

"No, of course not! I could never bring weapons like these through customs. But a few days ago we visited Mrs. Nam Bong, the former landlady, and dug them up from underneath a banyan tree in her backyard. Fortunately, nobody ever cut down the tree or built a house there." Smith opened the bag and showed Kiet.

"Here, take a look. It's been over thirty years, so they're a little rusted, just like the old bridge that leads to the rice paddies."

Kiet's hands trembled as he picked up one of the old rusted guns. He was so moved and emotional that he couldn't even manage to utter a "thank you" to Smith.

Then the couple got into the waiting car and drove off in the scorching midday heat.

Bach was left alone with Kiet in the restaurant now. She poured him a glass of water. Kiet seemed distant and lost in his thoughts. It took a little while before he smiled cheerfully again. He patted Bach on the head, like he used to when she was little.

"I can't believe that American!" he said, still surprised. "He hid my weapons under a tree without telling me. I went back to the creek the next day after the water had gone down and looked for them until my feet and hands were swollen."

"Did you steal the guns from the prison that afternoon?" Bach asked.

Kiet smiled. "Who else would it have been? But I got unlucky that day. The water was too fast and aggressive and the guards kept shooting at me. Bullets were flying over my head. Plus my legs started to cramp up as I tried to swim away."

"How many times did you steal guns?" Bach wanted to know.

"A few, I can't remember exactly. Everyone in the hamlet already suspected that it was me. And they were right." Kiet smiled again. "Bach, drink this glass of wine with me, okay?"

"What are we drinking to?" Bach asked, picking up the glass.

"We'll drink to the fact that Smith and I can be both enemies and friends at the same time."

Bach drank and emptied the glass. But she didn't drink to Kiet and Smith's specific situation. She drank instead to a belief she still clung to firmly, over thirty years after the end of the war: that in difficult situations people were still capable of showing some kind of natural kindness toward one another.

16 / LOVE AND WAR

NGUYEN NGOC THUAN

N guyen Ngoc Thuan was born in 1972 in Binh Thuan and currently lives in Ho Chi Minh City. He is a visual artist but has won several literary awards for his writing, including the Swedish Peter Pan Prize in 2008 for his children's book *Open the Window with Closed Eyes*. His story "Love and War" is notable for its postmodern, surreal style, rare in the tradition of socialist realism typical of most Vietnamese war fiction. While on the surface the story seems to function as a simple allegory for war and its destructive, all-consuming nature, the nuances of the narrator's feelings toward the unnamed cannibalistic female character—the woman he trusts and loves and continues returning to, despite the fact that she seems to be literally consuming him whole—complicate this overly simplistic reading. By the end of the story, the reader is left wondering, Who is the real enemy?

The rumors said she was a cannibal. So I wasn't exactly surprised when I woke up one morning next to her and discovered that I was missing one of my legs.

Did you eat one of my legs, I said, *while I was sleeping?*

She got angry and refused to let me sleep next to her again.

It can't be, I said, because I thought I really loved her. *I don't believe what everyone says. Your smile is so beautiful, your teeth are so white. You wouldn't use those teeth to bite me or those lips to suck my blood.*

But she was still mad at me.

I said, *When I asked if you ate my leg while I was sleeping last night, I was just kidding.*

She didn't believe me.

You are just like everyone else, she said. *You repeat the exact same things they all say.*

I said, *Well, now that I think about it, I actually must have lost my leg in the war. I must have forgotten,* I said. *The war was a long time ago, you know. Our country has gone through so many wars, it's hard to keep them all straight sometimes.*

A few days later, walking on crutches because I was now missing a leg, I came to apologize. She wasn't mad anymore and forgave me.

Having a bad memory is not a character flaw, she said. *And anyway, I know you're mentally deranged.*

Suddenly we were in love again, even more intensely than before. She even let me kiss her on the mouth.

That weekend, she let me sleep next to her again.

This time, she said, *you can sleep at my feet.*

Your feet? I asked.

Yes, my feet, she said.

Her feet were pristinely white like pieces of white jade.

Her feet were so purely white that I thought she must never use them for walking.

Her feet reminded me of a pair of delicate hands.

At midnight I touched her feet and felt a sudden shock, but also happiness.

After that I feel asleep. Contented. Fulfilled.

When I woke up the next morning and discovered that I'd lost my other leg as well, I had to ask her, *While I was asleep last night, did you eat my other leg?*

Immediately I regretted that I'd said anything. She was so angry that she began to shake. Her eyes filled with tears. She couldn't speak.

Finally she ushered me outside and shut the door.

I crawled across an empty verandah, feeling extremely sad. I knew then that I'd lost my pure trust in her.

I have lived this life, but I don't trust it.

I don't trust love.

I listen to the words of others instead of my own heart.

After she kicked me out I continued to sit in front of her door, hoping she would reconsider.

I continued to sit, and I continued to wait.

Meanwhile everyone kept repeating the rumor that she was a cannibal.

Finally, one rainy day, she opened the door and let me inside. Quietly she began cleaning the wounds of my severed legs.

I said, *It wasn't you, it was probably because of the war.* I said, *We have gone through too many wars—wars with the French, the Americans, and the Chinese.* I said, *I must have forgotten that I'd already lost both legs before I even met you.* I said, *It's all these past wars that have damaged our love for each other.*

Please forgive me, I said.

Please forgive war.

Please forgive everything that destroys our memories.

Or makes us not want to remember.

Or causes us pain.

Tears began running down my face as I spoke.

She said, *War isn't worth getting angry about.*

With that, I knew she had forgiven me.

War is a piece of shit, I said. *Dog shit.*

She laughed cheerfully.

She had apparently forgotten that we were in a fight, and so once again she let me spend the night.

She said, *Tonight I will let you sleep under the blanket with me.*

My heart leaped up into my throat, like on the day the South was liberated.

War has separated us, I said. *But peace will allow our hearts to blossom. As if our hearts were growing roses,* I said.

I love peace, I said.

And I hate war, she said.

Me too, I said.

When I woke up that third time beside her in bed, I discovered that my arms were gone.

I said, *Of course, I lost my arms and my legs in the war. I must not have remembered that. War is cruel,* I said. *It confounds me.*

Sweetheart, she said, *it isn't your fault. You have a bad memory, that's all. Nobody can hold a bad memory to blame.*

It's true! I said. *It's all war's fault. Goddamn war!*

I said, *We need to condemn the Americans. The French too,* I said.

And the Chinese! she said.

We must resist them, I said.

The Japanese fascists as well, she said.

I am so happy, I said.

She had never loved me this much before.

I said, *I'll print out pamphlets to inform people that we need to hate war. We must be antiwar,* I said. *War destroys our love for one another.*

She said, *Tonight I will let you put your head under my breasts.*

Under your breasts? I said.

Yes, she said. *Under my breasts.*

I lay my head underneath her breasts and went to sleep. I had never been so close to her heart.

The fourth time I woke up next to her, I touched my entire body and realized that my head was missing.

It's not a problem, I said. *It's only normal. Everyone loses their head after experiencing war. Besides, having a head only makes us crazier anyway,* I said.

War makes us crazy, she said.

She wanted to reward me for my trust in her love.

She said, *Tonight is a special night. I want to give everything to you.*

Give me everything? I said.

Yes, everything, she said.

My soul jumped. I lay down in her arms. I knew that I deserved this love. I had sacrificed enough in the war. It was a terrific reward for everything I had suffered.

Afterward I fell asleep.

Only people who are really in love can understand that when a woman chews a piece of your flesh, tearing it from your body, she is only feeling true love.

The fifth time I woke up next to her, I didn't bother checking what parts of my body were now missing. All I thought about this time was my love for her.

That is all I have now, this love. When it cools during sleep, I need to heat it up first thing in the morning when I wake up.

I also need to hate and condemn war more.

The Chinese, the French, the Americans . . . You were all cruel. I hate you!

I also hate those who have never gone to war with our country but plan to in the future.

Those are my last words. From a person who dies for love and war.

17 / THE PERSON COMING
FROM THE WOODS

NGUYEN THI AM

N guyen Thi Am was born in 1961 in the South Vietnamese province of Long An and earned her undergraduate degree in law in the former Soviet Union. She currently lives in Ho Chi Minh City and works as a successful businesswoman at a firm specializing in agricultural products. Although she is not a full-time writer, many of her short stories have been widely anthologized in Vietnam, and she is known for her minimalistic and subtle style. In "The Person Coming from the Woods," the spiritual world is treated as a normal extension of the physical world. Though she claims to be frightened at times, the narrator does not seem shocked or surprised to be visited by the wandering ghost of a fallen soldier. This is the reflection of a widely held belief in Vietnam: a person who has died in a violent, unnatural way, or a person whose body is missing, can never really rest in peace; on the contrary, their soul will continue to wander lost in the afterlife, stuck in a kind of tormented, restless purgatorial state.

After graduating from teacher training college, I was assigned to a school in the west of Quang Tri province, a remote and desolate area. It was a middle school with five classes and teachers who came from the lowlands; the majority of the students were ethnic minorities. The school principal had arranged for me to live with a math teacher named Ha who was about thirty years old. We shared a small house, the roof thatched with grass. It didn't look very sturdy. Sitting inside the house, I imagined that a strong wind could easily blow the whole thing away.

After class was over, we didn't really know what to do with ourselves in the evenings. In winter we would walk down to a creek and collect wood that had washed up on the shore and carry it back home. At night we burned the wood in a fire in the middle of the house to keep warm. Then we'd sit and stare at the flames, engaging in deep, serious thinking, as if we were philosophers.

One night, when it was getting close to bedtime, Ha sighed and said,

"I'm ugly and getting older, so it doesn't matter for me. But you're young and as beautiful as a goddess and have to teach and live here. It's such a waste."

I laughed. "My mother says that everybody has their own special fate. Maybe one day a man will come find me here."

"That could very well happen," Ha said. "You know, about twelve kilometers from here there's a border patrol station. Maybe a border patrol officer will propose to you."

Both of us laughed cheerfully; then we crawled into bed and lay under our blankets. We had trouble falling asleep. Eventually we slept for a bit and woke up again, then slept a little bit more. It was a long, restless night.

After two months, I started to notice that this area was really beautiful on brightly moonlit nights. When we opened the door on those nights, we saw mountains and hills drowning in the moonlight. In the distance, patches of white grass waved gently in the wind. It was at moments like this that Ha made her usual complaint:

"Shut the door! This place used to be a battlefield, didn't you know that? There are lost souls wandering all around here."

"I'm not scared," I said. "Why should I be? There's no anger between us."

Ha got into bed and covered her head with the blanket.

"Hang, please!" she moaned. "I'm begging you."

Finally I got up and shut the door, then crawled into bed myself. I could hear the strong winds outside blowing through the woods. I couldn't help but think that it might be fun if a border patrol officer out walking his rounds got lost and wound up here at our little thatched-roof house, talking with us, two young female teachers.

At the end of my first six months teaching at the school, I received a letter from my boyfriend. He wanted to end our relationship. His reason was simple: his family wanted him to get married because he was the only son. He couldn't marry me because I was living so far away. If everything had ended like that, it would have been fine. But with the letter he included a wedding invitation that had a note scribbled on it: "If possible, please make a visit back to your hometown and come to my wedding."

Tears rolled down my cheeks as I held his letter. It seemed obvious that he didn't care at all about my feelings.

That night, I woke up suddenly from a strange dream. My body felt hot and my throat was dry. I got up to look for a pill, then sat down next to the fire. Ha seemed to be in a deep sleep over in her bed. Maybe she was used to this lonely life by now. I stood up and opened the door. It was October. The sky outside seemed unusually high and full of stars. In the distance was a crescent moon, slipping slowly behind the mountains.

Then, at the foot of the mountain, I suddenly noticed the outline of a man holding a gun and walking with his head bowed. I knew that night hunters were common in this area. They often wore a small light on their forehead; when the light caught an animal in its path, we'd sometimes see the beam freeze, then begin to dance, and then hear the sound of a gunshot. Sometimes the hunters would stop by our little house to ask us to light their cigarettes or for a glass of water, or sometimes even to slaughter the animals they'd just killed. They could be extremely generous; sometimes they'd even give us a piece of meat that was still warm.

I'd been lost in my thoughts and hadn't noticed that the man was approaching our house. I could see now that he wasn't a hunter; he was a young soldier holding a gun and carrying a rucksack on his back.

He smiled.

"Hello, Miss Teacher," he said. "My unit has given me permission to return home for a short visit. May I rest here for a few minutes?"

I invited him inside and gave him a chair by the fire.

"Please, have a seat," I said.

The soldier took off his rucksack and sat down. I poured him a glass of water, which he drank enthusiastically. When he was finished, he put the glass down and warmed his hands by the fire.

"It's about seven kilometers from here to the main road," I said, "if you'd like to catch a bus to go to the lowlands. Do you know how to get there?"

"I've been living here for six years," he said. "I've been all over these woods." He paused for a moment and smiled. "Tomorrow I will visit my mother."

"How long has it been since you've seen your mother?"

"It's been six years."

"Why so long?"

"Because I haven't been able to make it back home. May I have some more water, please?"

I brought him more water and the soldier again drank voraciously, as if he hadn't had anything to drink in a long time. Outside, a lone forest cricket chirped loudly.

"Tell me about your hometown and your mother," I said, changing the subject. "I live far away from home, so I feel homesick too."

The soldier added more wood to the fire.

"My hometown is far away," he said. "In Ha Bac, near the Thuong River. There are many rice fields there. In the afternoons I used to go out to the fields to look after my water buffaloes and fly kites. I remember how the twinkling evening light used to mean that a monsoon was coming. The afternoon would look colorful and beautiful under the broad sky full of dark clouds. Then within a few minutes, the sky would go black, the winds would pick up, and it would start to rain. The kids who were out there taking care of the buffaloes would shout and run home."

"What about your family?"

"My father died when I was young, and my mother raised me and my younger sister by herself. My sister got married two years ago. My mother is a retired schoolteacher and lives alone now. I think she must miss me very much."

"Do you have a girlfriend?"

"I joined the army when I was eighteen and never had the chance to express my love to any girl. My unit is made up of all males, so there's nobody for me to fall in love with."

"Well, when you're on leave this time, maybe you'll meet someone. Who knows? But anyway, it's not a problem for men your age never to have fallen in love." I laughed. "Sometimes love causes nothing but misery."

"I'm not sure how happy a person is if they're in love. But without love, you feel very lonely. A person without love is like a statue. He wouldn't even be able to tell if moss started growing on his face."

The soldier's eyes suddenly became dark and cold. He turned to look at me, but I felt scared and turned away. Time seemed to slow down. The minutes went by very, very slowly. . . .

Suddenly Ha's young rooster crowed. Then a little while later, other roosters started crowing in the distance. The soldier stood up, hoisted his rucksack onto his back, and picked up his gun.

"Good-bye for now, Miss Teacher," he said. "I've got to catch the bus."

I stood up and saw him to the door. Outside, the crescent moon slipped suddenly behind a row of thick, dark clouds.

He took my hands in his and held them tightly. His voice quivered, broken, as he said, "Miss . . . Miss . . . May I kiss you?"

It was a natural reaction—I jerked my hands away, ran inside, and slammed the door. From the window, I watched the soldier walking away. Under the moonlight, his silhouette gradually became smaller. I wondered why he wasn't walking in the direction of the main road but toward the woods.

※ ※ ※

Two months later, a gray-haired woman accompanied by two young men stopped by our school and asked for a place to spend the night. I talked with her and learned that she was looking for the grave of a fallen soldier. Her son had died in this area during the war. She told me that one night she had a dream in which her son told her, "Mom, I must find a woman to love before I can come home to you." The gray-haired woman shared this dream with a medium, who then gave her some specific instructions:

"Find a paper doll crafted in the image of a young and beautiful girl. Take the doll and some rice and some salt to the river near the area where your son was killed. Pray and burn everything in that spot, then throw whatever remains into the river. Hopefully, his soul will return after that."

The medium insisted that the woman must follow these instructions exactly if she wanted her son to return home.

I went with the mother to the bank of the river. As I watched them set up a shrine and place the offerings on it, my body went suddenly all cold. The private in the photo placed on the shrine was the soldier who had come to our house on that night two months earlier.

I studied the photo for a while, then watched the ashes of the paper doll float down the river. The mother placed a wreath made of white flowers in the water, and eventually this too was consumed by the river.

The mother began to sob in the twilight.

"My dear son. You have someone to love now. Please come back to me. . . . My son . . . Please . . ."

As I left the riverbank, I felt like a sleepwalker. It was inevitable. I knew the thought would haunt me for the rest of my life: if I'd only let him kiss me that night, maybe he wouldn't have had to return to the cold, dark woods.

18 / OUT OF THE LAUGHING WOODS

VO THI HAO

Vo Thi Hao was born in 1956 in Nghe An and currently lives in exile in Germany. For nearly two decades she was a member of the Vietnam Writers' Association; in 2015 she resigned from that organization to protest the lack of freedom of expression in Vietnam. Her story "Out of the Laughing Woods" was well received when first published in 1991, and it was eventually made into a popular film. The portrayal of the group of women in the story as driven to a kind of hysteria after three years of isolated living at an army supply depot "deep in the ghostly arms of the forest" suggests the ways the war traumatized even those not involved directly in the actual fighting. The "laughing disorder" that apparently afflicts these women is likened to "the wild, cruel laughter of war." There is no real path to recovery, no hope of finding happiness during peacetime. The women have been irrevocably changed by the war and counted now among its millions of victims.

It was the dark green water of the creek that caused it.

All four of the young women charged with looking after an army supply depot deep in the Truong Son Mountains began losing their hair until every one of them was nearly bald.

When Thao, the fifth member of the group, arrived at the depot, the other four women were glad to see her. Thao had long, silky hair, which reached all the way down to her feet. They treasured Thao like gold and made sure the forest would never destroy her beautiful hair by giving her fragrant medicinal leaves to use as shampoo.

But the forest was too powerful. Two months after she arrived, Thao's beautiful hair began to turn thin and clumpy. Everyone cried except for Thao, who said, "There's no need to cry. I already have a boyfriend and he is very faithful. Even if I'm completely bald, he will still love me."

The other women stopped crying as they listened to Thao tell her story. Her boyfriend was a student at the University of Literature in Hanoi. His image came to Thao's memory from some distant place, but then he appeared clearly in front of all the women as a loyal prince.

Because the women loved Thao, all four of them also fell in love with this man, though in a strictly platonic way. This kind of love is impossible to explain in peacetime. Only those who have experienced war and utter loneliness and who have been on the precipice between life and death can understand it.

They had lived in the forest for three years, three rainy seasons and two dry seasons. It was now the third burning-hot dry season. Their supply depot was hidden deep in the ghostly arms of the forest. Every now and then a soldier would stop by to pick up supplies and clothes, then leave in a hurry. But they usually lingered long enough to flirt with the women. Their behavior was typical of men who had been living away from women for too long. Some of the soldiers would silently admire them as if they were queens, planting dreamy hopes that attached to the women's minds like cobwebs. But then the men would disappear and the women would be lonely again.

Gradually the violence of the battlefield crept closer to the remote army depot. The five women lived anxiously while the forest seemed indifferent, covering the ground with fallen leaves. The deep red color of the leaves was reflected in the bright, hot sky. The women dreamed of red at night while they slept.

One day around noon, three soldiers came to pick up some supplies. As they got closer to the depot they heard the sound of wild laughter. They stopped for a second, confused and maybe a little frightened. But then they recalled the stories people told about these woods and the witches who lived there and liked to throw parties from time to time. They kept walking, and as they neared the depot, one of the soldiers thought he heard something—probably a white gibbon, he figured, rustling off in the bushes. But as he got closer to the bushes a hand suddenly grabbed his neck. He heard the sound of wild laughter again as he struggled to free himself. The gibbon had a firm grip on him. Then he realized, to his bewilderment, that the white gibbon was actually a naked woman with unkempt hair and a haggard face. She laughed with her mouth open and head tilted up toward the sky.

The soldier's voice was stuck in his throat. He was barely able to call out, "Hien! Hien!" A tall, older-looking soldier came running. Hien was both scared and slightly amused when he saw his friend immobilized in the hands of a naked woman. He had heard of a disorder women sometimes suffered, something similar to this situation. Hien moved closer and signaled to his friend to stop struggling. Instead Hien advised him to be gentle and affectionate with the woman to make her calm down.

Then he left his friend there and ran up the steps of the watchtower to check on the other women. Hien found three women lying on the floor of the watchtower. They were writhing, crying and laughing at the same time, pulling their hair and tearing at their clothes. A woman who was younger than the others ran toward him, holding her head. She didn't have the laughing disorder, Hien could tell, but he knew she would soon suffer from it. Hien began to tremble as he stood in front of the naked, writhing women. He had witnessed plenty of death in his life as a soldier, but this scene overwhelmed him. He felt a part of him that had been dormant for a long time suddenly awaken and begin kicking around violently. He had the urge to disappear and forget everything.

But eventually he regained his composure. He thought he might know how to cure this laughing disorder that the women were suffering from. He vaguely remembered hearing about a particular treatment for it when he was a kid. He activated the safety on his gun, just to be sure to avoid any accidents, then brought the gun up to his shoulder and pointed it directly at the women.

"All right, you Viet Cong women, listen up!" he shouted. "Where are the supplies? Tell me now or I'll blow your brains out!"

It was like magic—all of a sudden the women became sober and silent. They looked around for a moment, slightly bewildered. Then, realizing what was happening, they grabbed their own guns and aimed them at Hien, ready to pull the trigger. But fortunately Hien's friend was watching from below.

"Don't shoot!" the other soldier cried out. "He's one of us."

The women noticed the star on Hien's hat and uniform and slowly lowered their guns. They looked at each other and seemed suddenly embarrassed to realize that they were naked in front of three male strangers. Terrified, they ran off into the forest, wrapping their bodies around trees and quietly sobbing. Even Thao—the only one not suffering from the laughing disorder—ran off into the woods. She really loved her comrade sisters and pitied the fact that they had never been in love. It wasn't until dark that the five of them returned to the depot and climbed up the watchtower.

The three male soldiers had already left. They'd scribbled a note on a page torn from a small pocket notebook: "Hello, comrades! We'll get our supplies from a different depot and send you a doctor. You must remember, our dear comrades, that this is war. Please forgive us. Farewell!"

A few days later, a nurse came to the depot and gave the women some white pills. But it seemed unnecessary; the laughing disorder had already passed. Now the women seemed calmer, though they looked as if they'd suddenly aged by twenty years.

After that people started referring to this forest as the Laughing Woods. Instead of using the approved secret code for the depot, people would say, "Today I'll go to the Laughing Woods depot to get my supplies."

A few months later the Laughing Woods depot was ordered to move to another location, closer to the battlefield. One day an enemy company attacked the depot. At the time, Thao was suffering from malaria fever and was unconscious. The other four women hid her under a secluded tree deep in the forest and returned to the watchtower to fight off the enemy. But this was no combat fairy tale. The women knew they couldn't win, so they used their last bullets to take their own lives.

Once the fever passed, Thao regained consciousness. The enemy had already withdrawn. All alone now, she buried the women painstakingly with her own hands, which were still weak from the fever. These women were heroines. Their names should have been printed on the front page of newspapers. Instead, this seemed like business as usual.

The night before the attack had been hot and suffocating. As they sat around chatting, one of the women had asked Thao to tell them again about her boyfriend. As usual Thao blurred fact and fiction in the stories about her loyal prince, and the women were captivated. But as they prepared for bed and Thao stepped into her mosquito net, Tham, the leader of the group, caressed Thao's face and said, "Do you think you devote too much love to him? I don't know why, exactly, but I'm worried about you. You're the only one among us who has ever really known happiness. When the war is over, you'll return to the city. Make sure you don't let men just love you out of pity."

Thinking back, Thao remembered that she had been upset with Tham for saying this. But now Tham and her other three comrades were dead. A bayonet had pierced Tham's chest. Before, when they'd bathed together in the creek near the depot, Thao had secretly stared at Tham's breasts and thought, *Venus's breasts cannot be more beautiful than hers.* She had wished that she had similar breasts.

Now Thao gently pushed the bodies of her comrades into the graves, covered them with a thick layer of leaves, then filled the graves with soil. She planted four pink crepe myrtle trees over the graves and watered them with what was left in her canteen. The arid soil sizzled as the water touched it. Steam hovered around Thao's legs.

※ ※ ※

Eventually Thao was taken to a military hospital to recover. While she was there, she learned that Hien, the soldier who had saved them from the laughing disorder, had been killed in combat. The rumor was that Hien's supervisor had commended his heroic sacrifice; the supervisor was on the verge of submitting the paperwork to Hanoi requesting that Hien be given the official honorary title of Hero when the political instructor came across the following lines from Hien's diary:

> I'll never forget what I saw in the Laughing Woods. Witnessing death was easier than seeing the scene in that forest, and hearing that sound—the wild, cruel laughter of war. It's terrible when women are involved in war. I would have died twice so none of them had to be in that situation.
>
> I shiver now as I think of my fiancée and my sister, laughing like those women, lost deep in an endless forest. . . .

The political instructor reported these lines immediately, and the military officials concluded that Hien, as it turned out, must have lacked true determination. This was typical, they said, of the petty bourgeoisie, the class from which Hien, who had been a student before the war, came. Hien's heroism, they said, must have only been a momentary impulse. "He's lucky we don't issue an official reprimand," the political instructor said.

So it goes.

Two years later Thao became a freshman in the Literature Department at Hanoi University. She was a different person than when she'd left for the depot in the Laughing Woods. Her eyes were like those of someone lost in a long dream, and her skin was pale because of the fevers she'd suffered when she was in the forest. Her hair, which had once been so luscious and beautiful and admired by the other women in the Laughing Woods, was now thin and falling out. When she smiled her face would finally show some spark of life. But she rarely smiled. In conversations she seemed distant and absentminded, and at night, alone in her bunk bed, she slouched over a notebook, writing entries in her diary, her thin frame weak and crumpled in on itself.

Thao often had two kinds of dreams. One was about her childhood, scenes in which she was a little girl again, wandering the streets of Hanoi finding treasures on the ground—a lost hairpin, an unclaimed boiled duck egg. In the other kind of dream she was back at the depot in the Laughing Woods; she saw clumps of her hair falling onto Tham's chest where the bayonet had left a scarlet wound. In the middle of this second dream she would often wake up screaming and clutching at the cold bed frame.

One night, unable to fall asleep, Thao looked around the room at her eleven roommates sleeping in their bunks. She guessed that they must be dreaming—their faces seemed happy and flushed with color. They looked so lovely. Their dreams must be far different from her own, Thao thought. She sighed, knowing that she could never really be part of this group.

Thao's boyfriend, Thanh—her loyal prince whom the women in the Laughing Woods had almost considered their *own* boyfriend— was in his last year at the same university. They went out on dates on Saturday nights and walked the moonlit streets lined with date palm trees. Thanh kept his word; he looked after Thao, but they didn't have much to talk about. They were often both silent, counting their steps as they walked, listening to the haunting sound of night birds flapping their wings as they returned to their nests. By nine o'clock, Thanh would dutifully bring Thao back to her dorm.

They acted reserved around each other, as if they both felt guilty about something. Thao looked forward to these Saturday dates with Thanh, but she also felt anxious. It was clear, she felt, that he saw her differently now.

She often thought back to the first time they'd seen each other when she returned from the Laughing Woods. Thanh was waiting for her at the station as Thao got off the train, a rucksack slung over her back. He looked astonished as he stood there looking at her again for the first time after so many years. He was speechless. Thao felt his eyes glance over her skinny body in the old military uniform, her pale lips and thinning hair. She started to cry out of self-pity. But Thanh realized he'd made a mistake and tried to comfort her and be extra affectionate. But this only saddened Thao more. She looked deep into his eyes and said,

"You never thought I would end up like this, did you?"

"I don't care how you look," Thanh said. "The most important thing is that you're back."

"Today maybe you feel happy because I'm back, but tomorrow you'll realize that loving a person like me will be a great sacrifice on your part."

"Please don't say that. I've been waiting for you for years!"

Thao paused. She adjusted the rucksack on her back and then once again looked deeply into Thanh's eyes.

"Let me free you from the burden of your commitment to me," she said finally, speaking very slowly.

"Don't talk like that," Thanh said, cutting her off. He took Thao's hands in his own and smiled. "Back together again after all these years, and already we're fighting."

Thao suddenly felt much better.

"Maybe I've become stubborn and aggressive after a few years in the war," she conceded.

Half a year had passed since then, and they still met every Saturday evening. One weekday, Thao went to find Thanh outside of his class to ask him something. While they were talking in the hallway, Thao noticed Thanh's face turn pale, then blush as he suddenly became quiet. Turning around, Thao saw a female student walking toward them. She had full, luscious lips and youthful rosy skin. She stared directly at Thanh as she passed by into the classroom. Once she was gone, Thanh tried to continue talking to Thao, but his hands trembled now as he held the balcony railing.

Thao understood what was going on. She hurriedly ended the conversation and left. Obviously Thanh and the girl were in love, although they had probably never admitted it to each other. They were classmates and spent plenty of time together. Everyone must have noticed that they made a beautiful couple.

She had become an obstacle to Thanh's happiness, Thao realized. He was only with her because of a platonic feeling of love and duty. There was no romance. She knew that if they got married, their life together would be tedious. Thinking about all this, Thao recalled Tham's words about her love for Thanh, the words that had felt like a warning delivered right before Tham was killed.

After the semester was over, Thao visited her hometown during the break. When she returned to Hanoi, she told Thanh that they needed to have a serious talk about the fact that they were not a good match. She told him that she'd found a new boyfriend and that he should stop thinking about her. Thanh listened attentively to what Thao said, but he seemed indifferent. He assumed she was lying to him. But then Thao started receiving letters delivered to the Literature Department's office every week; the letters arrived in a thick envelope with the words "To my beloved Mac Thi Thao" elegantly written on the outside.

Eventually, Thanh started to reconsider what Thao had said. He wondered now if maybe she was telling the truth. On the one hand, he felt angry at her betrayal; but on the other hand, he also felt a sense of a relief, as if he'd been relieved of a heavy burden. A month later he proposed to his classmate, and they got married that summer, right before graduation.

On the night of Thanh's wedding, Thao lay down on her bunk and lit a small oil lamp. She shielded the dim light with her hands, afraid that it might wake her sleeping roommates. They had started alienating Thao lately; it was as if they considered her diseased and therefore kept their distance, shunning her so she was left by herself in an isolated quarantine zone.

Thao spread the letters out on her bed and counted them. There were sixteen total, all unopened. Everyone in the Literature Department had condemned Thao for betraying Thanh. How could she betray such a handsome, faithful man?

Thao opened the first letter, carefully peeling back the sealed top of the envelope. She thought of Thanh. At this very moment he was probably comfortable and happy in the arms of his new wife. When Thao had been stationed at the depot in the Laughing Woods, she'd longed for a similar night with Thanh. It had once been the fire of desire that motivated her to make it out of the Laughing Woods.

The light from the oil lamp grew dim. It reminded Thao suddenly of a ripe, heart-shaped tomato. She cupped the lamp in her palms, squeezing the dying flame tighter and tighter, imagining the juices from the tomato running in waves of warmth over her hands and arms. She had the sensation suddenly that someone was tickling her. She began to laugh. Then it seized her whole body. As she convulsed with laughter, she flung her arms wildly, scattering the letters all over the room.

One by one, the other girls in the room started to wake up. They were scared and sat up in their beds. They listened to the laughter and, in the dim light from the oil lamp, saw the image of Thao writhing in a fit on her bed.

"She's hysterical," one of them said.

"She's gone insane," concluded another.

"We must take her to the doctor," another suggested.

But when they tried to urge Thao to come with them to the emergency infirmary, she refused to go. The roommates held her legs and arms and called to some male students down the hall to help them carry Thao to the infirmary, where she was forced to take a handful of white pills. Finally she fell asleep.

The roommates returned to their room and noticed the letters scattered all over the bed. One of the letters was opened and contained only a few lines:

I'll write to myself every Thursday night. Then on Friday I'll go to the Nga Tu So post office on my bicycle to mail it so I can receive my letter by Saturday afternoon.

I know this is silly, but it's what I must do so that Thanh will forget about me.

Oh Tham, my sister, I'm the only person left now in the Laughing Woods. There is no happiness for me anywhere.

Dear comrade sisters, rest in peace in the Laughing Woods! I will keep my promise to you all. I will make Thanh our faithful prince.

Girls in the Literature Department tended to be sensitive; Thao's roommates were able to figure out what had happened. They began to cry as they remembered that in the past few months they had alienated Thao and made her feel so alone.

At the first sign of dawn, the girls ran to the top floor of the dormitory, where Thanh had a room, and knocked eagerly on the door. Thanh seemed annoyed when he opened the door and saw them standing there. But the girls didn't say anything. They simply took him by the hand and led him to Thao's bed and the scattered letters. Silently Thanh read one letter, then the next and the next until he had opened and looked at all sixteen of them. Two-thirds of the letters were blank. Thanh's face was white; he looked as if he might collapse.

Hurriedly Thanh ran to the infirmary, but Thao had already left. The door to the room where she'd been sleeping was left ajar. The white sheet on the bed showed the imprint from where her small body had lain the night before after she'd been forced to take the sedative pills. The inevitable thought gave Thanh the sensation of choking: while Thao had been restrained here, treated like an out-of-control crazy person, he had been luxuriating in the happiness of being with his new woman.

Thanh walked to the hallway, then out onto the street. There was a strong, cold wind blowing across the city from the north. Yellow leaves floated in the air like butterflies caught up in a storm. As he walked, he couldn't escape the image in his mind's eye of a girl crushed by the cruelty of life, writing letters to herself at night by the dim light of an oil lamp. Suddenly he thought of a story he'd once heard about a type of sea bird that spat up drops of blood to build its pink nest; when the birds were worn out—when they'd spat up too much blood—they flew high up into the sky, then plunged themselves into the sides of rocky cliffs to die.

Thanh wandered past a familiar corner where on their Saturday dates he used to buy Thao sour plums with his modest scholarship money. Thao had eaten the sour plums enthusiastically without frowning, to make him happy, Thanh knew.

The fruit vendor was falling asleep, her head resting in her palm.

"Excuse me," Thanh asked, waking her up. "But do you remember the girl who often wears an old soldier's uniform? Have you seen her pass by here recently?"

The seller rubbed her eyes. "Well, yes, actually," she said. "You mean the girl who used to eat sour plums with you, right? She was here just a minute ago." The seller pointed across the street to the bus station. "I think she went to wait for the bus over there."

Thanh hurried to the bus station and looked for Thao everywhere, but she wasn't there.

Seeing no other choice, he returned to his new wife. Later he got a good job in the city, and they eventually started a family. Life went on as usual, but Thanh still thought of the sea bird and how small its wings must be.

*% *% *%*

Five years later, the alumni gathered at the university's main meeting hall. They wanted to relive their romantic pasts. At the party for the faculty of literature, Thanh chose a seat by the window, even though it was cold outside.

Maybe a magical thing would happen and Thao would actually show up. But how would she appear in front of him now? With a worn-out, exhausted body, or with dreaming eyes and a willow branch in her hands? Would she be wearing a nun's brown robes and greet him by placing her palms together and saying, "Amitabha"? Or would she appear as an elegant, wealthy woman wearing valuable jewelry? Would she be a talented journalist fresh off the plane from Saigon?

The party was loud and rambunctious. The wind blew noisily, like heavy footsteps. Pensively Thanh looked out the window, toward the main gate of the university.

"Oh, Laughing Forest! You have swallowed so much blood and tears. Why would you also steal my little sea bird?"

19 / THE SORROW WASN'T ONLY OURS

LUONG LIEM

Luong Liem was born in 1946 in Thai Binh and lives in the coastal northern province of Quang Ninh. As a soldier, he fought in the pivotal Tet Offensive of 1968 and served until the end of the war. He is the chairman of the Quang Yen Association for Victims of Agent Orange and works with the nonprofit organization Marin to search for the missing remains of Vietnamese soldiers who died in the war. He writes both short stories and poetry, and his work often depicts the hardships soldiers faced during and after the war. Like other stories that deal with the effects of dioxin poisoning, "The Sorrow Wasn't Only Ours" highlights how the war continued to harm and even kill long after 1975. The title of the story suggests the generational nature of the fallout from the war, particularly the lingering effects of dioxin poison, passed from veterans to their children born well after the fighting ended.

Back in elementary school, Dai and I were only friends. We loved each other, but it was innocent and platonic, the kind of love typical of two young water buffalo herders with mud-caked hands and feet. Still, we experienced passionate affection for each other.

Back then, we used to hold hands and run joyfully to a clump of bamboo trees or a corner of the rice paddy to catch grasshoppers to feed to my father's pet bird. As time went by, our love grew deeper. Years and years of our footprints marked the muddy road we had walked together to school. Everyone said our love was so strong, nothing could destroy it. But actually it ended up falling apart within the blink of an eye.

Who had caused this to happen? Was it Dai or myself? I felt extremely sad. My sadness was like thousands of sharp needles penetrating my young, weak heart. The wonderful dreams that Dai and I had nurtured over the previous ten years suddenly collapsed. There were no more smiles scented with blooming red orchids. What was left for me was just emptiness, which sent chills up my spine. Sorrow had come unexpectedly and left me with an emotional bleeding wound. My tears were everything. It seemed like I had become nothing but tears, endless tears that poured from my face and dissolved into the earth around me.

At university, Dai studied architecture while I studied economics. Although we'd gone to school in the same city, we hardly saw each other. We tried our best to meet at least once or twice a month. But by the last years of university, we were so absorbed in studying that we hardly saw each other at all.

In the last months of school before graduation, I left to do an internship in another province. When I returned to the city, I found out from my friends that Dai had been hospitalized. Hurriedly I ran to the hospital to visit him. I thought, *Dai will be excited to see me. I will rest my head against his muscular chest and listen to the beating of his heart.* But when I got to Dai's hospital room there was another girl sitting by his side. Dai looked at me indifferently, like a stranger he didn't recognize. I tried to talk to him, but Dai refused to respond. He stared blankly at something far away. I got angry and left.

After finals I went to visit Dai again. His body now looked gray and lifeless, like a pebble on the bank of a river. His eyes, which had once burned with energy, were now dry. He looked miserable, like he was wasting away. As soon as he saw me, Dai turned his face away, as if he hadn't even noticed I was there. If the romantic love between us was dead, there was still at least our friendship, our connection, our basic human compassion. Why was this happening? Whose fault was it?

After graduation I got a job at a coal company in the city. I was just a regular salaried employee, but I eventually got married and lived a decent life. My in-laws held somewhat high positions in the coal industry. My father-in-law was head of the Coal Equipment Import and Export Department, and my mother-in-law was in charge of the communal dining hall for one of the largest coal mines. We didn't have to worry about the basic necessities of life.

My in-laws let my husband and me enjoy our lives freely. We ate and bought whatever we wanted; we would just tell my mother-in-law how much it cost and she would pay for everything.

I thought that I would be able to enjoy this comfort for the rest of my life, but unfortunately it came to an end.

After my husband and I had lived together for three years, it was time for us to have children. Our parents wanted grandchildren to hold in their arms. In our fourth year together I got pregnant, which made everyone happy. Time went by slowly as I waited eagerly for my first child to be born. But before the end of the seventh month I suffered a painful miscarriage. I screamed and fainted when I saw the grotesque fetus covered in blood; not a human exactly, but not quite an animal either. My mother-in-law seemed even more horrified than I was. But she was able to stay calm. She held me in her arms and comforted me. "You can do nothing about it if Heaven doesn't let you have it. You'll have other chances. You and your husband are still young, so don't worry."

It happened again when I got pregnant the second time. I knew that my husband and in-laws were upset, but they still took good care of me.

But when I had a miscarriage the third time and the fetus came out flabby, as if it were just made of water, my mother-in-law started to scream and berate me.

"You have bad karma! Your parents must live a dirty, immoral life! You were only born to haunt and ruin my family. I want you to leave my son alone and move out immediately!"

"Why are you saying that about my parents? I can't have children because of my unlucky fate, that's all. It has nothing to do with my parents."

"How dare you talk back to me! Get out of here now!"

Listening to my mother-in-law's cruel words, I wanted to prove that it wasn't my fault, or that of my parents either. But what had happened was the evidence that I could not refute. I decided to stay quiet and swallow my resentment. But my husband, who had always loved and pampered me, started acting cold. He even brought home girls and had casual sex with them right in the bed that only he and I had shared. I requested a divorce. His family agreed immediately.

The day I left them was also the day I quit my job at the coal company. If I had stayed at the company, I would have had to face my unfaithful husband on a daily basis, and that wouldn't have allowed me to concentrate on anything.

Because for years I had been so occupied with my work and with the comfort and happiness of being the daughter-in-law of a wealthy family, I'd forgotten about my hometown, the place where my umbilical cord was buried and where my parents were longing for me to come visit. Before, my husband and I had driven a luxury car to visit them only once a year.

I came back to live with my parents, carrying with me the bitterness of my mother-in-law's false accusation. I was myself again, a typical rural woman. Dai, my first love, was still living there, and now I had to face him every day. At first I wanted to avoid him, but I didn't know how. I lived for myself and for today without thinking too much about the past because it would just cause trouble. But I wasn't sure why with each day that went by, I cared for Dai more and more.

After he finished university, Dai had been offered a job with a high salary and opportunities for promotion at a well-known construction company in the city. But he had declined the offer and requested instead to be a low-ranking state employee in our hometown. He eventually became the vice-chairman of the district.

Dai's life had remained the same over the years. He lived a simple and humble life, focused mostly on work. I loved him primarily for this reason. Because my love for him hadn't turned out as I had expected, I now had even more compassion for him. As the days went by, I never stopped caring for him.

But Dai acted very cold toward me. Whenever I came to see him, he was always cranky and tried to decline my help. But I didn't care. I still came to see him. I did whatever I could to help him, even if he scolded me and told me to leave him alone.

After moving back to my hometown to live with my parents, I eventually learned the reason Dai had rejected my love after his severe illness years ago. When we were growing up, Dai had been a handsome young man, with rosy skin and strong muscles. But suddenly, around the time we entered university, his skin started turning pale and his muscles became withered. After undergoing several medical exams, he was informed that he had inherited dioxin poisoning from his father.

Dai loved me and had sacrificed his life for me. When he found out about his dark future, he decided to reject me, thinking, *People are truly happy only when their lovers are happy.* Dai wanted me to have a happy family, so he had intentionally built a wall between us. I hadn't known about this before.

Now that I knew the truth, I loved Dai even more. But he kept rejecting me. I didn't know what to do. I tried to let time solve the problem and continued visiting him every day. As each day passed, he started to become less and less cranky. Then one day he sat down beside me and said, "Hoa, I let you go back then so you could enjoy your own happiness. But everything didn't turn out the way I wanted. Although I lived far away, I still knew about everything that happened to you. I love you very much. It's not your fault. It's the war's fault. Both of our fathers were exposed to Agent Orange and passed the effects of the dioxin poison on to their children. That's why you gave birth to such grotesque things. Now let's talk about us. We can't have children. We don't know what the future will be like for us. So let's just end our relationship now."

"Dai, your parents have already passed away, and mine will too someday. Only you and I exist. There is no reason for us not to be together and spend the rest of our lives together. I beg you."

Dai was moved by my words. Finally, days after this conversation, he agreed with my proposal and discussed the process for adopting a child. I was no longer anxious. On the contrary, I felt delighted, like a person walking on clouds. Our love had been rekindled.

Dai looked at me affectionately now. His deep eyes opened wide and seemed to brighten. Suddenly he embraced me tightly, so tightly that I felt my heart was breaking into pieces in his arms. His lips were warm against mine. I couldn't breathe.

20 / A MORAL MURDERER

LAI VAN LONG

L ai Van Long was born in 1964 in the central highland city of Da Lat and currently lives in Ho Chi Minh City. He is a news reporter for the *Ho Chi Minh City Police News* and has won many awards for his work as a journalist. In addition, he has published two collections of short stories and three novels. Several of his stories have been translated into Chinese, French, and Japanese, including "A Moral Murderer," his most famous story, which was highly controversial when it was first published in the early 1990s and cemented Lai Van Long's reputation as a provocative and fearless writer. The story deals with several issues that are considered "sensitive" by the Vietnamese government: the personal appropriation by communist officials of land previously belonging to the bourgeois class; peasants' disaffection with the propaganda of the revolution; forced political indoctrination in Marxist/Leninist thought; and the use of reeducation camps. More than anything, this story highlights the anger of the lower classes who felt betrayed by the empty promises of the revolution.

The following folk lyrics, which were associated with his memories of a distant past, now became his philosophy of life:

> A prince inherits his father's throne,
> While a Buddhist monk sweeps fallen leaves . . .

He didn't know when he had first memorized these lyrics and who had been the first person to sing them to him. All he knew was that when he was an elementary school student, the meaning of the lyrics evoked in him feelings of inferiority and aspirations for a better life.

He had survived thanks to his mother's years of suffering and hard work. She had been a street vendor, selling sticky rice from a bamboo basket, and she carried him—her child—with her all around town. She was penniless and had spent years looking for her husband, who was gone. She had no relatives. His mother's body became wasted and her eyes were sad, both of which made him pessimistic and quite reserved at school. He grew into a shy boy who tended to alienate himself from all social interactions.

In 1975 the roaring sounds of cannons and planes filled the air and the townspeople were bewildered. South Vietnamese soldiers, the last symbol of a regime that was about to be annihilated, took off their uniforms and tried to escape, lest the communists find them and exact revenge. For twenty-four hours, the city turned to anarchy—destruction of buildings, robbing, pillaging, and vengeful acts. Bloodthirsty people cried out cheerfully while others grieved their losses and hid quietly as they awaited what would come next.

He was sixteen then. He and his mother, the sticky rice vendor, divided the remainder of their uncooked rice into small containers because they needed to prepare themselves for the worst. He sat outside and guarded the front door of their dilapidated house and prayed for the safety of their shelter. However, his worries were unnecessary because those who had the guts and strength to become robbers were too busy destroying things, robbing, and shouting, especially when they ransacked big stores owned by wealthy families who had already deserted the city.

Three prisoners escaped from jail and used pistols to shoot and destroy the iron gate of a local judge's house. The door of the mayor's mansion was left wide open so that people could come in and share in the wealth that had formerly belonged to the mayor. The mansion's security guard ordered his fellow guards to remove an antenna from the roof and cart away a television set. They even used a GMC truck to move out all the valuables. When lawlessness reigned, violence and power became synonymous.

At noon the following day, tanks and military vehicles of the "other side" entered the city. The entire town rushed out to watch the communist liberators. Communist red flags with a gold star flew on the roof of the mayor's mansion and even above the most dilapidated huts throughout town.

At noon the day after that, order was restored after public loudspeakers announced a death penalty for robbers and pillagers. The peace of the first few days, characterized by anxiety, resembled a layer of fog covering the town. A change in history didn't make a huge difference for poor people, who eventually still had to worry about putting food on the table. Before, this part of town had been populated by hired laborers and working-class people who had had various kinds of jobs. Then the liberation occurred. The hired laborers, the construction workers, and the street vendors stopped doing what they had been doing, and everybody now had the same job, no exception. In the morning they all carried baskets and machetes with them and went into the woods. In the afternoon they traded their chopped wood for rice at the community hall.

The sticky rice vendor's son, who was in the tenth grade, dropped out of school and joined the town's proletariat. He collected wood and sold it as a street vendor. On his first day doing this, he felt embarrassed. Whenever he walked by an area where people knew him personally, he tiptoed and lowered his head. However, his mother was always by his side in times of tribulations and hardships, so he soon became used to his new job.

In July 1977 the government encouraged people to resettle in the New Economic Zones. He and his mother were selected for resettlement. According to the program, young people who were seventeen or older had to live together in the youth volunteer camp.

At 5:00 a.m., reveille sounded in the camp. Everybody enthusiastically had their morning exercise. Then a fire was lit in the kitchen and the smell of cooking sweet potatoes and maniocs filled the air. At 7:00 a.m. everybody was ready to go to work in the field. At 11:00 a.m. they had lunch—rice mixed with ground corn, pumpkin soup, and baked dried fish. At 1:00 p.m. they went back to work. At 5:00 p.m. they ate dinner right where they were working. At 7:00 p.m. they worked the night shift until 9:00 p.m. In the evenings when there was not enough electricity or there was a storm, they gathered for political instruction. Thousands of people sat by a fire listening to one person lecturing on "Pavel and the October Revolution."

If there had been no afternoon of October 21, 1977, he—the son of the sticky rice vendor—and thousands of other people would have become the Pavels of the New Economic Zones. But that was not his fate, because it turned out to be an unforgettable afternoon. He who had been fatherless suddenly had a father.

His father returned in a military Jeep with a driver and bodyguard. He had the look of a prideful hero. His hair was gray, bald above the forehead. He wore a faded uniform, and his dark skin indicated that he was an experienced man.

When they were finally reunited, his father and mother both cried. He was astonished and became madly happy due to such a wonderful surprise. Just a one-minute rendezvous between them erased eighteen years of longing and desperation.

The secretary of the village, who had the rank of captain, and the commander of the Youth Volunteer Association paid his family a formal visit for the first time. They lavished compliments on him when they shook hands with his father, a lieutenant colonel they referred to as "Comrade" and he called Dad.

He was very surprised at the commander's obsequious behavior because one morning not long before, the commander had criticized his squad for not completing their duty, reprimanding them with harsh words: "You guys are remnants of the former regime! You prefer dancing and drinking over working in the rice paddy! All of you must work harder!" But now, good fortune had knocked on his door and given him a father who appeared quite late in his life but made significant changes.

His father, Mr. Suu, was able to rescue him from Squad 1, Platoon 3, Company 9 of the Youth Volunteer Association, as well as his mother from her shacklike house roofed with eight pieces of tin, the standard housing for citizens resettled in the New Economic Zones. His family now moved back to town, where his father "offered" him and his mother a luxurious mansion as a gift. The words "Villa Pensée" were engraved in a piece of marble across the front gate.

When they threw a party to celebrate the new house and the family reunion, Mr. Suu got drunk and formally announced, "Thank you, comrades, for offering this 'Revolution' house to us. The district leader, who had the rank of major, used to be the owner of this mansion. His father was my father's boss prior to the August Revolution, and thirty years ago, I was the servant of his pampered son named Sang. I was fed two meals a day just to wash, groom, and feed his valued horses. Comrades, as you can see"—his father pointed to the back to the house—"the district leader didn't give up his obsession with horses when he moved here from the central highlands. That five-compartment horse stable over there stands as clear evidence of his bourgeois lifestyle. Have you guys been able to help Sang get rid of his horse obsession in the reeducation camp?" Laughter echoed all around. The alcohol got everybody high, and so did the feelings of victory.

That afternoon, eighteen years after his birth, the son firmly believed that he would have a more fortunate destiny.

And he was right. He was compensated for his previous hardships; he was able to continue his education. If the word "compensation" had carried its full meaning, he would have become a history researcher, as he had always wished. But a new "offer" was made, and now he had to drop out of college at the end of his sophomore year in order to become a worker in an automobile manufacturing factory in the Soviet Union.

Rather than sit in a lecture hall and library enriching his knowledge so he could eventually become a member of the intellectual bourgeoisie, he would become a factory worker, a job where he didn't have to use his brain. After a few years, he would be able to buy an electric rice cooker, an iron, and pots and pans, and take them back with him to Vietnam. In addition, he would have the "background of a worker who had been trained in a socialist, technologically advanced country in the use a five-kilogram hammer." This was one of the reasons why, with no hesitation, he became so excited about going abroad. So he went.

Meanwhile his parents stayed in Vietnam and worked diligently. After many years of fighting in the war, Mr. Suu now lived in the luxurious mansion that had once been owned by his former boss, the enemy of the working class. Mr. Suu gained an insightful appreciation for the victorious revolution in which he had participated. He enjoyed the mansion, "booty of war."

Although he was a quiet person and rarely revealed his feelings, his wife sometimes caught him standing at the front door, touching the marble columns on the front porch. Mr. Suu once said to her, "When my father and I were the servants of Sang's family in Hue, we always stayed in a storage room or a buffalo and horse stable, and we did not dare set foot in the house. A maid did all the cleaning. There was no place there for men like us. We would be beaten if we stepped with our mud-stained feet on the tile floor."

Mr. Suu's wife then told her husband about her years of living miserably in other people's homes. "They threw us out and refused to give us shelter. I could put up with it, but I felt sorry for our son. He couldn't invite his friends over because where we lived was not what you would call a real home."

"The only way to stop generational poverty and servitude is by joining the revolution," Mr. Suu stated quietly, a triumphant declaration to put an end to suffering.

A few years later, Mr. Suu was promoted from lieutenant colonel to colonel before his retirement. Half of his life had been dedicated to the revolution, and as a reward he and his family now lived in a very nice house. Mr. Suu thought there would be nothing to worry about. Although social status and privilege affected all social relationships, Mr. Suu, a retired officer, only cared about his own "privilege" within the territory of the Villa Pensée. In other words, he now had enough time to enjoy his privilege within the limits that society dictated.

The mansion still had its original architecture. Right next to the fence at the back garden was the five-compartment horse stable. A few hundred steps from the stable was an A-shaped, two-floor house with dark purple walls and a jade-green floor. The balcony was supported by a row of pillars tiled with white, black-veined marble. There was a beautiful 2,000-square-meter garden in front of the house. The walkway was covered with white pebbles all the way from the gate to the garden, which was divided into two sections: on the left was a tennis court and on the right was a flower garden and a pond with an artificial island in the middle of it.

Around the pond were willow trees with branches drooping grace-fully until they nearly touched the water. At the center of the gar-den was a water fountain in the shape of a mermaid, and next to her were statues of two little boys.

The design of the grounds of the mansion was indeed "art for art's sake," as the bourgeois class would say, and it was useless to Mr. Suu, a retired military officer, so he decided to change it.

First he converted the pond into a fertilizer pit; then he cut down the thick conifer and willow trees and removed the concrete from the tennis court to clear space to grow sweet potatoes. He planted poles in the ground around the mermaid statue, tied wires to the mermaid's head, and connected them to the newly planted poles and branchless willow trees nearby; this he used as a sturdy trellis to grow pumpkins and gourds. Because the soil had never been used to grow anything, it had a lot of nutrients and his veg-etables grew very fast. He and his wife also began raising several pigs. Eventually they converted the Villa Pensée completely into a self-sufficient communal farm.

Then, in mid-November 1988, Mr. Suu received an unexpected letter:

Saigon, November 3, 1988

Dear Mr. Truong Van Suu,

After thirteen years in your reeducation camp, I have been released. Over the last ten years, you have paid no rent for living in my Villa Pensée. Isn't that more than enough for the "blood debt" that a "puppet of the American imperialists" has to pay?

Soon my wife and children will join me here from France, and we will file the legal paperwork to reclaim ownership of the house that you are now living in. I am writing to you in advance so that you will not be surprised and will have enough time to prepare everything. This is

the law of a civilized society, of course. I assume that a high-ranking
officer like yourself will understand.

You and I are not strangers, so I hope that you will not create any
difficulty for us in this matter.

Thank you, and I wish you well.

Lam Quang Sang

Mr. Suu was more surprised that not long after this, he was requested by the authorities to verify the facts presented in the letter.

Six months later, around noontime, a shiny new car entered the Villa Pensée. Three elegant, wealthy-looking people got out of the car and walked directly toward Mr. Suu, who was standing against a pillar and looking at the street. A big, tall man with gray hair, wearing a pair of gold eyeglasses and a gray suit, extended his hand for a handshake and said,

"If I remember correctly, you must be Mr. Suu. It's been thirty years . . ."

"Yes. It's me, Mr. Sang." Mr. Suu used his right hand to shake Mr. Sang's hand and his left hand to push the door open. "Please come in."

"I probably don't need to repeat what I said," Mr. Sang said.

"Of course not. So when will you move in?"

"In fifteen days," Lam Quang Vinh, Mr. Sang's son, replied rudely.

"In fact, we didn't intend to make this request, but you have ruined this house too much," said a woman wearing a blue dress, a white fur jacket, and lots of valuable jewelry. She spoke in an intentionally demeaning tone because she saw sweet potatoes growing in the tennis court and pumpkins and gourds in the flower garden.

With the help of the authorities, everything was settled to make sure each party's requests were satisfied. In short,

1. The plaintiff was compensated with a small amount of money equal to the cost of Mr. Suu and his wife's labor invested in gardening and raising pigs for the last three years.
2. While waiting for a new house, Mr. Suu and his wife were "allowed" to reside temporarily in one of the compartments of the horse stable.

Both parties agreed to comply with these conditions.

Under Mr. Sang's ownership, the mansion was restored to its original beauty, as well as its elegant, artistic, and bourgeois look. The mansion became the headquarters of The Viet-kieu Trading Company and symbolized the restoration of bourgeois power. The attractive word "Viet-kieu," associated with dreams of huge investments in U.S. dollars, became irresistible to some communist opportunists who had once subverted the former regime with their own blood.

Two months after the grand opening of the company, thanks to the use of the word "investment" in an advertisement, cars with various kinds of license plates came frequently to visit the Villa Pensée. People said that once, when the chairwoman of the company had donated thousands of dollars to renovate a military cemetery, the vice president of the province had, by mistake, called her "Comrade." The following day, the news talked about this incident as if it were a thank you to her from thousands of fallen soldiers in their graves.

Things like that happened every day, and Mr. Suu witnessed all of it. At first he was not very pleased, but gradually, thanks to the influence of propaganda, he told himself, *It has been fifteen years. . . . We're all Vietnamese anyway.* He even lost hope in the authorities' promise to move him and his wife out of the horse stable and into a new house. He stopped feeling angry about it. There had been promise after promise, but nothing happened. Then one day the president of a suburban ward, after taking into consideration Mr. Suu's situation, gave him a piece of land on the outskirts of town. The only problem was finding the money to build a house.

Mr. Suu wrote to his son in the Soviet Union to ask for help. His reply was full of complaints, and no money was enclosed: "Dad, you don't understand how I live, work, and earn money here. But let me tell you this: Stop hoping, because I am just a 'slave' abroad."

In order to prove that his passion for horses had not been killed by thirteen years in the reeducation camp, Lam Quang Sang selected ten horses from various regions of the country and raised them on the grounds of the Villa Pensée. Every day he paid people to cut grass for the horses. He paid so well that many people wanted the job. Mr. Sang said that he was simply "helping" people, especially those who had known him in the past. Eventually Mr. Suu and his wife were hired to be in charge of cutting grass for the horses; they worked to save enough money to build their own house.

The victorious colonel, Mr. Suu, appreciated the generosity of Mr. Sang, a defeated major, and with his "military dignity" he guaranteed Mr. Sang high-quality grass. It seemed Mr. Suu had forgotten that he had once done this kind of work before, forty years earlier.

When Mr. Suu was able to save about two-thirds of the money needed to build a new house, his son returned, completely empty-handed after seven years of working abroad. He admitted to his parents his own mistakes and unwise behavior due to his attempts to "save face." His father did the math in his head and could estimate how much money his son had spent to keep his own "dignity" abroad. He had lived, essentially, with the extravagance of a rich person.

The son rested for one week and then decided to help his parents financially so that they would no longer have to smell horse manure every day. He went door to door looking for work, but no place needed to hire the kind of labor he did, so he, an expert in swinging a five-kilogram hammer, trained in an industrially advanced country, was jobless.

There was no other option left for him, so the son followed in his father's footsteps: he too began cutting grass to feed Mr. Sang's horses.

※ ※ ※

It was a roasting hot afternoon. The father, the mother, and the son were soaked in sweat. The sugarcane grass was tall and overgrown, up to their chests. Its leaves were sharp, leaving scratches on their faces. Since his return, the son had been angry and frustrated due to his unemployment. He cursed: "Life is unfair. Some people always have a wonderful life while others suffer permanently."

"If you're tired, go home first. Dad and I will try to fill up another sack of grass and go home later," his mother said in a loving tone, as she always did.

"You two go home whenever you want. I'm leaving," he replied without looking at them and walked away.

He walked through the gate of the mansion and toward the back of the house. A car honked at him, urging him to step aside. He didn't care. He kept walking. The car kept honking.

"Are you deaf?" asked Lam Quang Vinh, Mr. Sang's son, sitting behind the wheel.

He saw Vinh's angry face through the window. A girl sitting next to Vinh in the car frowned to express her anger.

There was a second car trailing Vinh's, and the people in it leaned out the window to curse him.

He turned back his head angrily.

"What?"

"Motherfucker!"

The first car accelerated and galloped as if to kill him, as if he was nothing more than an insolent, low-class bastard. The cars

stopped suddenly and everybody got out and started threatening
him violently. Vinh was the fastest—he kicked Mr. Suu's son very
hard in the chest, which made him buckle over with pain. The
others stood around looking at him derisively. He staggered toward
his home in the horse stable, leaving behind the contemptuous
laughter.

"Tie him up! What a bastard. Somebody call Policeman Hung
for me..."

His head was reeling. He went to his father's bed and found a
pistol, something his father had saved for him. The pistol was brand
new and fully loaded. He checked the gun to make sure it worked,
then left and kicked the door closed behind him. He saw his father's
jar of herbal moonshine that was still half full, but there was no
need to drink it now. The hatred he had been harboring in his heart
for over twenty years had already turned into courage.

He held the pistol firmly in his hand and walked toward the
mansion where he heard loud, cheerful voices. He stood with his
legs spread wide at the center of the open door to the living room
where people were talking cheerfully, drinking, and smoking.

There were four men flirting with four lewd women. "They"—
both the old and new bourgeoisie—were luxuriating in wealth,
and it was they who threatened ill-fated people and made them
suffer.

Bang! Bang!

He began shooting. Bodies fell on the floor, knocking over the
things in the room.

Finally he shot the last man, who was the most detestable. He
was wearing a pair of sunglasses, his gaze fixed up at the ceiling;
his arms drooped lifelessly over the edge of the table where he'd
fallen. Lam Quang Vinh, the prideful Viet-kieu vice-chairman of
the company, was dead.

Bang! Bang!

He shot Vinh once more in the sweaty forehead.

Bang!

And he shot Vinh again, creating a large bloody hole in his fore-head. Vinh's body, in a custom-made suit, fell on stacks of beer cans and glasses. Blood, alcohol, and saliva were all over the couch, the glass table, and the clothes of both the survivors and the dead.

Some of the girls in the room had only been grazed by the bullets, and some were completely unharmed. But everybody was scared and dumbfounded, seeing corpses stacked one on top of the other.

Everything happened and ended so quickly. In the end, the loud voices of the people in the room were nothing compared to the sounds of shooting and the noise of things breaking.

After he took care of the business, the murderer walked to a wine cabinet and took out a brand-new bottle that still had a bright yellow seal. He used the grip of the pistol to break the bottle neck and threw back his head to take a long drink. He then used the last bullet to shoot the portrait of an old man wearing a loose traditional outfit, a circular headdress, and a French bracelet on the wall. The old man was a member of Mr. Sang's family and represented its past.

※ ※ ※

"Were you drunk?"

"No."

"Then why did your breath smell of liquor?"

"I drank after I did it."

"Do you feel remorse for what you've done?"

"Why would I feel remorse for something I had planned twenty years ago?"

"Why didn't you use the last bullet to shoot yourself, like many people would have?"

"Because I wanted to use it for something more important."

"And what was it?"

"I had to act on my grandfather's behalf and get his revenge."

"Can you become a moral person again?"

"Only a truly moral person has the courage to fight back against generational oppression. I don't want 'the prince to inherit his father's throne.' My father tried to take care of this matter by joining the revolution, but I have my own way of doing things. Freeing oneself from an oppressive fate is a moral thing to do, at least for me. And if I have any children, they will never have to cut grass to feed horses, like the three generations before them."

PERMISSIONS AND ACKNOWLEDGMENTS